# The 18th Brigade

# CONRAD JONES

GerriCon Books Ltd

First published in Great Britain in 2008
by
GerriCon Books Ltd
Orford Green
Suite 1
Warrington
Cheshire
WA2 8PA
www.gerriconbooks.co.uk

A CIP Catalogue of this book is available from
the British Library

ISBN: 978-0-9561034-3-7

First published by GerriCon Books Ltd. 12/2008

Printed and bound in Great Britain by
the MPG Books Group

CHAPTER 1

# BAGHDAD'S BLOODY SUNDAY

September 16th, 2007, approximately 12.08pm in an upmarket secure section of the occupied Iraqi capital. It was a steaming hot day and the temperature was climbing over one hundred degrees. Hathem al-Rubaie was a young medical student following in the footsteps of his illustrious parents, his mother an allergist, and his father a famous pathologist. The family could have fled Iraq at any point following the allied invasion, but they chose to remain and help their countrymen try and rebuild their war ravaged nation. Hathem was hungry already, despite the early hour, because his family was fasting in observance of the Muslim holy month of Ramadan. They were fighting their way through the traffic on the way to their respective jobs, sharing the same vehicle to save money.

"Pull in here. I will walk the rest of the way, this traffic is getting worse every day," Hathem's father pointed to a gap in the traffic and his son followed his direction by sliding the rusty white Opel into a space next to the kerb. A cacophony of honking horns objected to the manoeuvre, and Hathem answered them with his middle finger raised.

"Hathem! That is so rude. I did not send you to medical school to learn how to be an uncouth yob," his mother scolded him playfully and slapped the back of his head gently.

"Don't forget to pick up your sister's university application forms, I promised to fill them in with her later on," his father turned and kissed his wife goodbye, and then kissed his son on the cheek. He yanked open the car door and scrambled out of the old vehicle into the searing heat. Another horn blared loudly, urging

Hathem to move on. Hathem watched his father struggling out of the passenger seat, preparing to walk away into the crowd, never once thinking that he would never see him in this world again.

"I will be glad when things get back to normal and we can use the BMW to get to work, this car is so embarrassing," his father slapped the roof and turned into the throng, gone. The family had parked their much newer German coupe in a lockup garage for safety reasons. Anyone driving a prestige motorcar was likely to become the victim of kidnap by militant extremists, even if they were Iraqi. Anyone in a government post or in a position of responsibility was fair game for the numerous religious militias that were terrorising the occupying forces and fellow Iraqis alike.

"The way things are going it will be as old as this thing before we can drive it safely on the streets of Baghdad again," his mother muttered from the back seat.

"We are safe while we are living in the green zone mother," Hathem reassured his elderly parent.

"Safe my foot, we are prisoners in our own country, and that is all we are," she started to rant, which was her favourite past time. He watched his mother waving her arms as she spoke, emphasising her argument, and it made him smile. Hathem loved his aging parents dearly, not just because he was their son, but also because they were such honourable people. They always put others first, always thinking of someone else's feelings before their own. That was why the family had remained in Iraq when most of the wealthy people left like rats deserting a sinking ship.

"We are privileged guests of the interim government mother, outside of the green zone is a nightmare, you should count your blessings," he answered her as he pulled the Opel back into the heavy traffic. They crawled forward to the Nisour Square, where a traffic cop rushed in front of their car with his hand raised, stopping the traffic.

"Oh my word, what is going on now?" his mother cried, distressed at being delayed again.

"I can see a convoy approaching," Hathem craned his neck to see what was happening.

"I don't see why they have to stop all the traffic for them to pass un-hindered, as we all have somewhere to be."

"They are escorting government officials, mother," he answered.

He pressed the clutch pedal down disengaging the gear, but the car still crept forward almost imperceptibly. Hathem had mentioned that the clutch cable was wearing badly, but his father had brushed off the issue as unimportant. It had lasted ten years so it would be alright for another few yet, or so he thought. Hathem smiled as he remembered his father's lecture on the failing economy and how even replacing a single clutch cable before it snapped completely was a waste of Iraq's limited resources. The car juddered as the clutch plate engaged itself momentarily.

"Stop your car, there is a convoy coming through," the traffic policeman shouted at Hathem.

"It is stopped," Hathem protested pulling on the handbrake to counteract the failing clutch.

"Don't you shout at my son, we're doctors you know," his mother wound down the window and stuck her head out to scold the police officer. Status was everything in the Middle East, and doctors were far higher in the food chain than a lowly traffic cop, who wasn't even allowed to carry a weapon, despite the increasing number of them being targeted by suicide bombers.

"Be quiet Mother, he's only doing his job. I told father that the clutch was failing," Hathem tried to calm her, but the heat and hunger was making her taut.

Hathem looked toward the oncoming convoy. The sight was an ominous one as four armoured vehicles hurtled through the crowded streets, leaving a billowing dust cloud in their wake. The armoured vehicles were topped with huge 7.62-millimeter machine guns, each one manned by a single soldier. He didn't recognise the uniforms, but there were so many combatants in Iraq now that it was hard to know what country any of them were from, unless they sported a flag somewhere.

The convoy rattled into the intersection without slowing down or caring a jot about the surrounding vehicles, which Hathem thought was reckless to say the least. The convoy was only twenty yards in front of the rusty white Opel when the handbrake cable snapped, and the failing clutch engaged the plate momentarily. The old car juddered forward a yard, prompting the policeman to run to it in a panic and try to stop it moving any further.

"Stop the car you must wait for the convoy to pass," he bellowed at the top of his voice, showing off his authority to the passing heavily armed troops. He blew loudly on his whistle.

"I've told you not to shout at us, we are doctors," Hathem's mother leaned out of the vehicle and shouted back at the policeman.

"For Allah's sake man it moved a yard and no more," Hathem shouted at the official. The heat and hunger was getting to him too.

A second Iraqi policeman ran to the other side of the car and grabbed the front wing with both hands trying to stop it moving forward again. Hathem couldn't believe his eyes at the drama being created by these two Iraqi traffic cops. They were obviously new volunteers, not even dressed in full uniforms yet. They had ill fitting jackets on and their own dirty trousers and shoes. Many of the new Iraqi police didn't have full uniforms yet. Hathem raised his hands in despair and punched the steering wheel. The horn blared loudly.

It was then that he noticed the convoy had come to an abrupt halt directly in front of them. All four huge machineguns were pointed toward the white Opel. Hathem stared in disbelief. He was about to step out of the vehicle when the first armoured truck opened fire, and four massive 7.62 high velocity bullets ripped into Hathem. The windshield exploded in a shower of lethal glass shards as the other three machine gunners joined in the melee, turning Nisour Square into a killing zone.

Hathem's mother sat in the back seat and screamed as she realised that her son's exploded head was in her lap. The car rocked violently as the heavy machineguns shredded it. She threw herself between the seats and covered her son's ruined body with her own, trying to protect her only son, her pride and joy, her precious legacy. Bullets smashed into her back pulverising her internal organs and shattered her bones as they exited her and then entered her already dead son. The vehicle was completely destroyed when a heavy round pierced the fuel tank and turned it into an inferno. The petrol tank exploded lifting the vehicle four foot into the air. The intense heat welded mother and son into one bizarre cinder, no longer recognisable as humans to the naked eye.

By the time the machineguns had stopped firing sixteen innocent people in Nisour Square were dead and over fifty others maimed and seriously injured. To this day, despite investigations by the FBI, and the US military, no one has been disciplined or charged with their unlawful killing.

CHAPTER 2

# BAGHDAD'S BLOODY SUNDAY

September 16th, 2007, approximately 12.08pm in an upmarket secure section of the occupied Iraqi capital. It was a steaming hot day and the temperature was climbing over one hundred degrees. A joint troop of American Blackwater men, and British 18th Brigade employees were manning a primary personal protection convoy. Primary is the word used to describe military commanders, government officials, embassy staff of members of the allied state department staff. There were a huge number of diplomats and VIP's in Iraq, working to rebuild the government, organising the military operations and developing a lasting infrastructure that would have longevity. Protecting these people in a theatre of war as dangerous as Iraq is a critical but thankless task. The Islamic extremists were targeting officials at every opportunity with suicide attacks and the new phenomenon of road side bombs.

There were one hundred and eighty thousand American troops fighting the insurgents in Iraq. Close personal protection required one hundred and sixty thousand well trained, highly experienced soldiers to keep the extended operational staff alive. The allies had no other choice but to employ professional mercenary soldiers as the protection squads. In both Iraq and Afghanistan there are more mercenaries than regular soldiers. Blackwater and the 18th Brigade are two such private security firms used by the American government.

Sergeant Mel Hickey was manning a turret gun, a task he despised. The intense heat combined with the dust cloud from the leading armoured vehicles left his throat feeling red raw all day long. He had pulled a twelve hour protection shift, which entailed carrying government officials to and from the main interim government buildings in the centre of the green zone. Mel was an ex-Royal Marine Commando, one of the most elite fighting forces on the planet. He served fifteen years in the Marines before the temptation of becoming a highly paid mercenary in Iraq became too great to resist. He had a wife and three young children to consider. He joined the 18th Brigade and earned more money in a month in Iraq than he could in a year as a regular soldier in the British Army. Mel had seen some of his old soldier buddies while he had been on duty a few weeks before, but they had nothing but contempt for him. One career Marine who had served alongside him for ten years or more actually spat on his shiny new mercenary combat boots, and then walked away from him without saying a single word. The incident had hurt his feelings badly, he was still a Royal Marine deep inside, but he had the opportunity to build a substantial nest egg and secure the financial future for his young family. 'Surely they could understand his motives'.

The armoured truck jerked violently as it hit a pothole, shaking him from his thoughts. He heard the driver and the crew inside the vehicle laughing and joking at his expense as he was thrown around like a ragdoll in the turret.

"Pass me the water up you bloody clown," Mel shouted into the hull of the armoured truck.

"You're supposed to be concentrating on the traffic," a voice answered and a camouflaged arm appeared through the hatch holding a metal flask of water.

"I'm choking to death on Iraqi sand up here," he shouted back and took a long swig of the cooling liquid.

"Keep your eyes open, we're approaching Nisour Square," the driver called out.

Sergeant Mel Hickey took another mouthful and then dropped the water bottle back down the hatch. The square was a major intersection and as such was an ideal point for a suicide bomber to be lurking, or to position a car bomb. He grasped the handles of the 7.62-millimetre heavy machinegun and swung it through one hundred and eighty degrees on its pivot, eying every vehicle as a potential target. They were approaching the junction at speed when the lead vehicle braked suddenly. To his left he saw a rusty white Opel crawling slowly toward the convoy. He swung the machinegun toward it. The driver of the vehicle raised his hands violently and shouted something about Allah. The hairs on the back of the ex-Royal Marine stood on end, and tingles ran down his spine, droplets of cold sweat soaked into his tunic. The back window of the car opened and a female passenger was screaming at a man half dressed as a traffic cop. It looked like the man was trying to push the old car toward the convoy. Another man joined him and pushed the other wing of the vehicle. The horn blared loudly.

In a split second he identified the group as suicide bombers. The car was packed with explosives and two men half disguised as traffic policemen were pushing the vehicle into the convoy. The driver of the rusty old Opel shouted 'Allah', his death knell, and Sergeant Mel Hickey opened fire.

# CHAPTER 3

# WARRINGTON/ ENGLAND/ VIGILANTE

Two years later a rusty old Volkswagen estate car pulled into a disused car park, not far from the town centre of Warrington. Warrington is a large satellite town close to the cities of Liverpool and Manchester. It is the commercial centre of the North of England. The supermarket that the deserted car park had once serviced had long since ceased trading, and plywood boards covered the windows and doors. The car's headlights beamed across the dark lot, revealing tall weeds that had grown through the decaying tarmac. He could hear some of the stronger plants thumping against the sills as the car crawled slowly toward the deserted building. The car came to a halt in the space furthest from the road, and closest to the derelict Kwiksave, where the yellow glow of the streetlights couldn't penetrate. The battered old estate looked at home parked next to the crumbling building, hidden in the shadows. He turned off the engine and it spluttered into silence. A waft of diesel exhaust fumes drifted into the ancient vehicle, and mixed with the cloying smell of petrol that already pervaded through it.

He twisted slightly in his seat, and looked toward the town centre. A symmetrical line of streetlights snaked off into the distance. To the left, two hundred yards away, was a sportswear warehouse, with a small gymnasium attached to it. There were half a dozen empty cars parked in front of it, their owners were probably still pumping iron inside. On the same side of the road, the dark structure of a concrete multi-storey car park loomed, its interior too dark for his eyes to penetrate. Across the road on the right hand side was a trendy bar called Times Square. The lights inside were burning brightly, and the deep boom of a bass line carried through the chill night air. Apart from two burly bouncers outside the bar, the streets were empty. He studied them for a few minutes, trying to identify them. The two doormen had the customary shaved heads, short black padded bomber jackets, and dark combat trousers. One of them was wearing black gloves, and he was clapping his hands together in an effort to keep his hands warm. The other had high laced Doc Martin boots on, and he was kicking them gently against the wall, to keep the blood flowing into his frozen toes. Even from this distance he could see their breath billowing in the cold air.

He didn't recognise them, so they weren't Brigade men. Most of the pubs and clubs in the town centre were protected by Brigade security personnel, and most of them knew him well. The last thing he needed now was to be recognised. It was going to be hard enough fooling the town centre CCTV cameras, without bumping into acquaintances, who could later become witnesses. He had been running through this plan in his head for months, and had completed one dry run the night before to iron out any snags that he might discover. It had gone smoothly. Time was ticking away for him, and he had to take control of the situation. It had to be done tonight.

He opened the door and carefully swung his legs out of the vehicle. He knocked something over. A rusty old coke tin clattered across the tarmac. In the dark shadows of the car park it sounded like a thunderclap to him. He held his breath and froze, as if becoming very still would make him invisible. The can stopped against the prickly stem of a tall thistle. He twisted his head round and looked toward the two bouncers. They were oblivious, as the bass lines boomed, drowning everything else out. His heart slowed back to its normal rate, and he breathed deeply to steady his nerves.

He placed both hands on the door frame and heaved himself out of the car. His strong muscular arms pulled him forward onto his legs, and he steadied himself for a moment. He reached back inside the Volkswagen and picked up a joke-shop mask. He stretched the rubber old man mask over his big bald head, wrestling the eye holes into place. He placed a floppy old felt trilby hat on top, and a pair of spectacles finished the homeless man disguise. He walked briskly, if not a little unsteadily, toward the side of the derelict supermarket, what little light there was, completely diminished the further he progressed, and he stopped to peer into the inky blackness. As he walked he counted his steps in his head, one, two, three, four and five. He reached out and blindly felt around, until his hand touched the cold metal mesh of an abandoned shopping trolley, which he had left there the previous evening. His fingers moved swiftly along the metal until he found the plastic handle. He pushed the trolley toward the back of the estate car, with the wheels squeaking and the metal basket rattling as he went. Anyone watching would see a smelly old homeless man carrying his entire life in a discarded shopping trolley.

He fumbled for the boot lock and pressed the button in, the lock clicked open. Quickly he reached inside and grabbed a camping gas cylinder. It was full and the weight took him off balance slightly. He placed the gas bottle into the trolley and then steadied himself, before reaching in for a second cylinder and repeated the process. Next he lifted three, five litre petrol cans out, and placed them in the trolley with the gas canisters. There was a cardboard box containing the rest of his components, which he placed on top of the trolley before covering them all with a grubby old quilt.

Finally he grabbed a large stuffed toy rabbit from the boot, one of the ears was missing, and he plonked it, sat upright in the trolley. He was ready to proceed, but he had to destroy any evidence that he may have left behind. From his pocket he retrieved a book of matches, and a cigar, which he lit. He pulled the soothing smoke into his lungs, and stared at the glowing tip until he was happy that it was lit properly. Then he opened the match book and placed the burning cigar inside, before folding the cardboard flap over it; he then placed a paper clip over the match book to hold the burning cigar in place. He leaned into the boot and his knee clicked loudly as it buckled slightly, throwing him off balance again. Like lightening his left arm shot forward and gripped the roof of the car, powerful muscles and sinews held his weight, while he regained his composure. He placed the smoking improvised fuse on the wheel arch, and then turned on the valve of another camping gas cylinder. It hissed loudly as the highly flammable gas began to pour into the rusty old estate.

He closed the boot and it clicked audibly as it locked. Then he turned and pushed his wobbly shopping trolley out of the shadows and into the fluorescent glare of the town centre streetlights. The metal basket rattled as it bounced over the uneven tarmac of the deserted supermarket. He reached the kerb, and stopped to allow a bus to continue its journey toward the newly built terminus, which was five hundred yards to his right. The bus driver, who was massively overweight, was wearing a regulation salmon pink shirt, which made him look like a human space-hopper behind the wheel. The bus was completely empty of passengers as it cruised by him.

The bouncers' gaze followed the path of the bus as it passed by them, but they didn't give any more than a cursory glance to the scruffy tramp crossing the road, with his shopping trolley. He reached the other side and bounced the trolley up the kerb, it rattled loudly and then settled back down as he pushed it toward a small shopping precinct. The precinct was also known as Times Square, like the bar built on its periphery. It was late, and it was freezing cold, no one was around. He looked up and down the deserted streets. Behind him the town centre monitors were situated on top of the streetlights, and he was beyond their viewing range now. In front of him was the entrance to the precinct. The pavement was made from shiny red house bricks, set into the ground like tiles. There were two low brick walls, one on either side of the wide pathway, built in a funnel shape, narrowing as you reached the entrance.

On the left was a set of double glass doors, which led up a set of stairs to a bank, and some offices. The office suite was on the first floor and it extended over the precinct entrance, creating a tunnel beneath it, through which the shoppers had to pass. On the right was a health food shop, which occupied the length of the entrance tunnel, before it opened out into the square plaza beyond. The plaza would be covered by cameras, but he wasn't going that far. He had business with the people that ran the bank and their associates in the offices next door. He had exactly five and a half minutes before the cigar ignited the matches, which would in turn ignite the propane and blow the car to bits.

The double doors had aluminium frames, and double glazed units fitted into them. He took a hand held power drill, and placed it into the keyhole. The tungsten drill bit made short work of it, and in less than six seconds the latch was detached. It clattered

11

onto the floor inside the porch. Quickly he pushed the door open. The porch area was twelve feet by eight feet, and a wide hessian door mat covered the floor, spotted with discarded chewing gum. At the end of the entrance area was another set of thick glass doors, and the staircase was beyond them. He reached under the stuffed rabbit and grabbed a canister of petrol. Then he unscrewed the top and threw the canister against the doors at the far end. He repeated the process with the other fuel cans, before placing the propane cylinders near the door, and switching on the valves. The gas hissed loudly and he kicked the bottles over rolling them down the narrow entrance hall. There was less than two minutes left.

He grabbed the cardboard box and took out a thick wax church candle, which he lit outside in the fresh air, away from the spreading flammable fumes. He glued the candle to the inside of the box; it was still burning as he folded the lid loosely closed. Then he pushed open the glass doors again and placed the box on the floor inside. The box stopped the gas coming into contact with the naked flames just long enough for him to escape. He calculated that he had about forty seconds.

The shopping trolley rattled loudly as he pushed it away from the precinct, not that anyone was around to notice. He had just reached the bus terminus when the Volkswagen exploded in a ball of flames.

# CHAPTER 4
# LOCKING STUMPS

Terry Nick was the leader of the 18th Brigade. The Brigade had begun life as an extreme right wing organisation, with a penchant for violent racist assaults, destroying immigrant owned businesses, and a string of homophobic attacks. The Brigade and organisations like it had been formed as offspring from an organisation known as the National Front in the seventies. Initially the NF had been formed as the medium for Britain's racists to vent their fury at the tide of immigration which swamped the country in that decade. Years later the leaders of the NF realised that mainstream politics was the way forward, and they distanced themselves from violent extremist right wing factions of the organisation, which led to the birth of groups like the Brigade.

The Brigade realised that their organisation was attracting a lot of ex-military personnel into its ranks, and they used their members to operate a large security firm which controlled the door security in over ninety percent of the bars and nightclubs in the North West of England. Control over the doors gave them ultimate control over the sale of drugs within. The Brigade employed over three hundred of its hardcore members, as door security guards, bouncers, and general muscle. Each man was hired out at eighty pounds sterling, per night shift. That equates to a legitimate turnover of one hundred and sixty eight thousand pounds per week, or close to nine million pounds a year. Not bad money for a bunch of racist, Nazi loving thugs. Of course the profit from the sale of drugs, and the protection money they charged the drug dealers, was worth ten times that figure.

In recent years Terry had orchestrated Brigade Security and

expanded its security business on an international scale. They placed tenders for the contracts to police stadium pop concerts and music festivals all over Europe. Their ranks had been swelled by dozens of ex-service men, veterans of Iraq and Afghanistan. Terry Nick had seen the potential of using highly skilled ex-soldiers as personal body guards, and he touted them for extremely lucrative contracts to protect visiting rock stars and celebrities, along with several high profile politicians. He had opened communications with American mercenary companies, who provided protection for high ranking officials in war zones. There were hundreds of contracts for mercenary security firms worth billions of pounds. Terry wanted to steer the Brigade away from its drug business, and turn it into a professional mercenary outfit. He had been successful at keeping the two parts of the business very separate, and few of the hired muscle who worked on the doors knew anything about the international close personnel protection business.

The Brigade owned the empty first floor of a pub on the outskirts of Warrington town centre, called The Turf and Feather. Terry Nick used it as his administrative base, somewhere where everyone knew that they could find him, his office. Many of the Brigade members used it to socialise, as well as their employer's base, much to the detriment of the pub's regular customers. The Turf was an unusual building. The ground floor was built from dark house brick, but the upper living quarters and the roof were clad with olive green corrugated metal sheets, which joined at odd steep angles. The architects dream was an optical nightmare. Despite its odd design it was once a busy pub, always packed with the local residents, who lived nearby. Situated in the centre of a private housing estate it had a captive audience to service. Unfortunately, since the arrival of dozens of shaven headed bouncers, most of whom sported swastika tattoos beneath their ears, the locals had become intimidated, and voted with their feet. Only a hard core of serious drinkers still frequented the pub, and they were always on their best behaviour when Brigade men were in close proximity.

Terry Nick was sitting outside the pub on a wooden picnic bench, smoking a menthol cigarette. He had a habit of playing with the gold loop, which pierced his left ear, and he was unconsciously twisting it through his fingers as he talked. A miniature gold boxing glove hung from the earring, both decoration and a warning. Terry was duly elected leader several years earlier, after the untimely demise of his predecessor. Just turned fifty, he was old enough to be respected for his experience, but still young enough to be feared as a fighter by his younger colleagues. He was six two, lean, wide at the shoulders and narrow at the hip. His big hands were marked with a mosaic of scar tissue, war wounds from decades of bouncing in pubs and clubs.

He hadn't always been a racist it just sort of crept up on him as he got older. When he left school he had started up a small market stall business selling fake sports branded tee shirts and tracksuits. In the seventies and eighties people loved to walk round open air markets. Bargains of every description could be obtained, from tomatoes to tumble driers. At the time a wave of Pakistani immigrants entered the United Kingdom, and seemed that they all wanted to become market traders. They were very shrewd businessmen, and suddenly nothing was priced at ten pounds or five pounds anymore. They became nine pound and ninety nine pence, and four pounds and ninety nine pence respectively. The pricing culture of the whole country changed almost overnight. Working closely alongside the influx of ruthless foreign traders had a twofold effect on Terry Nick, firstly it made him bankrupt, and secondly it turned him into a racist bigot. Recent years had allowed him to revisit his entrepreneurial side, as he nurtured their international protection business, and tendered for more and more lucrative contracts. His links with Blackwater in America had been the making of him, launching him and the 18th Brigade from small time security firm with criminal activities into an international multi-million pound operation.

It was late, dark and cold, but since the introduction of the smoking ban in July 2007, you either smoked outside or didn't smoke at all. His faded denim jeans were offering little protection from the cold, and he pulled his leather bomber jacket closed, and zipped it up to the chest. There was an electric heat lamp attached to the wall above the benches, a feeble attempt by the stingy landlord to pacify his smoking clientele. It was having no effect at all.

Three Brigade Lieutenants sat with him; all of them dwarfed Terry Nick. His much younger companions swallowed dianabol tablets like candy, and stacked them with daily nandrelone injections. The combined effect increased their muscle mass to frightening proportions. The majority of the 18<sup>th</sup> Brigade's membership looked exactly the same, pumped up skinheads, covered in tribal tattoos and Nazi insignia. Their appearance was incredibly intimidating to those outside of the organisation. FBI investigations into Nisour Square exposed that most of the Blackwater soldiers habitually used anabolic steroids.

"It's last orders Terry," a tiny barmaid appeared, barely five foot five in her shoes, a short dark bob framed her pretty face. Despite her petite frame, she took no messing about from the regulars, Brigade men or not. She was a second set of ears and eyes for Terry Nick, and she reported any shenanigans that she heard behind the bar to him. Terry and his colleagues couldn't hear the bell outside, which signalled closing time, so she always ventured out into the cold to tell them.

"Thanks darling, bring us another round out please," Terry replied. His voice was deep and gruff, like he had gravel in his throat. He was a very dangerous man, but a very charming one too. Terry wouldn't tolerate any of his affiliates swearing in the vicinity of the pub barmaids, and if they didn't use their manners, please and thank you, then there was hell to pay.

"Are any of my lads still in there?" he asked. He made the point of buying his employees the last drink of the night, if they were still in at closing time.

"No Terry, Dave and Norman were the last ones out, and they left half an hour ago, both absolutely skittled, as usual," she replied laughing as she went. The tiny barmaid scurried off back inside the pub to get the drinks. The four skinheads watched her walk away; tight black ski pants accentuated her slender frame. She seemed to know that they were staring, and she wiggled her hips as she walked.

"Those two are always pissed," said one of the Lieutenants, breaking the silence.

"Why do you think we call them Dithering and Headbutt, one can't walk straight and the other one has crashed into more walls than Mr Bump."

The group started to laugh, and they picked up their pint glasses and finished their beer. The road which ran past the pub was deadly quiet. Only distant traffic noises could be heard, drifting several miles on the breeze.

The sound of two car engines racing toward the pub became apparent. The roads were quiet at this time of night, and apart from the pub and the housing estate, there was nothing else around. The car park at the front of the pub was hidden from the main road by thick hedgerows, but the beam of two sets of headlights shone, lighting up the trees that surrounded the pub. The engine noises growled as they approached, and wide bore exhausts exaggerated the throttle sound. There was a deep thudding sound as the bass lines of a car stereo were amplified through a boom box. The vehicles were hidden from view by the tall hedgerow which grew around the perimeter of the car park. They heard the cars screech to a halt, beyond the bushes, and then loud voices could be heard over the booming music. Then the cars screeched off again.

"That sounds like trouble to me," Terry said, standing up from the bench. His colleagues followed suit, and they walked away from the smoking area, four pairs of high combat boots stomped in unison toward the car park.

Terry Nick walked toward the front door of the pub. A white framed, hexagonal conservatory acted as the pub's foyer. As he reached it the tiny barmaid was bringing their pints of beer out to them. He raised his hand, signalling her to stop, and pulled the front door closed tight, without saying a word. The barmaid looked at the swastika tattoo on his hand, and although she had seen it a thousand times, she still wondered why a nice bloke like Terry Nick had marked himself with such an offensive emblem. Through the conservatory window he pointed to the lock with his finger. The tiny barmaid did as she was told and locked herself in the pub. Then she ran inside, and peered through the window, curious as to what was going on. Terry Nick didn't frighten easily.

# CHAPTER 5

# DITHERING DAVE & HEADBUTT NORMAN

Dave and Norman were two of the oldest and smallest Brigade members. They were both in their fifties, and they were both habitual heavy drinkers. In the early seventies they were part of the first British hardcore racist group, The National Front. The group was set up predominantly by right wing conservatives, who had had enough of the tide of black and Asian immigrants that had entered the country. At that time, Britain was in the throes of a severe recession, over three million were unemployed, and every year a new batch of school leavers joined the back of the dole queues. There was an atmosphere of desperation all over the country, but especially so in the inner cities. Racial tensions exploded across the country, and some of the worst race riots ever witnessed erupted in London, Liverpool and Birmingham. The riots spread through towns and cities all over the United Kingdom. Dave and Norman affiliated themselves with the right wing Nazi skinhead groups that sprung up out of the riots. When they first joined up they dressed in the stereotypical skinhead clobber. Bovver boots, drainpipe faded denim jeans, Ben Sherman shirts, and short Harrington jackets. Twenty years on they were still dressed the same way.

They had stuck to their racist values all through their adult lives. The National Front dwindled into obscurity during the nineties, and was replaced by more acceptable mainstream political parties like the British National Party, who had a number of elected representatives at Westminster. The extreme members of the rightwing took umbrage with the new politically correct BNP, and joined associations like the 18th Brigade. Eighteen signifies the first and the eighth letters of the alphabet, A and H, representing the initials of Adolph Hitler. The Brigade had no practical use for the two aging drunks in their day to day business, but they used them to organise members' administrative duties and complete paperwork. Terry Nick had a soft spot for them, and they were generally highly thought of by the younger members. They were both quick witted in their rare sober moments and even funnier after six pints.

Most of their days were spent propping up the bar of the Turf, and today was just like any other. They left the pub before last orders and wobbled down the path, which led to the housing estate where they lived. The path meandered through the estate, and shoulder high hedges ran down both sides of it. Every hundred yards or so, the path branched off, allowing access to the houses on either side.

"We didn't say goodnight to Terry," Norman said, as he staggered to the left and crashed into the bushes. He screwed his face up tightly at the last minute to stop the branches poking him in the eyes.

"We didn't did we, because you're pissed, that's why," Dave answered, pulling his wobbly friend out of the bushes, and directing him back down the path.

"I'm not pissed, and if I am, then you're arseholed, because I can drink you under the table," Norman said offended. He stopped for a second to look sternly at his drinking partner, and then he lost his balance and toppled into the bushes again.

"Of course you can, that's why you're on your arse in the bushes, and I'm picking you up off the floor," Dave grabbed him by the scruff of the neck and pulled him back to his feet. His knees buckled slightly and then he seemed to regain his balance again. They set off down the dimly lit pathway, holding each other upright.

"We didn't say goodbye to Terry did we?" Norman repeated himself.

"Shut up you pisshead, here have a cigarette," David took two Lamberts from his packet, lit one and gave it to his unstable friend. Norman took a deep drag on it and then watched the swirls of smoke leaving his mouth as he exhaled. The streetlight ahead was out, and the path became almost pitch black. The burning end of their cigarettes glowed deep red in the dark.

"What do you think of that little Mandy bird behind the bar?" Norman wobbled as he tried to make conversation. The dark scared him slightly and talking helped.

"She's alright, all the curves are in the right places, not that you've got any hopes of finding out anyway you dirty old man," Dave teased, laughing and spluttering on his cigarette smoke at the same time. He coughed up phlegm and spat it into the bushes.

"I hope you choke to death, you cheeky bastard," Norman countered, and slapped his friend hard between the shoulder blades.

"Well, who are you kidding? She's half our age, and I think Terry has a bit of a crush on her anyway, better steer clear or he'll break your legs," Dave said, he coughed again and his chest rattled. Thick green phlegm came up from his lungs, sounding like it was choking him. He cleared his throat of the thick mucus and spat again.

"I'm not scared of him, anyway he'd have to catch me first," Norman chuckled and then staggered right. He hit the bushes and then fell backward onto the tarmac. His arms and legs stuck up in the air, like a giant infant on a changing mat.

"You really are a fucking nuisance," Dave said bending down to pick his friend up off the floor. He could barely see him in the gloom.

"I haven't had anything to eat today, that's why I'm a bit more pissed than you," Norman moaned on the floor and then he grunted as he was pulled up to his feet again.

Norman tried to dust himself down a little, and he started to whistle tunelessly. Dave had a grip of his arm and his grip tightened suddenly. Norman looked at Dave, but Dave was looking down the path toward the next streetlight. There were three figures standing across the path, each one was hooded, and their faces were hidden. Norman looked behind them and there were four more figures approaching from the rear. Three of them were hooded and hidden, but the front man wasn't. He was tall, over six feet, and he was black. He was broad and athletic, and he was moving with a purpose toward them. His hands were gloved, with leather sparring mittens, and in his right hand was a wicked looking blade. It was the type of knife sold in fantasy weapons magazines, gilt edged curved steel blade attached to a handle, which was spiked to act as a cruel knuckle duster.

"What the fuck is going on?" Norman shouted, trying to sound intimidating, but the men advanced from both directions. He stared at the blade with wide eyes, and his jaw hung open in fear.

"Have you got any idea who we are?" Dithering Dave growled as the black men drew nearer.

"We knows exactly who you is man," said the man at the front of the group. He smiled, exposing stained misshapen teeth, but there was no humour in his smile, only venom. The glint off one gold capped tooth at the front seemed out of place surrounded by decay. The wicked curved blade flashed as it reflected the yellow light from the streetlights, and the slashing noises carried on long after the screaming had stopped.

# CHAPTER 6

# WARRINGTON/ VIGILANTE

The bus terminus was nearly new, and was built as a statement of intent by the borough council, to demonstrate that they were dragging Warrington kicking and screaming into the twenty first century. A plate glass facade thirty feet high curved in an s shape, forming the front of the building. Inside was a brightly lit space, high ceilings and white marble tiled floors. As far as bus stations go, this was first class. The tramp left his shopping trolley at the door, and it swished open as he approached. He held the stuffed rabbit under his arm for effect. There were only a handful of people waiting for their last bus home, some too drunk to notice, and some too tired to be bothered about the scruffy vagrant as he headed for the toilets.

He entered the gents' lavatories, more reminiscent of a five star hotel than a bus terminus. White polished tiles and stainless steel fittings, and the heavy pungent odour of strong disinfectants, had replaced urine stinking, graffiti covered cubicles. The cubicle furthest from the entrance was empty, and he crossed the white tiled floor, being careful not to slip, and pushed open the door. Once inside he pulled off the mask and floppy trilby in one swift movement. He slipped off his jacket, and retrieved a plastic shopping bag from the pocket. The jacket, the mask and hat, all fitted inside the bag with ease. He left the tattered rabbit on the toilet pan, looking forlorn, and then headed back into the deserted terminus, looking like a normal bus passenger.

Blue flashing lights flashed, and the sound of police sirens blared as the emergency service raced to the scene of the burning Volkswagen. He froze and watched them speeding past. The headlights of an empty bus approached the bay that he was walking to, and he jogged awkwardly toward the exit door so that he could board it. He reached the door and lost his balance again. There was a metal bar fixed to the wall to aid the disabled passengers, and he shot out a strong arm and grabbed it, stopping himself from toppling over. He regained his balance and stepped forward. Just as he stepped outside there was an enormous whoosh sound, followed by a loud explosion, as the gas bottles in the bank's foyer ignited. It had taken longer than he'd anticipated for the gas to reach the candle, and he made a mental note to adjust his calculations next time.

# CHAPTER 7

# THE TURF AND FEATHER

In the not so distant past, 18th Brigade men sensing imminent danger would have rushed to an arsenal of hidden firearms, in order to defend themselves. However in recent years the Brigade had been infiltrated numerous times by Britain's security services, leading to the arrest and incarceration of many of its senior members. They were constantly under police observation, and Terry Nick knew that the Turf and Feather had been rigged with spy cameras eighteen months ago, so they used it as a base, and nothing more. That was another reason why he spent most of his time outside in the beer garden smoking, where he could conduct his business away from the prying eyes of the law. Their weapons were well hidden, and well dispersed, but were too far away from the Turf to be of any use now. He wouldn't make the mistake of putting all their eggs in one basket, or give the authorities a reason to arrest them for possession. There were no weapons of any description allowed to be carried in the Turf, and if Terry Nick discovered otherwise then the offenders were in deep trouble. The soldiers that he deployed in Iraq and Afghanistan were supplied with weapons upon arrival in the country they were employed in.

There was a squealing of tyres on the main road, as the two hatchbacks turned into the pub car park. Their headlights illuminated the entire area, and the air was filled with the throaty exhausts and the boom base of their stereos. They skidded to a halt side by side fifty yards in front of the four huge Brigade men. Terry Nick was blinded looking into the headlights, and he couldn't make out who was in the vehicles. The music stopped. Terry looked across at his men, and made a quick mental assessment of the situation.

Two hatchbacks fully loaded equalled a maximum of ten men, but more likely eight, four in each. His three lieutenants weighed in at nearly twenty stones each, and they were battle hardened fighters. Even unarmed they were an awesome group of men. Terry smiled his best smile, and stepped toward the vehicles, making a display of not being afraid of anyone. Automatically his lieutenants stepped forward with him, all about ten feet apart, as they advanced in a line, silent and menacing.

The doors of the two cars opened and shadowy figures emerged from the vehicles. Two men exited from the first car; then there were three, then six and finally seven in total. They walked slowly to the front of the cars, silhouetted by the headlights. They were all tall, over six foot, but very slim. They reminded him of stickmen, long gangly limbs and narrow shoulders. There was silence as the two groups faced off.

"I've come to tell you that your interests in Manchester have been placed under new management, init, your services are no longer required init," one of the silhouettes spoke in a very distinctive accent.

There was a combination of Jamaican yardy, and Salford Manchester, twenty first century gangsta language that was spreading across the country like a plague. All of a sudden the teenagers and criminal elements of Britain were talking like black hip-hop artists. The problem was that even the would-be white gangsters and drug dealers were using the same accent, so without seeing the colour of their skin, Terry couldn't distinguish who they were. Their physique was very distinctive though, and it reminded him of the trip to Kenya he had once made. The Kenyan men are all short, but their Somali neighbours were all built like beanpoles. The taller men from Somali were preferred as security guards and policemen.

"Well, that's very kind of you to come all this way to tell us, however I'm afraid we require a period of notice before we terminate a contract, and it's usually about fifty years," Terry walked slowly to the left hand side, trying to peer through the dazzling lights. The huge skinheads started laughing at their leader's sarcastic humour.

"That's very funny, init, but there's nothing funny about it. I'm giving you an opportunity to keep your interest on this side of the county, but your Manchester business is now in our hands," the same voice replied.

Terry Nick caught a glimpse of the man doing the talking. He was tall and black skinned, wearing a tight skullcap that became a veil at the back of his head, some kind of Muslim thing that Terry had seen on American gang films. His features were sharp, high cheekbones and an angular jaw, long thin nose bone. He was convinced they were Somali.

"I don't think you heard what I said. I don't think you understood what I said because you can't speak English properly, init! What the fuck does 'init' mean lads?" Terry spoke slowly and carried on moving slowly forward, and to his left. His lieutenants were moving to the right hand side in a line, trying to get beyond the glare of the headlights. The skinheads chuckled again at their boss's cutting remarks.

"I think it's a black thing Terry, init," the skinhead furthest to the right said, joining in the charade. His boots kicked a discarded pint pot, and it clattered across the tarmac. He reached down and picked up the glass, and then he hurled it toward the glaring headlights. The shadowy figures stepped aside and the glass shattered on the bonnet of the car behind them.

"I weren't sure if you would be cordial about it or not, init, so I took the liberty of offering you an incentive to walk away peacefully," the voice became more Jamaican as if he were emphasising the accent on purpose for effect. He moved quickly, and tossed something toward Terry; it dropped onto the tarmac with a wet thud. Terry leaned over and inspected it. His face turned a deep purple colour, as his blood pressure went through the roof. Anger was rising from the pit of his stomach, threatening to consume him. He knew that he had to keep control of himself, as the stakes had just been raised. He stared at the severed hand; it was small and male, and there was a Liverpool Football Club ring on the middle finger, just like the one Headbutt Norman always wore. Terry Nick stood up and stared at the silhouette, his face was like stone, and the veins in his neck were pulsing.

"You have no idea what you've just started, I'm very pissed off now, but I guess that was always your objective," Terry nodded his head slowly, wishing he could get his huge hands around the man's throat.

"I hope you have got the message, we don't want a war, init, and we know that this isn't personal, it's business, init," the black man waved and the men started to get back into the cars.

"I'll look forward to discussing 'business' with you under different circumstances next time," Terry Nick growled, trying to maintain his composure. One of his Brigade men walked over and picked up the severed hand. He recognised the ring and then tossed the appendage to the next man in the line. It dawned on them one by one what had happened to Headbutt Norman.

"You're as good as dead you black cunt," the Brigade man next to Terry Nick shouted. He spat toward the headlights.

The black man who had been doing all the talking stopped in his tracks. He stepped to the side of the vehicle beyond the lights, where he could be seen properly. Terry knew he was definitely Somali now that he could see him. The Somali smiled an evil smile. Rotten teeth, gold caps, and distinctive green eyes, Terry would have no problem tracking this bastard down. The Somali stopped smiling, and reached inside his leather jacket. He pulled out a Mac 10 machine pistol, and clicked off the safety. The sound of the metal breech engaging carried across the car park, signalling that it was ready to dispense death at the rate of nine hundred bullets a minute. He pulled the trigger and sprayed the front of the pub with high velocity bullets. Glass shattered and sparks flew as the nine millimetre rounds blasted into the pub Terry Nick and his men dived spread-eagled on the tarmac, and covered their heads with their hands, as if they could stop a bullet.

Terry looked up and his heart stopped a beat. He sucked his breath in sharply and a low moan came from his throat. He watched what was happening instinctively, even though all he wanted to do was close his eyes, and make it go away. Mandy, his favourite little barmaid was watching them through the pub window, but the light inside was reflecting off the glass, making it difficult for her to see anything. She was screwing her eyes, and pressing her forehead against the window to get a better view when the machinegun opened fire. The back of her head exploded as two fat nine millimetre bullets ripped through her skull, liquidizing her brains, and spraying the pub dart board with grey matter. She didn't even have time to scream.

The gunfire stopped, and then the car doors slammed closed.

Terry stood up as the two hatchbacks sped off the car park, tyres squealing and spraying grit behind them. One of the hatchbacks screeched to halt as it reached the main road, and a lone man climbed out of the passenger door. He ran to the back of the car and opened the boot, reached inside and dragged a bloodied body out. The he repeated the process and dumped a second battered corpse on the road, before jumping back into the car. Terry Nick heard laughter and then the deep booming noise of a bass line as the cars sped off into the night.

Fearing the worst Terry walked over to the bodies. It was a shocking sight. He could barely recognise his two colleagues, because their injuries were so bad; their faces slashed open across the mouths, from ear to ear. Their noses had been cut in half vertically, deep to the bone. The only way he could tell who was who, was because Headbutt Norman's hand had been cut off. He stared at them in disbelief, and anger twisted his stomach in a knot. Then he noticed bubbles in the thick congealing blood around Norman's mouth, miraculously he was still breathing.

"Has anyone phoned an ambulance?" Terry growled and took off his belt. He wrapped it tightly around the top of Norman's injured arm, trying to stem the flow of blood from the wrist.

"They're already on the way Terry," one of his men answered as he knelt down and felt for a pulse in Dithering Dave's neck. He took off his jacket and placed it over his bleeding friend to keep him warm; his pulse was very weak. The sound of a siren wailed in the distance, and they prayed that it was heading their way.

"They've shot Mandy! The fucking bastards have shot Mandy!" Dano shouted at the top of his voice. He was one of the biggest and hardest members of the 18th Brigade. He ran in a tight circle like a man demented, and he booted a parked car as hard as he could. The car door buckled as if it were made of cardboard, under the force. Dano stepped back and kicked it again. The window shattered into a thousand pieces. Hot stinging tears ran down Dano's face as he kicked the car a third time, anger and frustration, mixed with a feeling of helplessness, had sent him into a steroid rage.

"They are fucking dead, when I get my hands on them, they are fucking dead, I'll going to rip their fucking heads off with my bare hands," he reached down and grabbed the sill of the car beneath the centre column, and heaved. The car tossed onto its roof with a deafening clatter, and the sound of breaking glass, as the remaining windows shattered as they imploded. He kicked the upturned vehicle again and it span slowly ninety degrees on its roof.

"What are we going to do Tez?" asked one of the lieutenants. He stood watching his friends bleed on the car park, as the sirens grew louder. A second and third siren joined the first, approaching from a distance away.

"I want you to telephone our men in Manchester, and let them know what has happened. Tell them to get tooled up and expect trouble from the Yardies. Then once Headbutt and Dithering are in an ambulance, it's time to pay the piper for the tune that he's just played."

# CHAPTER 8
# MANCHESTER / SOMALI 'YARDIES'

Somali drug gangs had been prevalent across the United Kingdom for a number of years. Every year saw their numbers grow, fed by both legal and illegal immigrants. For some strange reason they had taken on the mantle of Jamaica's gang culture, and called themselves 'Yardies'. Yardie is a term stemming from the slang name given to occupants of government yards in Trenchtown, a neighbourhood in West Kingston, Jamaica, and made famous by Bob Marley in 'no woman, no cry'. Trenchtown was originally built as a housing project following the devastation caused by Hurricane Charlie. Each development was built around a central courtyard with communal cooking facilities. Due to the poverty endemic in the neighbourhood, crime and gang violence became rife, leading the occupants of Trenchtown to be stigmatised by the term Yardie. Now the name was bandied about, and applied to any organised black gangs, Jamaican or otherwise. The Somali gangs of Manchester found the tag romantically endearing, so they stuck to it.

Omar was the new leader of the Yardies. He was from the bullet riddled streets of Mogadishu, and had carried an AK47 as soon as he was old enough to pick one up. He had travelled in the back of a cargo container for nearly three weeks to reach the United Kingdom, almost dying of thirst en route. The civil war in Somalia had reached fever pitch, and there was a huge bounty on Omar's head, several rival gangs were out to kill him, and it was only a matter of time before they succeeded. He made his way to Manchester, where he joined members of his extended family. His fearsome reputation had preceded him, making the leader of the Yardies at that time, extremely nervous about him, and he viewed his arrival as a threat. Within two weeks of stepping onto the pavements of Manchester, Omar had killed the Yardies gang boss and his bodyguard. In his mind it was just natural selection, the strongest survive, and the weak die.

Omar was typical of his race. He was six feet three inches tall, but only weighed eleven stones. His face was elongated, like a caricature, high cheekbones, and distinctive green eyes. The skin on his face was smooth, almost stretched over his angular bone structure. He was certainly not a handsome man. He was a frightening man. When he smiled he showed decaying teeth, rotted by years of chewing Somali drug weeds. His two front teeth were capped with gold, which only highlighted the rotten dentures surrounding them. His hands were unusually long and bony, and his palms were pale pink in contrast to the deep black colour of his skin.

"Where are we heading?" asked the driver of the car. Loud music was thumping from the speakers. A man in the back of the car passed Omar a burning joint. Omar squeezed the cardboard roach between his finger and his thumb, and inhaled the cannabis fumes deep into his lungs. He rocked his head to the music, and inhaled again.

"Take me to my Judie, I feel the need for some good loving," Omar said, exaggerating his Jamaican gangsta drawl. He smiled displaying his stained teeth, and his gold caps glowed in the darkness.

The driver looked hard at Omar for a second, his adrenalin was pumping from the evening's violence, which was effecting his better judgement. He indicated to turn right onto the motorway that would take them back to Manchester. A huge white metal sculpture towered above the slip road.

"We've just started a war Omar, you can't seriously want to go to see your Judie," the driver was shaking his head as he spoke. He banged his hand on the steering wheel aggressively.

Some of the Yardies thought that trying to muscle out the 18th Brigade was a little premature, to say the least. Omar's shock tactics had impressed some of the gang, and alienated some of the others. The Brigade had been in control of door security for decades, which ultimately gave them a stranglehold over the drugs trade. They said who could sell drugs, and who couldn't. They also took a huge slice of the profits, in return for the exclusivity to sell drugs within the premises that they protected. Omar wanted to expand his drugs business into the city centre of Manchester and to do that he had to negotiate with, or oust the Brigade. He chose to do the latter.

"I mean they will come after us now man, init, we need to get ready for them," the driver continued giving his advice, shaking his head for effect. He only stopped talking when he realised that Omar was glaring at him with those deep green eyes. The evil smile had disappeared from his face, and his eyes bored into the driver.

"You know what I mean though, init?" the driver asked nervously. "All I'm saying is we're all buzzing now Omar. We've just dropped the h-bomb on the Brigade, and the night is still young, they'll come back at us man, init."

Omar remained silent and took a deep drag on the joint. He held the burning smoke in his lungs, enjoying the effect of the drug, soothing his rising anger, and clearing his muddied thoughts. The men in the back of the car watched in silence. The atmosphere was tense, electric, like the sensation just before lightening strikes, dark and oppressive. The baseline boomed as Omar exhaled the smoke toward the driver, leaning toward him as he did so. The driver took his eyes off the road for a moment and looked at Omar, and there was madness in them that chilled him to the bone; a cold calculating glare, which gave little away. The driver turned his attention back to the motorway, wishing that he had kept his mouth shut.

Omar took his blade from inside his coat. It had been crafted by a fantasy weapons factory that specialise in ornate, craftsman built knives. The long narrow blade curved wickedly, razor sharp on one side, and serrated on the other. It was designed to rip and tear the internal organs of a human being, a most horrendous way to die. The serrated edges cut and pull delicate flesh, piercing intestines that could never heal naturally, because of the infections that would ultimately follow. The designs come from the well practised art of 'shank' making in Americas prison populations. He gripped the handle and turned the blade slowly, and the dashboard lights glinted from it. A bead of sweat ran down the driver's cheek, but he didn't take his eyes from the road. The handle wrapped around Omar's fist, creating a terrible knuckleduster, made from brass spikes. Omar tapped the forefinger of his free hand onto the spikes one at a time. The last one pricked his finger and a small bead of blood formed on the tip. He put the injured finger into his mouth and sucked the blood from it. Omar never took his eyes off the driver as he caressed his evil blade. The men in the back remained in complete silence. No one spoke, and no one moved for fear of upsetting their volatile leader. He pressed the window button and flicked the used joint stump out into the night. Red embers flashed past the window as the wind took it. He put the blade back inside his pocket and the atmosphere lifted tangibly. The driver seemed to relax slightly, although sweat was running down his forehead freely.

The hatchback reached the end of the M602, at the Salford junction. The set of traffic lights was on red and the car pulled to a halt, their colleagues in the car behind flashed their lights. The driver's cell phone rang. He looked at Omar for permission to answer it, still frightened by his leader's behaviour. Omar nodded his head and looked out of the window at the wing mirror. He could see the driver behind holding his cell phone to his ear, obviously calling them.

"What's up?" the driver answered. The driver behind asked a question that Omar couldn't hear.

"I'm taking Omar to see his Judie, init," the driver said in reply to the unheard question. The driver's eyes flicked left momentarily when he spoke, looking for a reaction from Omar. Omar was still staring at the wing mirror. There was silence for a minute as the driver behind spoke again.

"Look man, I'm just doing what I'm told to do, so if Omar want to see his Judie, then Omar will go and see his Judie, init," the driver was getting flustered. He was trying to talk without being stabbed, and concentrating on the traffic lights which were still red. The motorway was deadly quiet, and only one other car was at the junction.

"Fuck you man! You can talk to the man himself, init," the driver was shaking as he handed the cell phone to Omar, "Louis wants to speak with you man."

Omar ignored the cell phone and turned from the window. He stared into the driver's soul with his piercing green eyes.

"What's he saying?" Omar hissed.

"He wants to know why you're going to see your Judie right now," the driver's hand trembled and his lip quivered as he spoke. He swallowed hard and it felt like he had a golf ball in his oesophagus.

"I'd better explain it to him then." Omar said as he opened the door and climbed out.

"Omar! Don't hurt him man, he's just asking a question," the driver shouted after him, but he was already gone. He could see Omar in the rear view mirror striding toward the car behind. Omar's driver and the other men opened their door and scrambled out to follow him.

"What's you bitching about blood clot?" Omar said as he approached the car. The driver had the window wound down and he was blowing smoke out of it.

"Nothing is bitching Omar, I'm asking what are we doing next, that's all," he answered in a matter of fact manner, shrugging his shoulders. He blew smoke from his nostrils, and then inhaled again.

The lights changed to green and the car behind them sounded his horn, frustrated by the fracas that was blocking the road. Omar stuck his middle finger up at the driver and snarled at him. He leaned into the second hatchback, pushing his face right against the driver's forehead.

"What do you think the Brigade is going to do next man?" Omar snarled.

"They're going to come back at us, init," the driver answered, keeping his gaze away from his enraged boss.

"And does anyone think that they can take the Brigade on in a fair fight?" Omar turned and addressed his affiliates stood behind him on the road. Everyone looked at the tarmac avoiding his piercing eyes. No one replied.

"Do you have any idea how many fucking skinheads will be tooling up now to come for us?" Omar turned back to speak into the hatch back.

"What's wrong with you? Why don't you answer me questions?" Omar slipped back into Jamaican drawl, as he glared at his men. Still no one answered him.

"If the cat has got your tongues, then I'll explain the situation for you, and then we all know where we stand, init," Omar shouted.

"The Brigade has over three hundred full time soldiers, another two hundred on standby, and that is just here in the North West. Those men are all ex-army; some of them are mercenaries in Iraq. Do you want to square up to them?"

The traffic lights changed back to red and the reflection seemed to glow in Omar's eyes, making him look demonic. The driver of the car stuck behind them gunned his engine in frustration. Omar glared at him, and he lifted his foot off the gas.

"They are linked to stinking mercenaries all over the world, and I mean all over the world," he turned and looked at every man in turn as he spoke. "Do you think we can stand up toe to toe with them?"

No one answered.

"In less than an hour all their door security in Manchester will be armed and ready to fight, an hour after that every spare man that they have will be trawling every bar and cat house that we own looking for us. Do you want to go and wait for them to turn up, and then hope that we get lucky?" Omar spat the question out.

No one answered.

"We are going to lie low tonight, I'm going to see my Judie and you all need to do the same. If you go where the Brigade can find you then you is on your own, init," Omar pointed a long bony finger as he spoke.

The lights changed to green, and the car behind them gunned the engine again. He sounded his horn, a long extended blast. Omar looked at his men and said, "Do you understand me?" as he walked toward the car that was stuck behind them. His men were nodding their heads in agreement as it made sense once it was explained to them. Their boss had survived decades of guerrilla warfare in Mogadishu. He knew how to hit and run, wear your enemy down without losing your own men.

"I'm sorry we kept you waiting but I had to teach my men a lesson," Omar said as he approached the frustrated driver. He smiled and showed his rotten teeth, a twisted evil grin.

The driver wound the window up to deter the approaching Yardie boss from reaching inside, but he hadn't locked his door.

Omar lurched forward before the man could realise what was happening, and he snatched the door open. The driver tried to scrabble away from his attacker, but the seat belt held him in place. Omar reached inside and grabbed him by the hair. He slammed the driver forward, smashing his nose into the steering wheel. The driver tried to scream but blood rushed into his mouth, making it more of a gurgling sound.

"Please! Don't hurt me," the man gagged, blood and saliva sprayed the windscreen.

"Take the seatbelt off," Omar shouted.

"What? Why, I don't want to," the man protested weakly.

Omar slammed his head forward again. The rim of the steering wheel split the driver's lips, and his front teeth protruded from an ugly gash.

He gagged again, and then fumbled with the belt catch, and he pressed the red button which made it click open. Omar heard it click and dragged him from the vehicle. The driver grabbed the centre column trying to stay in the car. His summoned his last vestiges of strength, trying to stave off the onslaught. Omar kicked the writhing body below the rib cage, knocking the wind from him. More blood sprayed from his broken nose and split lips, as the breath was forced from his lungs. He gasped for his breath, a thick mucus gurgling sound rattled in his throat.

"Please! I'm sorry," his voice was muffled, barely audible.

Omar slammed the car door shut on his fingers. The man screamed and released his grip on the car. Omar opened the door, and then slammed it shut again. The driver's fingers were bloodied stumps, the nails cracked and split, his breathing was becoming more erratic, making him sound like he was drowning in his own blood. Omar took his blade from his jacket, and he grabbed the battered driver by the chin. His long bony fingers held the man's face in a vice like grip, as he carved his nose into two, lengthways, from his forehead to his top lip. The driver let out a blood curdling scream as the cold blade cut him to the bone, slicing the cartilage like butter, scraping his bones and ripping the soft tissue.

Two sets of headlights appeared in the distance from the motorway behind them, forcing Omar to stop his cutting. He put the knife inside his jacket and ran to the hatchback. His men looked visibly shaken by what they had just witnessed as they scrambled into their cars. They all knew that their boss was violent, but it had reached frightening levels in the last few hours. It seemed that his anger could be unleashed in any direction, at anytime.

Omar didn't look as if his pulse had even quickened, and he seemed calm and collected, as he cleaned his precious blade on a piece of chamois leather. The tyres on the hatchback squealed as the Yardies headed into Manchester to lie low. The Brigade would be on their way soon.

CHAPTER 9

# THE 18ᵗʰ BRIGADE

Terry Nick watched the paramedics working on his friends. The tarmac around Headbutt Norman was covered in blood. Terry wasn't sure how much blood a man had in his body, but he thought that most of Norman's was on the floor. The makeshift tourniquet he had made with his belt to stem the bleeding had saved Norman's life. Dithering Dave was groaning as the ambulance men applied emergency dressing to his terrible face wounds. His cheeks were flapping open exposing his teeth and gums, and Terry cringed at the sight. He turned back toward the pub, where the police were talking to Dano and the other lieutenants. The police had put up a tape cordon around the entrance, protecting the crime scene inside, where Mandy's body still lay. Forensic teams were pulling on white paper suits, ducking beneath the tape and entering the pub. The windows were all shattered and the jukebox could be heard playing an Oasis tune called 'cigarettes and alcohol'.

Terry stayed a safe distance from the police. He was in earshot of their questions, and his men were being professionally vague. The only time information was given to the police was when it suited the Brigade, usually removing someone from a rival outfit off the streets, and sending them to spend some time at 'Her Majesty's pleasure'. The last thing he wanted to do now was talk to them. He was fond of Dithering and Headbutt, and he'd had a thing for young Mandy. Nothing had ever happened between them, because she was much younger, and he was unhappily married, but there had been chemistry between them.

There were often violent attempts made on their business interests, it was just par for the course in the security industry.

38

Rival criminal organisations had jostled for territory for as long as history can remember. The more territory a gang covered, the more business opportunities there were. Gangs often caused trouble inside rival territory, trying to oust the current gangsters, but this was different. Terry mulled over the evening's events and tried to make sense of it all. The man with the bad teeth and the machinegun was Somali, he was sure about that, and he had stipulated that they were moving in on their Manchester business. Terry knew that there were Somali gangs around the Moss Side area of the city, but he had little to do with them. They were mostly small time drug dealers who supplied the local black youth with crack cocaine and heroin. The Somalis were Muslim, and drugs were not generally accepted by Islam, but like any religion, parts of it can be conveniently disregarded when it suits.

There had been rumours that a Somali gang leader and his bodyguard had been murdered somewhere in Moss Side. Terry remembered some of his police contacts talking about it, a year or so ago. The victims had been carved up badly, and their bodies dumped in the road where they lived as a warning to others. There was always someone being shot in the city. It had gained the name, 'Gunchester' in the press as gun crime became more prevalent, but he remembered that particular case because of the level of violence that had been used. Even hardened police detectives with years of service had never experienced anything so severe. The men had been tortured for an extended period of time, it wasn't like a normal hit, and the injuries were similar to those he was looking at now.

It wasn't much to go on, but it was a starting point. He decided that he would get rid of the police, alert his men that were working in Manchester that there could be attacks, and then head into Moss Side, which was the area that the Yardies controlled.

It sounded like the Somali gangs were trying to expand their business into the city centre itself. Terry was always open to negotiation after all the drug dealers paid a hefty tax to the Brigade, in order to be allowed to operate. He had been shot twice in the foot years before during a dispute with Russian Mafioso, and he still carried the limp. Brute force was not always the best option, but in this case he was left with absolutely no other option. The Somalis must have watched the Turf and Feather for a period of time, to be able to identify who would be 'Soft Targets'. It was obvious from their surveillance that Dithering and Headbutt were older and smaller than their colleagues, and that they staggered out of the Turf about the same time most evenings, drunk. The Somalis had tracked them and then set a trap for them. Then they had cut so badly that Terry wasn't sure if they would live or die. Looking at the injuries, and how bad the scarring was going to be, they would be deeply affected by them for the rest of their lives. Sending a harsh message was one thing, but cutting someone's face in half, and removing their hand was a few steps beyond acceptable, even in his violent world.

"We need a word with you and your men Terry," a police officer approached, interrupting his thoughts. Terry knew him vaguely as he was on the alcohol licensing team, which investigated both the landlords and the door security guards whenever there was trouble. They had the power to grant and revoke licences at a stroke. Terry would have to be cordial, and try not to rock the boat. The security business paid his men's wages, and it was the number of men employed that made the 18th Brigade a force to be reckoned with. The truth of the situation was that he didn't really have that much information to give to the police.

"Do you need us to come into the station to give statements?" Terry asked cordially. He took out a menthol cigarette, tapped it on the packet, and lit it with a Zippo lighter. There was a Nazi swastika engraved on the lighter, and the policeman stared at it. Terry clipped it shut, and put it back into his pocket, eyeing the policeman as he did so.

"I think it would be for the best, under the circumstances," the policeman replied, trying hard to hide his disapproval.

The local police knew that the Brigade were responsible for stirring up racial violence all across the country, but they rarely gave them the opportunity to prove that they were to blame. On the other hand they also provided excellent information from time to time, and maintained order in the premises that they controlled. There was never any trouble in Brigade monitored pubs and clubs, no one dared. There were also rumours that the Brigade men were being protected by the establishment, and numerous Brigade employees had walked out of custody avoiding any criminal charges against them.

"We'll be there at nine o'clock sharp tomorrow morning, along with our legal team," Terry answered crisply, leaving no room for negotiation. He walked toward his men, who were watching from the cordon.

"I think we need to interview you and your men tonight," the policeman flushed red, anger rising.

"I think that you need to be looking for a black man with a Mach10 machinegun, not talking to us, there's nothing to tell," Terry carried on walking away.

"I don't want to arrest you Terry but if you refuse to co-operate then I'll have no choice," the policeman raised his voice and followed on his heels.

Now everyone was watching the standoff, the police and the Brigade men. It would be a battle of wills to determine which leader was going to back down, of course the police held the upper hand, but technically Terry Nick and his men were only witnesses.

"What are you thinking of charging me with? Being in possession of bleeding employees, maybe?" Terry turned to face the policeman, and stared into his eyes. They were similar height, but Terry was twice as wide as the lawman. He puffed out his chest muscles to increase his girth.

"Look here, two of your employees are seriously injured, and a poor young barmaid is dead because she was in the wrong place at the wrong time. Technically you are not suspects, but don't think for one minute that it's not your fault. Why else would someone come here and shoot up the pub?" the policeman spoke very calmly, but there was venom in his words when he cast aspersions of blame.

"So charge me then, how about 'being shot at with undue care and attention', or 'ducking a machinegun bullet under the influence of alcohol', I'd love to see you make anything stick officer."

Terry Nick leaned forward and touched noses with the police officer; both men were crimson with anger, both not wanting to back down, he continued.

"I have said that we will cooperate, and we will be at the station tomorrow morning at nine o'clock to answer any questions that you have."

"What about the explosions in the town centre earlier?" the policeman dropped in the question like a psychological bomb. He thought by springing the question that he could catch the Brigade leader off guard.

"What fucking explosion?"

"The explosion at the Blackstallion's bank, behind Times Square."

"What are you talking about?"

"The bank that was in the newspapers last week, the same bank that has been accused of funding Islamic militants in Afghanistan, or do you not know what I'm talking about?" the policeman was starting to lose his temper and several of his officers moved closer to the two men as they argued.

"Now you listen to me plod. Two of my men are bleeding on the car park, and one of my friends has been shot through her head by a gang of black men, probably Somalis. None of which was provoked in anyway. I haven't got a Scooby doo what you are talking about any banks being blown up anywhere, do you understand me?" Terry hissed the last sentence, and placed his big hand on the policeman's chest.

"Terry Nick I'm arresting you for withholding information, and you don't have to say anything, however, anything that you do say will be written down and later given in evidence. Anything you fail to mention at this stage may be used later against you in a court of law, take them in," the officer had had enough.

Half a dozen policemen surrounded the Brigade men and tried to handcuff them. The lieutenants held their huge arms straight and tensed up their steroid built muscles. There was no way the policemen could put the cuffs on without breaking bones first. Dano laughed as two officers struggled to force his arms behind his back. None of the Brigade men fought back at all, they just tensed their arms.

"Do you think they need to go to the gym Terry?" Dano laughed, as they were far too strong to be forced into compliancy.

"I think that you have made your point fellahs, I'll tell my men to go in quietly, if I can make one phone call," Terry smiled at the police officer in charge, and held his hands out for them to cuff him.

The policemen became increasingly frustrated and the Brigade men were read the same rights that Terry Nick had been, and they were bundled away to a waiting police van. The investigating officer needed to maintain his position of authority. He was an experienced police officer, and had dealt with offenders for decades. When he mentioned the explosion in the town centre, he noted that there wasn't even a spark of recognition in the Brigade leader's eyes.

# CHAPTER 10

# WESTBROOK/ VIGILANTE

The bus turned off a dual carriageway onto Cromwell Avenue. He looked out of the window into the darkness, and the reflection of the interior of the empty bus made it difficult to distinguish the world outside. He cupped his hands against his face and the glass, so that he could get a clear view into the night. On the corner stood the Peace Centre silhouetted by the moonlight. He could see the red glow of a fire in the town centre behind it, which gave the building an eerie glow. It was an unusual building clad with wood. Its roof was set at angular slants. He remembered why it had been built, way back in his mind's eye. The day before mother's day, 1993, the Irish Republican Army had attacked his home town with two bombs, and murdered two young boys, out shopping for presents. The Peace Centre had been built to commemorate the tragedy. That had been part of the reason why he'd joined the army. A feeling of affront, being attacked for no real valid reason, made him want to serve his country.

That was a long time ago. It seemed to be a lifetime ago. He had served two tours in Iraq and two tours in Afghanistan since then. Now he was back in civilian clothes again, and trying to adjust to life outside the army. It wasn't working out very well at all. The country was still at war in two countries, but all anyone wanted to know was who had won Big Brother, or Strictly Come Dancing. His army friends were still being shot up and blown up, but no one seemed to care. Every day on the news there would be a report of another improvised explosive device killing his colleagues. He couldn't understand why the newsreels were still calling them improvised. There was nothing amateurish about a hand built weapon that could penetrate British armoured plate. Perhaps that was why the news played things down so much, because they didn't want to tell the public that our most advanced battle tanks and armoured personnel carriers could be destroyed by using old discarded ordinance and a copper disk. It sounded crazy, but he had seen the damage that the formed copper disk created. The explosive is shaped and drives the copper disk fast enough to punch a hole in the armour. Once inside the targeted vehicle the copper disk bounces around inside at six thousand feet per second, like a lethal pinball, cutting through flesh, and smashing bones like a hot knife through butter. The folks at home couldn't understand how our armoured troop carriers were being knocked out week after week by improvised devices. The reason was that the word improvised made it sound like the explosive devices were built by Afghan chicken farmers, unfortunately the technology involved was deadly simple, and incredibly effective. The Taliban mujahideen were far from chicken farmers. They had been at war since the Soviet Union invaded them in the eighties, and two generations of young men had never known anything but how to fight a guerrilla war against invading white Christians. Whether they spoke Russian or English was irrelevant.

The fact was he was still at war in his mind. His men were still fighting in the deserts far away, and no one seemed to care. As his time out of the army progressed, he became incredibly bitter. He felt that feeling of helplessness that he had felt as a young boy when the IRA attacked his home town. After everything he had been through he had gone full circle, and ended up back where he started. It all became too much when a local foreign bank was exposed for sending weapons and supplies to Afghan Taliban fighters, under the guise of food parcels for orphaned children. That was the final straw that broke the camel's back. He would not stand by while the enemy raised money for supplies in his own back yard. They were buying the bombs and bullets that would be used to kill his men next week in the deserts of Afghanistan.

He had dusted himself down and stopped feeling sorry for himself. It had been a revelation to him, a new mission. Now he would fight alongside his men again, but he would fight the enemy in his own backyard, and there were plenty of them to target. Suddenly, there was another flash in the sky, which lit up the darkness for a second. Another gas canister must have exploded inside the bank. He smiled to himself, and then checked how far the bus had travelled toward his destination.

The bus turned a corner and he could see the multiplex cinema lit up in the distance, his target lived behind it. He pressed the stop button, and the bell rang above the driver. He gripped the handrail with his powerful hands, and his strong arm muscles pulled him upright. The bus slowed to a halt and the concertina doors swished open to allow him to alight from the vehicle. He checked his balance before he stepped down from the bus awkwardly. The moonlight was illuminating the areas that the yellow glow from the streetlights didn't reach. He pulled his collar tight as the cold night air bit into him, and he could see his own breath as he exhaled. He checked himself again and then set off into the night; he didn't have long before his target would appear.

# CHAPTER 11

# LIVERPOOL

It was getting close to midnight and the streets of Liverpool were busy. Drunken revellers walked arm in arm, and wobbled from one bar to the next. Music of every genre played, and tunes from a thousand bass speakers vibrated across the city. Jay was stood on the door of Flanagan's Apple, a three storey Irish bar on the world famous Mathew Street, home of the Beatles. The area maintained its sixties image, by keeping cobbled streets that were lined with live music bars. An Irish band was playing to a packed crowd inside, fiddles and flutes were driving the beat. Four lithe young women walked toward him. They were half dressed, wearing short skirts and cropped tops which exposed firm tanned flesh. All four sported diamante belly button jewellery, which emphasised their tan. They walked past the long queue of people that were waiting patiently to get into the pub, and came straight to the front of the line, high heels clicking on the cobbles. Jay smiled at their cheek and shook his head, as they approached him.

"Hiya Jay, can we come in please because we're all bursting for the toilet," a tall brunette pouted as she spoke, her lip gloss glittered in the dark. He'd got her phone number from her a week earlier, but when he'd tried to ring it there was no such number available.

"Oh, I see it's hiya Jay can we come in please? When it suits you, you can be as nice as pie, can't you," he laughed and clapped gloved hands together excitedly, enjoying the power to allow access or not.

"Please Jay! We're bursting for the loo! Pretty please with a cherry on top," she flirted again, pulling a hard done to face.

"You gave me the wrong phone number last week," he raised his eyebrows, and faked a stern expression. The girls all started to giggle as they realised that their fake phone number plot had worked again. They did it every week, unsuspecting men buying them drinks all night, and then passing off the wrong phone number at the end of the evening.

"I'll give it to you tonight big boy ........and my number too," she teased. Her friends all giggled again as Jay stood aside and let them into the Irish bar. He slapped the brunette on the buttocks as she passed by, and she squealed with delight and laughed again.

"Hey mate, we've been waiting here for twenty minutes now, and they've just walked in, it's not fair," the young man at the front of the line moaned indignantly. He had a tight skinny rib tee shirt on and slim white sunglasses, despite the fact the sun had gone down hours ago.

"Well now you've been wasting your time then haven't you?" Jay looked down at the young man from a great height, and took an instant dislike to him. Jay was the Brigade General in Liverpool city centre; He had just returned from a six month contract in Iraq, and he oversaw the Brigade's business interests in the city, reporting only to Terry Nick. He was huge, incredibly muscular, shaven headed, and his neck was twenty inches round.

"What do you mean I've wasted my time?"

"I mean that you're barred."

"What do you mean I'm barred, that's not fair, I've not done anything," the young man inflated his chest trying to appear assertive in the face of the giant doorman.

"You're barred for wearing white sunglasses at night and for being a first class twat........ Now do yourself a favour and go before I lose my temper," Jay grabbed him by the ear, twisting it and dragged him out of the queue. The other revellers laughed and cheered as the man fell over on the cobbled street.

Jay's cell phone buzzed in his pocket. He took the phone out and waved to his colleagues on the door to take over the entrance.

"Hello. Jay speaking," he answered, not recognising the number on the screen.

"Jay, it's Terry Nick. We have got a major problem, and I need you to sort our men out tonight," Terry said, from the custody suite at the police station.

"Why mate? Where are you at?"

"I'm helping the police with their inquiries."

"What's going on Terry?" Jay asked as he walked away from the door to find a quiet spot.

"Headbutt and Dithering are in hospital, and it doesn't look good," Terry explained.

"What happened to them?"

"They were jumped down the path, on the way home. They've been carved up pretty badly, Norman had his hand cut off."

"Who would do that to those two old timers? Bloody hell they're harmless," Jay said shocked by the news, which didn't make sense at all.

"I'm not positive, but I think the leader was a Somali, from Manchester, they're after our doors over there. They shot Mandy with a Mac10," Terry continued.

"What the fuck was Mandy doing there?"

"She was watching from inside the Turf, and they sprayed the front of the pub."

"Is she...?"

"Yes, she took two in the head," Terry sounded choked.

"I'm sorry mate, I know you two had a thing for each other," Jay said, instantly regretting that he had.

"She was just my friend, that's all," Terry corrected him, his voice becoming stern again.

"Yes I know, I am just sorry that's all, she was an alright girl," Jay recovered his thread.

"I need you to warn the lads in Manchester, and get over there and make sure no one does anything stupid."

"I'm not sure I understand," Jay said.

"Tell them to keep their eyes out for anyone looking like they could belong to a Somali gang. There were only two car loads when they arrived at the Turf, so I'm assuming that there are plenty more of them still in Manchester, so tell them to keep their eyes and ears open, but not to go looking for anyone," Terry said, aware that he was being listened to by the policemen around him in the custody suite.

"Are the police listening to you?" Jay caught the drift.

"That's correct," Terry answered.

"Okay, now I understand, do you want us to talk to anyone that is associated with their gang, if they are already in our premises?"

"I think that that would be the best policy in this case," Terry answered, sounding perfectly innocent.

"Okay and you think they are a Somali drug gang?"

"That's correct," Terry said.

"Do you reckon they're from Moss Side?" Jay knew where all the black gangs operated, but he wanted to be sure.

"That would be correct too, as an educated guess anyway," Terry couldn't be absolutely certain, but he was as close as damn it.

"I'm assuming that the police are all over this, and we need to be discreet," Jay continued.

"That would also be correct, and I would expect a balanced approach to this," Terry added cryptically.

"How come they have arrested you if you're witnesses?" Jay asked.

"Do you remember that bank in the town centre being in the papers last week?"

"The Blackstallion, I read something about them sending money to Afghanistan?"

"That's correct, well someone went to town tonight and blew the fucking thing up," Terry said it slowly.

He didn't know if any of his Brigade men were actually responsible. It was just the type of thing they would be involved in, but no one carried out a mission like that without it being sanctioned by the Brigade hierarchy. There had been incidents of younger members taking it on themselves to act unilaterally, but they were rare. The Brigade had a fragile business to operate which needed to be licensed in order for it to exist. Attracting unwanted police attention was the last thing Terry would want to happen. When the Brigade launched an attack on an immigrant target, then it was well planned and well thought out. Nothing was left to chance, and no evidence was left behind that could incriminate their organisation.

"What? I didn't know we were hitting them," Jay said genuinely surprised.

"Are you sure about that Jay?"

"Of course I'm fucking sure, are you telling me the police think it's us?"

"Yes they do, that's why I'm in here, withholding information, apparently," Terry still wasn't sure who had done it.

He couldn't tell from Jay's voice if he'd known about the attack. It could just as easily have been anyone who had read about the story in the news papers. The whole country had been up in arms overnight. There were mass withdrawals of funds from the bank the following day, and the television cameras showed long lines of angry customers waiting to follow suit.

"Look Terry, I don't know anything about it, but someone does. I'll put the word out now that we are under the microscope for torching the bank. Someone must be bragging about it somewhere. It shouldn't take long to find out who is responsible. Is your legal brief on the way to the police station?"

"I only have one phone call so I need you to sort that out for me too," Terry explained.

"No problem boss, you take it easy in there. I'll get onto it right away," Jay started walking back toward the Irish pub to make arrangements.

"One more thing Jay," Terry said.

"Yes, go on boss."

"No guns," Terry whispered.

"What do you mean?"

"You know what I mean, no guns, they're very dangerous and we have enough eyes on us at the moment," he whispered again.

"Okay, I understand, take it easy."

It would only take a few calls for the Brigade men in the city centre of Manchester to be placed on red alert, and to be made ready for any more attacks. Then a few quiet words in certain ears, several searching questions to the right people, and they would be told who belonged to the Somali gangs and who didn't. If any of them were drinking in Brigade protected venues tonight, then they were about to wish that they'd stayed in.

# CHAPTER 12

# WESTBROOK/ VIGILANTE

The rear of the cinema complex was unlit, apart from the moonlight. He kept to the darker shadows at the edges of the car park as he skirted the lot to reach his surveillance spot. There were thick bushes next to a service road, which led into a nearby shopping centre, and superstore. Beyond the service road was a quiet cul-de-sac, consisting of a dozen four bedroom detached houses, all made from brown house bricks, with slate roofs, and spacious lawns front and back. He checked his watch as he neared his spot. It had taken just twenty minutes from the bus station to here, and he had allowed twenty nine minutes, so he should be slightly early according to his calculations.

The bathroom light came on in one of the houses that he was watching; frosted glass distinguished it from normal rooms in the building. He could see the silhouette of a male standing close to the bathroom window, probably in front of the toilet, sloped shoulders and a paunch could clearly be distinguished. He counted the roofs across from a big oak tree, one, two, three, and it wasn't the right house, and that wasn't his target. It was a false alarm but there was time yet.

The alarm monitoring company that worked for Blackstallion bank had a three phase response to any alarm contact. First of all, when the gas explosion ignited, the alarms bells would have been triggered, sending a message via the phone lines to the monitors. The monitoring company would then notify the police and fire departments of the alarm having been triggered. Each step of the process would take some time. He had allowed ten to fifteen minutes for the emergency services to respond, at which point they would confirm if the alarm was a genuine break in or a fire. The third part of the monitoring company's response was then to call the bank's listed key holders, who then had to respond by attending the premises.

He had allowed twenty nine minutes minimum for the key holder to be woken up. Then the key holder would have to dress and get organised, grab his car keys, and then drive down the service road directly past the spot where he was waiting. The plan had been timed to absolute perfection. A well organised military operation, just like the ones he'd led in Iraq and Afghanistan on numerous occasions. Only this time he was the freedom fighter, not the invader. He was the one using guerrilla warfare to achieve his aims, in his own country. It was his hands that had created and painstakingly built the improvised explosive device that was hidden in the thick foliage, waiting for its target to pass.

# CHAPTER 13

# MANCHESTER

Jay parked his Honda Blackbird in an empty parking bay opposite a Manchester pub called Tommy Ducks. It was a landmark pub in Manchester because it stood completely alone. The only remaining survivor of a Victorian terrace, long since demolished. It had been saved because it was a listed building of historical interest. The exterior walls of the pub had been decorated with green ceramic tiles, much more akin to a gent's toilet than the outside of a pub, and the windows were made from stained glass. It was set back in a quiet part of the city centre, but only a few hundred yards walk from the main hustle and bustle. Jay always parked here, because of its close proximity to the city centre's pubs and bars. He pulled the bike up onto its stand and opened the lockbox on the back of the powerful motor cycle.

He removed a thick metal wheel lock and threaded it through the back wheel and frame, before securing it. Jay checked that the coast was clear in either direction; he could hear music from Tommy Ducks but the main entrance was hidden from view around the opposite side. There was no one in sight. He reached into the lockbox and removed a nine millimetre Berretta, and shoved it down the back of his faded jeans, covering the handle over with his leather bomber jacket. Terry Nick had told him, no guns, but Terry Nick was banged up in a urine stinking cell in Warrington somewhere. He had also told him that someone had shot little Mandy with a Mach10 machinegun, and cut Headbutt Norman's hand off. If there was ever a time when he needed to carry a gun, then it was tonight.

Jay was old enough to remember the terrible race riots that tore

Liverpool apart in the late seventies. Huge parts of the city became a war zone as immigration combined with mass unemployment proved to be an explosive cocktail. He had been attacked at school by a gang of black pupils, mimicking what was happening on the streets of their city every night. A week before they had played football together every dinner time in the school yard, but now a line had been drawn in the sand. Jay had become a member of the racist skinhead organisation, the National Front, less than a week later. Six months after that he had joined the army, and three months later he was starting his first tour of Northern Ireland.

A stretch limousine drove by, an elongated Hummer, sprayed powder pink, its windows all blacked out. It seemed to pass him for ages as he wondered who was inside. His mobile buzzed in his pocket and disturbed him from his thoughts.

"Hello," he answered, watching the red taillights of the Hummer fading round a bend in the distance.

"Jay, it's Danny Holley. Are you in town yet?" the voice asked.

"I've just got here now, I'm behind Oxford Road McDonalds, why what's up?" Jay answered.

He had put the Brigade men in Manchester on alert before he'd left Liverpool, hoping that they would have some useful information before he arrived. Although it was a big city, everyone knew everyone else's business, especially where guns and drugs were concerned.

"We've put the word out all over the city and I've just had a call from our boy's on Canal Street, and they reckon there's a couple of Somalis pissed up, bragging about how their gang is about to take over the city centre," Danny Holley explained.

"Is there now? Well that is exactly what we wanted to hear," Jay started walking toward the bright lights of Oxford Road. There was a set of traffic lights on a busy crossroads and a McDonald's restaurant on the corner, Golden Arches glowing brightly in the darkness. Beyond the burger giant the nightlife was still in full swing.

"I thought you'd be happy about that. Have you heard anything about Headbutt and Dithering?"

"No they're both still in surgery, and it doesn't sound too good to me. Norman lost his hand."

"I heard that, what the fuck is that all about?" Danny Holley sounded angry, as did the rest of the Brigade when they heard about the earlier incidents.

"I'm not sure, but Terry reckons it was done as a message, a warning that they were taking over the city centre doors and we are supposed to just walk away quietly," Jay explained.

"This lot have got a fucking nerve haven't they? They'll get what's coming to them, and make no mistake about that," Danny Holley snarled.

"No one is to touch them till I get there Danny, which bar are they in?" Jay picked up his pace and nearly fell over a drunken tramp rifling through the litter bin outside McDonalds. "Get out the way!"

"What?" Danny asked confused.

"Nothing, I wasn't talking to you. Which bar are they in?"

"They're in the Phallic Palace on the canal," Danny answered.

"Great name! Who thinks these things up?"

"Some bloody big poof probably, if they move the boys are going to bell me, and then follow them. They're chomping at the bit to do these bastards Jay, just give us the word and they're toast," Danny snarled again.

"Tell the lads to keep their eye on them till I get there, and not to do anything," Jay spoke slowly and clearly to make himself heard over the increasing volume of music as he approached the main drag.

"No worries Jay, everyone knows what the score is. I'm two minutes away from the bar myself," Danny said.

"Is everyone tooled up?" Jay asked.

"All the bars are covered, stab vests on everyone, but no shooters right?"

"Right, no shooters, for now anyway," Jay felt the cold steel of his Berretta against his skin as he walked.

"I'll see you there in two minutes."

"Danny, before we get there mate, there's something else we need to sort out, but it needs to stay hush hush," Jay changed his tone, trying to draw Danny Holley into his confidence.

"What's the problem Jay, you haven't got an ex-boyfriend in the Phallic Palace have you?" Danny laughed to himself and thought he was funny.

"Shut up you moron, this is serious!" Jay berated him.

"Sorry mate, I'm only having a laugh," Danny answered sheepishly, trying to stop laughing.

"Terry Nick has been lifted by the police," Jay started.

"How come?"

"Do you remember all that stuff in the papers and on the telly about the bank in Warrington that was sending money for weapons to Afghanistan?"

"Yes, we were going to bring it up at the next meeting, someone needs to sort them out," Danny was back into snarling mode.

"Well, it looks like someone already has sorted them out. Have you heard anything about it?" Jay pried.

"No, nothing. Why what's happened?"

"The bank was blown up earlier tonight, and Terry is in the frame for withholding information," Jay continued fishing for information.

"Do you think it's one of ours?" Danny seemed surprised.

"I don't know what to think to be honest with you, but we need to ask questions discreetly, keep your ears open in case the culprit starts to brag about it, but don't broadcast it or the police will think we're covering it up," Jay said.

"Okay Jay, bloody hell what a night this is, see you in two minutes," Danny answered.

Jay cut off the call and slipped his phone into his jacket pocket. He reached the traffic lights and pressed the button to cross the busy road. There were black hackney taxi's whizzing past him every few seconds, crossing the road would be impossible at this time of night unless the lights turned to red. To his right he could see a long line of people waiting to get into a popular vodka bar called Revolution, most of them looked like the last thing they needed was vodka. The lights changed to amber, then green and a beeping sound signalled that he was safe to cross. He jogged across the road and slipped into a narrow alleyway, which took him through to Canal Street.

This part of the city was known as the gay village because of the number of gay bars that lined the canal. It had become a popular venue for homosexuals and heterosexuals alike, and the Brigade monitored all but two of the bars. The two bars that were not covered by the Brigade were reggae bars aimed at a predominantly black clientele. Jay looked to the right as he stepped onto the canal side. The walkways on both sides of the canal were cobbled with dark stone, and full of people enjoying the flamboyant atmosphere of the gay quarter. A rainbow of neon lights reflected off the dark waters of the canal. The village had a carnival feel to it, seven nights a week, which kept the pubs and bars busy. Two men walked past arm in arm, looking a little worse for wear, one of them sported a village people handlebar moustache, which made Jay chuckle to himself. 'Who said there's no such thing as a stereotype' he thought.

About one hundred yards to his left, he could see Danny Holley standing on the cobbled street, talking to two of their doormen. Danny wasn't as tall as the Brigade men he was talking to, but what he lacked in height he made up for in girth. He had a barrel chest, and a matching beer belly, if trouble ever flared he was like a human bulldozer. All three of them were smoking cigarettes and the conversation was becoming animated. Jay walked toward the men and watched one of them poking Danny in the chest aggressively. They saw him, coming through the crowd, and Danny broke away from the trio to meet him.

"Alright Jay," Danny put out his hand in greeting. He looked perturbed.

"Alright, are they still in there?" Jay shook his hand, and noted that beads of sweat were forming on Danny's brow.

"Yes, they're well pissed apparently, they've been buying everyone shots of rum, and flashing money around like it's going out of fashion. They've been winding the doormen up all night too, nothing heavy enough to throw them out, just niggling comments every time they walk past," Danny explained.

"Why aren't they drinking in the black clubs across the canal?" Jay could hear the unmistakable rhythm of a Bob Marley tune drifting from the bar opposite.

"Apparently they're not welcome over there, there's been a lot of hassle between the rival gangs in Moss Side lately, and the doormen won't let them in, in case they cause trouble," Danny nodded his head toward the black doormen across the canal. They were big men, wearing tons of gold bling around their necks, and dark shades.

"Someone should tell them it has gone dark," Jay commented

on the sunglasses, as it was one of his pet hates, sunglasses at night, and even worse Bluetooth ear pieces when you're not driving. Now that is a killer.

"It looked like you were having a row with Brendan when I walked up the road," Jay enquired about the animated conversation he'd witnessed, and broached the subject gently at first.

"Yes, I was asking about that bank incident and he got a bit lippy," Danny pulled deeply on his cigarette as he explained. He shrugged his shoulders to excuse the argument as unimportant, but he looked nervous.

"What was he lippy about? Does he know something about it?" Jay took a stick of chewing gum from his pocket, peeled off the wrapper and rolled it into his mouth. He stared at Danny looking for a reaction.

"I'm not too sure, but they have heard some details from the fire bomb in Warrington, Brendon has a friend in the fire service. He told them that whoever set the fire bomb had a detailed knowledge of improvised time delayed fuses, and that the bombers had set the vehicle that they arrived in to explode almost simultaneously, probably ex-military," Danny explained.

"So why would that piss Brendon off?" Jay asked confused. There was something missing from the conversation. He wasn't being told the whole truth.

"His brother has just come out of the army, served in Iraq a couple of times I think," Danny shrugged again, becoming very vague, and a bead of sweat ran down his cheek.

"So what?" Jay pressed the issue.

"Look, I just asked him if he knew anything about it, and he bit my head off," Danny explained.

"I don't see the connection. Why would that piss him off Danny?"

"Because his brother has been to a few of our 18th Brigade meetings lately, he's got a real problem with the rag heads, apparently he's suffering from post traumatic stress syndrome, having counselling and stuff. So I asked him if he thought his brother might have done something on his own back."

"I thought I told you to be discreet," Jay said sternly. He nodded his head as Danny spoke, encouraging him to open up with the truth.

"It was just an idea, after all the firemen think the bomber has military knowledge, and Brendon's brother is all fucked up," Danny looked aggrieved that Jay didn't appreciate his investigation skills.

"He isn't fucked up Danny, he's just come back from a war. How many of our members have been in the forces?" Jay asked lighting a cigarette.

"I don't know, probably a few," Danny blushed being grilled like this made him feel uncomfortable. Jay was much smarter than he was, and he was making him feel inadequate.

"More like a few hundred," Jay said, inhaling deeply on the soothing smoke. He watched the door of the bar behind Danny intently, and a tall black male walked out unsteadily to have a cigarette. As the heavy glass doors closed behind him the music became instantly quieter.

"Sorry Jay, I was trying to help," Danny said turning to see what Jay was staring at.

"We'll talk about it later," Jay said pushing past him. The sidewalk was empty except for the tall black man.

Moments later Brendon opened the front doors and stepped outside. Brendon was tall and lean, his shoulders were always hunched and his head and neck angled forward slightly giving him a hyena appearance. He was known within the Brigade as a loose cannon, showing little or no respect for the organisation hierarchy. It was only the sheer size and brute force of the Brigade's lieutenants that kept him in line. He looked toward Jay as he approached and indicated with the nod of his head that the black man was one of the Somali Yardies.

Jay weighed up the situation mentally. The Yardie was tall and skinny, his skin was deep black and almost gloss. He had shoulder length dreadlocks held back in place by a wide Alice band, which stretched from his forehead backwards. He was wearing a Manchester United replica team shirt and black denim jeans. The Yardie smoked his cigarette which was in his right hand, and his left hand held his cell phone. As Jay approached him the mobile phone rang. Jay stepped toward Brendon, waiting to see what happened, before making a move. The Somali answered the phone and walked a few yards away from the noisy club, finding a spot where he could hear the caller. He threw the cigarette away and stuck his index finger into his ear hole, blocking out the noise.

The telephone conversation started off jovial, but within a few minutes the Somali was becoming very agitated with the caller. He looked confused and annoyed. Jay had a sneaking feeling that the caller was telling him to get out of the city centre. Maybe the Yardies were warning their affiliates that the Brigade would be looking for them. The Somali's persona changed completely from being a confident drunk to a paranoid and agitated man. He was mid conversation when he turned toward the club. His eyes locked with Jay's stare. Suddenly he realised that the three huge doormen were watching him intently, and he stopped talking immediately, lowering the cell phone slowly, as if sudden movement could provoke an attack.

Jay moved first, sensing that the Yardie was suddenly aware of the danger he was in. He was only a second faster, but it was enough to block the Somali's escape. The man bolted but Jay hit him at speed, wrapping his huge arms around his skinny frame, lifting him from his feet like he was a child. Jay held him in a brutal bear hug, preventing him from shouting out, and squeezing the breath from his lungs. The Somali kicked his feet in mid air trying to break the suffocating hold but to no avail, he was well and truly held. Jay carried the man quickly down the side of the bar into a dark alleyway, out of sight from the revellers on Canal Street. The Yardie's frantic struggling was becoming more feeble by the second, lack of oxygen was sapping his strength. He was baring his teeth and his eyes had become wide and bulbous. Once they were safely out of earshot from the canal area Jay released the Somali, and he collapsed in a heap on the floor, gasping to bring air back into his lungs. Brendon took a step toward the prone figure and kicked him square in the groin. The Yardie doubled up in agony, and he vomited on the floor, almost choking to death in the process as his oxygen starved lungs screamed for air.

"I need him to be able to talk Brendon," Jay said, pushing him away from the Yardie.

Brendon snarled at Jay with a twisted sneer, and he tensed as if he were about to attack his much bigger colleague.

"Don't even think about it Brendon, I'll pick you up and break you in half before you can say sorry," Jay smiled at Brendon as he spoke, but there was no humour in his voice.

"No offense meant Jay, I'm just wired that's all. This fucker and his mate have been winding us up all night," Brendon spat his words and kicked the Yardie in the back. The toecap of his doc martin boots snapped two bones in the man's rear rib cage. He coughed and vomited again struggling to regain his breath.

"I'm not going to tell you again Brendon," Jay stood between the Somali and the young skinhead. "Now go back to your door, and keep your eye on his mate, I want them both."

"Great, I get to miss out on all the fun," Brendon sneered again and spat on the Somali as he turned and headed back into the bright lights on Canal Street. He flicked Jay his middle finger when he was out of reach, a final defiant gesture before he did as he was told, and then he kicked over a crate of empty beer bottles angrily. The crate split and the bottles smashed across the dark alleyway. Brendon giggled like a big kid as he kicked the scattered bottles everywhere.

"Follow him Danny and make sure he doesn't mess this up," Jay turned angrily to face Danny Holley.

"Do you want us to bring the Somali back here?"

"No, not unless he tries to leave, and I don't want the world and his wife to know what is going on Danny. Do you remember discreet Danny?"

"Yes, I get the message Jay, discreet." Danny Holley jogged down the dark alleyway, crushing the broken bottles beneath his considerable weight as he headed into the neon lights.

Jay turned his attention to the Somali on the floor. He had stopped vomiting and his breathing was becoming more regular, although he was still curled up in a foetal position. The smell of acidic vomit mixed with half digested rum was pervading the alleyway. Jay grabbed an empty aluminium beer barrel and dragged it toward the Yardie. He flinched waiting to be hurt again, and relaxed a little when Jay used it as a makeshift stool.

"You're one of the Somali gang from Moss Side," Jay didn't ask a question, he told him. The Yardie looked up at Jay, his eyes white in the darkness, but he remained silent. He looked around wondering where the other skinheads had gone.

"It's just you and me, no one is going to hurt you. I want some information that's all," Jay spoke flatly, no anger or aggression in his tone.

"I'm not in any gang man, I'm a student, init," the Somali spoke for the first time, and he had already given himself away as a 'wannabe gangsta'.

"That's funny because you have been telling your friends that your gang is going to take over the city centre. Are you going to invade the math's class first maybe?" Jay said sarcastically.

"I'm not in any gang man, init," He repeated. He wiped the sick from his mouth with the back of his hand, looking at the residue he grimaced, and spat on the floor.

"I haven't got a great deal of time to fuck about, you see some of my friends have been badly hurt by your gang tonight, and one of my friends was shot in the head, and she was a pretty girl too," Jay looked behind him up the alleyway and spoke as if what he had said was of little importance to him.

"I told you I'm not in a gang, I'm a..........oomph!" he didn't finish his sentence. Jay moved like lightening for a big man and stomped on the Yardies chest. Once again he was gasping for his breath. Jay sat back down on his beer barrel and waited for the man to regain his composure. Tears started to run down the Somali's cheek, glistening as they reflected the neon lights from the end of the dark alleyway. His cracked ribs were beginning to hamper his breathing.

"I need to know the name of your boss, and where we can find him of course," his voice was as affable as ever, like he was talking to his favourite auntie.

"They would kill me man, you know that, init," the Somali sniffled as he spoke, all bravado had gone.

"They might kill you if they knew that you had told me, it's possible. If you don't tell me then I will kill you, and that is an absolute certainty," Jay took the used chewing gum from his mouth and rolled it between his finger and thumb. He aimed it at the Yardie and then flicked it at his face. The chewing gum hit him in the middle of the forehead, making him flinch in fear.

"You have got thirty seconds, and then I'll shoot you. I can always go and start on your friend in there, he may be more cooperative," Jay cocked his head indicating toward the back of the pub. He reached behind his back and removed the nine millimetre from his waistband. He clicked off the safety, which made a loud metal click in the darkness, and then he noisily slid a round into the breach. The Yardie tried to crawl backward on his elbows, digging his heels into the floor to drive him away from the gun. Jay stood up quickly, grabbed the metal beer barrel with both hands and hurled it at the Somali. He made a muffled cry as it struck him, and it rolled noisily down the alley.

"Ten seconds left," Jay pulled his sleeve to look at his watch.

"I don't know his name man, init."

"Five seconds left," Jay ignored the Yardie's pleas.

The Somali pulled his knees into his chest and wrapped his arms around them to protect himself. He was groaning loudly as he curled up, hiding from the gunman stood over him.

"Three seconds, two seconds, one second, you're dead," Jay pointed the gun barrel against the Yardie's elbow joint, digging it into the flesh.

"Okay okay! Please don't shoot, His name is Omar, I don't know his surname, we just call him Omar, init," the man spoke in garbled English.

"Where would I find this Omar character?" Jay pushed the barrel hard against his elbow joint.

"He has a Judy on Peppermint Street, that's all I know man, init," the Yardie was still curled up tightly.

Jay stamped hard on the Somali's head with the heel of his combat boots. He squealed and released his knees, moving his arms over his head. Jay took a steel suppressor from his jacket and screwed it into the barrel of the Berretta. He pressed the silenced gun against the back of the Yardies exposed knee joint and squeezed the trigger. The bullet ripped the joint apart, smashing the kneecap into shards of bone which were drilled through the surrounding muscle tissue like miniature arrowheads. The Yardie opened his mouth in a silent scream, and a throaty gargle was the only sound that came out.

"You're telling me lies, and you have five seconds to tell me the truth before your other knee goes," Jay spoke in the same affable manner, no malice, no anger or aggression in his voice, which made him far more frightening.

The Somali was writhing on the floor sobbing. He was grabbing his shattered knee trying to hold his precious life blood in, but he was failing badly, blood pumped between his fingers soaking his black jeans.

"I'm telling the truth man, his Judy lives at the park end of Peppermint Street," the Yardie could barley put a sentence together between the sobs. He grimaced and rolled onto his back, writhing in agony.

"You forgot to say, init, at the end of your sentence," Jay mocked him.

"It's the truth man, It's the god's truth," he said through gritted teeth.

Jay grabbed the foot of the injured leg and twisted it violently. The shattered joint snapped completely and he turned the foot three hundred and sixty degrees. The Yardie tried to roll with the injury to soften the excruciating pain, but he couldn't. Jay dropped the floppy leg on the floor, the foot completely reversed on its self, and the Yardie screamed like a banshee.

"I'll give you one more chance to tell me where to find Omar, and then the other leg goes the same way as that one," he stamped on the ruined limb and the Somali screamed again. He burbled something that Jay couldn't understand.

"I can't understand what you're saying," Jay said calmly. He righted the beer barrel and placed it close to the writhing Somali. He was gibbering incoherently, trying to twist his leg back to its normal position but the pain was too much for him.

Jay pointed the Berretta at his other leg and the Yardie's eyes widened in absolute terror.

"Salford Towers, she lives at Salford Towers, man," he raised his hands to ward off another bullet.

"Is that the tower block on Cross Lane?"

"Yes, she lives on the fourth floor, number forty three," his words came out between deep gasps of breath; he was slipping into tachycardic shock.

Jay pointed the gun at the Somali's head and pulled the trigger. A fat nine millimetre bullet smashed through the brow bone leaving a ragged hole in the centre of the forehead. By the time the flattened bullet had finished bouncing around inside the skull his brains had been liquidised into grey mush. Death was instantaneous.

# CHAPTER 14

# WESTBROOK/ VIGILANTE

A bedroom light flicked on. He counted the houses again, one, three, four, it was his target's home. He waited long seconds before the first light came on downstairs. His target was on the move. He shifted his weight and nearly lost his balance, only lightening quick reactions saved him from taking another tumble. He shot out a strong arm and grabbed the thick branch of a bush, steadying him. He kept a hold on the bush as he bent over and switched on a remote detonator. A small red light glowed in the darkness. He stood upright and walked in the shadows toward the back of the cinema. The sound of an engine starting in the cul-de-sac indicated that his target was on the way as planned, responding to the alarm company's notification.

The target was a Saudi exile, Rashid Ahmed. Rashid was the first born son of an incredibly rich family, who lived in the holy city of Medina, in the Hejaz region of Saudi Arabia. Medina is the burial site of the great prophet Muhammad, Muslim faith states that a prophet must be buried where he leaves the mortal world, and so a beautiful mosque was built on the site of his home where he died. A walled city was built around the holy grave in the twelfth century, beyond the walls people live in low houses with gardens and plantations which spread across a fertile river delta. Rashid's family was intimately linked to the innermost circles of the Saudi royals, and they benefited greatly from the relationship by being granted very lucrative construction contracts, that involved building the country's network of motorways.

Rashid was sent to university where he studied engineering, but his degree was given to him because of his family's status, rather than for his academic achievements. He was lazy and arrogant, an exceptionally unpopular student with both the professors and academia alike. Things didn't change much when he completed his degree. He walked into a senior position in his father's company, but his incompetence and arrogant demeanour led to a series of disasters. Rashid wouldn't ask for the advice of the more experienced engineers in the company when he was confronted with something beyond his capabilities, and when his many mistakes were highlighted his terrible interpersonal skills compounded the issues further. His father realised that his eldest son was becoming a liability, and he demoted him to a menial desk clerk position, and forced him to revisit his engineering studies. Rashid became more reclusive than ever, and threw himself into his religious studies with fervour.

At about the same time the Soviet invasion of Afghanistan was becoming headline news, and Muslims the world over travelled to fight alongside the Taliban mujahideen. Much to his father's dismay, Rashid joined them. He was attracted by the glamorous ideal of being a religious freedom fighter, a soldier of Islam. The harsh reality of the war in Afghanistan however was far from glamorous, and he soon realised that he was a better engineer than soldier. He left the mujahideen in their mountain hideouts, and used his substantial wealth to bring arms into the country, selling them on at a profit to the Afghan rebels. It seemed that he had at last found his niche in life's rich tapestry.

At the end of the Soviet invasion Osama bin-Laden brought a delegation of senior mujahideen leaders to meet the Saudi royals. Their purpose was to offer the Saudis a ready-made army of Afghanistan veterans based on their soil in Saudi Arabia, ready to fight any aggressor. The Iran, Iraq war was over, but the Iraqi's looked poised to invade Kuwait, which brought their armies too close to Saudi Arabia for comfort. The Saudi royal family always portrayed themselves as devout followers of Islam, however they did not want an army of Islamic extremists camped on their doorstep. The deposal of the Shah of Iran by extremists was still a recent memory, and a warning to the regimes of Iraq and Saudi that extremism could destroy them if they allowed it to take root in their countries. The royals chose to protect themselves from Saddam's sabre rattling in Kuwait by inviting American troops to be based on their soil. It was a decision which echoed across the Muslim world like a thunderclap.

Offended by the decision, Osama bin-Laden and his affiliates were banished from Saudi, and Rashid went with them. His father disowned him, not wanting his son's action to tarnish his relationship with the Saudi royals. Rashid had made a fortune of his own during the war, as the arms trade is a very lucrative business to be in, especially during an armed conflict with the duration of the Afghanistan war. He also had a rich vein of contacts that he had made during the conflict, which he continued to utilise through the nineties. In early two thousand he used a false identity to enter the United Kingdom, where he created a financial institution which masqueraded as a high street bank. He used his huge financial assets to sell loans to people with poor credit ratings, obviously at extortionate interest rates, and he doubled his fortune in less than two years.

When the allied troops entered Afghanistan to topple the Taliban, Rashid once again began to sell arms to them. It was the actions of a disgruntled employee which brought his illegal activities into the public domain, and started the nation's backlash against his bank that was dominating the country's newspapers and television reports. The publicity had led to him being arrested and interviewed by the Terrorist Task Force, which were an elite Special Forces unit, set up to deal with Britain's growing number of extremist cells, from both ends of the scale. Rashid had been in the arms trade long enough to cover his tracks well and there was little solid evidence to prove that he was involved in anything except banking. The public's confidence in his institution however was shattered, and there was a week long run on the bank which wiped out its share value on the stock market.

The adverse publicity and allegations of sending arms to Afghanistan Taliban fighters, which would be used ultimately to kill British troops wasn't just bad for business, it had also attracted the attention of some very dangerous people.

# CHAPTER 15

# MANCHESTER

Danny Holley and Brendon stood near the front doors of the Phallic Palace, and watched the remaining Yardie. Brendon was pacing up and down; his shoulders stooped making his appearance even more menacing to onlookers. He had a permanent snarl on his face, which was his shield against the world. If you always look angry then not many people bother you, especially when you're big built with a shaved head and swastikas tattooed beneath the ears. The Somali was oblivious to the attention he was receiving. He was a tall slim man with very narrow shoulders, and a shaved head. His skin was deep black as only African skin can be. He had a white hooded top on and faded blue jeans, and on his feet he had a pair of brown canvas flip flops, which showed the skin on the soles was pale pink in contrast to the rest of him.

The Yardie was holding court at the bar to a group of young women. He leaned over the bar to make himself heard and ordered another round of Tequila slammers. The fact that his friend had been missing for nearly twenty minutes still hadn't dawned on him. The drinks arrived on a black plastic tray, small shot glasses filled with potent clear liquid. The group of girls cheered as they were set down on the bar. The barman showed off in front of the young women spinning a salt shaker like he would do with a cocktail glass, and then he placed the salt pot and a bowl of lemon slices next to the glasses. The Somali began to distribute them amongst the group of giggling girls. He took his time, holding each one individually and pouring a pinch of salt onto the back of their hands. Once the salt had been distributed he handed each woman in turn a small slice of lemon, then they all clinked their glasses and cheered again.

The Yardie downed his Tequila and put the glass on the bar, grimacing at the sour taste. The girls giggled again and followed suit, each one of them screwing their faces up at the taste. The Yardie's expression changed and he turned around looking for something that wasn't there. He looked drunk and confused. Suddenly he realised his cell phone was vibrating in the back pocket of his jeans. Laughing he pulled the cell phone out and placed it to his ear, he cupped a hand over the other ear trying to shut out the noise of the music, but he couldn't hear the caller. The Somali put a long arm around one of the girls and hugged her jovially, making his excuses for having to leave the party, and headed for the front door. As he passed the huge Brigade doormen he grinned sarcastically and made a gun shape with his fingers, cocking his thumb as he opened the doors.

Danny Holley was right behind him as he stepped outside, and Brendon followed. The Yardie put the phone to his ear and was about to speak when Danny Holley punched him hard in the back of the neck, where the spine meets the skull. The phone clattered across the cobbles toward the edge of the canal as the Somali's legs buckled. Brendon grabbed him before he collapsed and the Brigade men bundled him down the alleyway. They had only gone a few yards when Jay appeared out of the gloom.

"Where's your van?" Jay asked Brendon.

"At the bottom of this alley, It's behind the club on Oxford Road," Brendon replied.

"Tie him up and put him in your van, we might need him later on, and make sure nobody sees you," Jay walked past them toward the bright lights on Canal Street.

"Where's the other one?" Danny Holley asked, noting that there was no sign of the second Yardie.

"Don't worry about that Danny, just get him to the van," Jay didn't turn round, as he barked out his orders.

"He gets right up my nose," Brendon complained as he dragged the unconscious Somali deeper into the alleyway. His van was parked at the other end, and there was no chance of passing potential witnesses.

Jay stepped onto the cobbled canal bank and looked both ways, trying to think straight. There was a group of young men crossing a narrow footbridge which led to the far bank, and the reggae clubs. He walked after the young men, staying about ten yards behind them. The group were obviously drunk and in high spirits. One of them had a distinctive tiger print tee shirt on, and was as camp as Christmas. They approached the door of Marley's bar, and the dulcet tones of the reggae master drifted across the canal, mingling with tunes from a dozen other venues. The group of young men walked in unhindered by the bouncers. The black doormen saw Jay approaching and they nodded a cautious greeting. There was a mutual hatred between the Brigade men and the black bouncers, but they had to work on opposite sides of the canal three hundred and sixty five days of the year, so they tolerated one another, plus Jay was huge, which always helped.

"Did you see the young lad in the tiger print tee shirt?" Jay looked through the glass of the front doors, and pointed to him.

One of the black doormen was standing next to an alcove, which was set back into the wall. It had a tall barstool inside it for the doormen to sit on when things were quiet. Above the stool was a wooden shelf. Jay spotted two mugs of steaming coffee on the shelf and a stack of old bodybuilding magazines, and some newspapers.

"I can see him, why what's the problem?" the doorman next to the stool said moving away from the alcove.

"I've just called the police, and barred him from over the Phallic Palace across the canal. He's dealing fake Ecstasy tablets, real nasty stuff, put two young girls in the general hospital last week. He's bad news, him and his mates, you'll have the law all over you if you don't get rid of him," Jay lied through his teeth.

The black doormen eyed Jay suspiciously from behind their mirrored sunglasses, and then looked at each other.

"Let's get them out, we don't need the police searching the place," one of them said. The second bouncer nodded and pulled open the door, sliding his huge shoulders through the gap. His partner nodded a silent thank you to Jay, and then followed his colleague into the club.

Jay took two steps backward, manoeuvring his huge frame to the entrance of the bouncer's alcove. He pulled his jacket up at the back and removed the nine millimetre Berretta from his waistband, and hid it beneath the stack of bodybuilding magazines.

He noticed with interest that a one-time Mr Olympia winner from Warrington, Walter O'Malley was posing on the front cover. Jay knew him well and had trained in his gym for a while. He took the magazine and stuffed it into his jacket with a mind to read it later, and then placed the rest of them on top of the pile that was hiding the gun.

He stepped away from the reggae club and walked toward the footbridge. On the other side of the canal bridge Jay saw Danny Holley and Brendon walking out of the alleyway laughing; they high fived each other and went back inside the Phallic Palace. Jay crossed the footbridge quickly, and halfway across he dropped the silencer into the murky brown water; with a dull plop it disappeared. He walked toward the alleyway but stopped when something on the floor near the edge of the canal caught his eye. There was a mobile phone on the cobbles, the screen was flashing on and off, bright green, and it vibrated gently alerting its missing owner that someone was calling. Jay bent down and picked it up. There was no one around close enough to see. He looked at the flashing screen and smiled. The name of the caller was Omar.

# CHAPTER 16

# WESTBROOK/ VIGILANTE

He heard the distant engine noise change as the vehicle was put into gear, and then saw two beams of light penetrating the darkness as the target switched on the headlights. The beams swung left to right across the cinema car park as the black Porsche Cayenne headed toward the narrow service road, which led away from the cul-de-sac. He reached the back of the cinema and headed for the rear fire escape door, and slid his fingernails under the metal bevel which ran down the middle, acting as a weather seal. The door had been left so that it looked closed, but it had not been locked, and when he tugged gently on the bevel the door clicked open. He entered the long dark passageway which was situated at the rear of the cinema, leading to the projection booths at the back of the auditoriums, and then turned to look back to the service road. His knee clicked and gave way, and he grabbed the doorframe to stop himself from falling. The Porsche was less than fifty yards from the explosive device in the bushes.

He took a cylindrical remote from his pocket; it looked like a battery, and he placed his thumb over the button at the top. The Porsche pulled almost level with the bushes when he pressed the button and closed the cinema doors at the same time triggering the IED, or 'improvised explosive device' as the British press called them. Military personnel called them IFD's or improvised formed devices, which was the more descriptive name for this type of bomb. He had used a thick piece of steel, cut into a square, which had once been part of a salad bar in a restaurant, as a base, and then he'd tacked a two foot section of a car exhaust pipe to it at a perpendicular angle.

The exhaust pipe was then packed with a home-made explosive material, which was popular with Britain's modern Islamic terrorists. Hydrogen peroxide, which is a hair bleach, and brown cooking flour, when mixed together in the correct quantity make a powerful explosive material. The London tube and bus bombings on the seventh of July 2007, which killed over fifty commuters from all walks of life, were a sad endorsement of how effective it could be.

He knew only too well how to utilise its potential. The open end of the exhaust pipe was packed with a conical copper lump, which he had hammered into shape using every day plumbing pipe.

The effect on the Porsche was similar to the impact delivered by any other military road side device. The explosive material causes a devastating blast wave, which can only escape its confined space in one direction, toward the copper lump. The copper projectile is then propelled at six thousand feet per second toward the target vehicle, which in this case belonged to Rashid Ahmed. At that point the combined speed and density of the copper means that it can easily penetrate armour plate, so the Porsche wasn't really a challenge. It ripped through the metal door like it was made from rice paper, flattening the projectile on impact, and making it both fatter and flatter. Then the red hot softened metal bounced around inside the Porsche turning the driver into so much flesh and blood splatter that it took the forensic units three days to bag it all. The force of the blast had buckled the Porsche in half lengthways, making it impossible to open any doors or windows. It was only dental recognition that identified the driver as Mrs Mira Rashid Ahmed.

# CHAPTER 17

# MANCHESTER

"Hello, where have you been man? I've been trying to ring you for an hour, init," the voice of the caller said, when Jay answered the cell phone that he had found on the floor.

"Am I speaking to Omar?" Jay asked laughing, and he wandered toward the alleyway at the side of the Phallic Palace.

"No, I'm using Omar's phone, init, who is this?" the voice replied angrily, confusion made the man's voice rise in pitch.

"Oh sorry, I've not explained have I? I found the phone on the floor; do you know who it belongs to by any chance?" Jay goaded.

"It's Lewis's phone man, init, where did you find the phone at?"

"I found it on the floor," Jay pretended to be thick.

"Where did you find the phone on the floor man?" the voice spoke slowly.

"In Manchester, I've found it on the floor in Manchester," Jay bit the back of his hand trying not to laugh.

"Are you winding me up man? Put Lewis on the phone man," the voice became angry again.

"I can't I'm sorry," Jay carried on enjoying the charade.

"Why not?"

"He's a bit tied up at the moment I'm afraid," Jay choked back a snigger.

"What about Michael man, is he with Lewis, init?" the man was becoming frustrated again. He still wasn't sure if his colleagues were just drunk somewhere, messing him about on the phone.

"Michael has got a really bad headache man, init," Jay tried to put on a strained Jamaican accent goading the caller even further.

"Who is this man, and all your bullshit? Put Michael on the phone right now man," the caller shouted down the phone.

"I really can't do that because he has a terrible headache, you see I put a nine millimetre bullet through his brain, and you can tell Omar that his days are well and truly numbered," Jay cut the call off, and then punched three numbers into the phone, nine, nine, nine.

"Hello emergency, which service do you require?"

"Police please," Jay stepped into the darkness of the alleyway.

"Hello Police emergency, how can we help?"

"I want to report a shooting on Canal Street, there was a fight outside Marley's bar and the bouncers dragged a man down the alleyway next to the Phallic Palace, and then there was a gunshot, send the police quickly please," Jay cut the call off, and then hit the 'power off' button, making the cell untraceable.

# CHAPTER 18

# THE TERRORIST TASK FORCE

John Tankersley was the lead officer of the Terrorist Task Force. He was an ex-special forces' operative, selected to head up a taskforce which had been formed to combat the growth of international terrorism. They were neither police nor military, and they answered directly to the Minister of Defence. Their brief was to identify terrorist cells and remove them from existence, by whatever means necessary. John Tankersley was an eighteen stone fighting machine, trained in mixed martial arts, and a natural marksman and weapons expert. Everyone that worked with him called him 'Tank'.

Tank had been stationed in Liverpool with the Terrorist Task Force since 1991. As a younger man he had completed a six-year stint in the British Army and was almost immediately sent to serve in Northern Ireland. He was quickly selected for a position with Special Forces before joining a mixed task force that combined military personnel with civilian law enforcement officers. Tank had joined the armed services as a seventeen-year-old boy just out of high school. He was always a well-built young man, naturally bigger and stronger than most boys his age, and he was picked for the army boxing team. Tank was a fit young soldier and he quickly became a talented pugilist. In his first competitive bout he had come up against a much older opponent from the Paratroops regiment. British Paratroops regiments have a fearsome reputation and the men that serve in those divisions are fiercely proud of their regiments. The boxing matches that were organised between different regiments held a lot of kudos, and regimental pride is always at stake. Despite his strength, Tank was not expected to win. His opponent was bigger, stronger and more talented. The fight was held over six three minute rounds and Tank had stood toe to toe with his bigger opponent every round, not appearing to feel the blows from the heavier man. No matter what combinations the talented paratrooper hit Tank with he couldn't make any head way against the younger soldier.

"It's like firing a pea shooter at a fucking tank! I've hit him with my best shots and he's still standing." his opponent had said after the third round. That was it. The nickname stuck, Tank.

The nickname suited him more now that he was older than ever before. Tank had become a keen martial arts exponent trained in Thai-boxing and Brazilian wrestling. The effects of combining the powerful kicks and punches of Muay-Thai kickboxing, with the lethal chokeholds and lock techniques of Brazilian Jujitsu were devastating. John Tankersley was a one-man demolition squad. He had lifted weights three times a week religiously since leaving school and had increased his muscle mass since joining the Army. His shaved head and muscular physique had an intimidating effect on most of the criminals he encountered. His Glock 9mm scared the rest.

The uniformed police division had called the Terrorist Task Force in to investigate the incident at Westbrook, as soon as they realised that it was a roadside bomb that had caused the explosion. Forensic teams had already cordoned off the area by the time Tank and his team arrived at the scene.

"What are all those people doing there?" Tank asked as he climbed out of his black Shogun.

He was pointing toward a crowd of about a hundred people who were milling about near the back of the cinema, watching the police process the scene. Tank checked his watch. It was half past one in the morning, and a little late for a group of passersby to be gathering.

"They're the cinema goers from the late show, which finished just after midnight," a uniformed officer greeted him and answered his question.

"Why haven't you cleared the area?" Tank asked grumpily. He couldn't tolerate incompetence.

"All the cars on the car park belong to them, customers and staff. We didn't know if you would need to keep them here for forensics or not, so we asked them to wait," the officer shrugged, a bit put out by the big man's attitude.

"I can see from here that the blast came from those bushes that are charred at the end of the car park," Tank pointed again.

The bushes adjacent to the destroyed Porsche were illuminated by spotlights, which had been brought in by forensic teams, and they were clearly burnt. The officer looked at the bushes and then looked back at Tank, blankly.

"Whoever set the detonator walked past all those cars toward the cinema, therefore they're evidence. Get rid of all those people. Give them a receipt for their vehicles, and tell them to go home, and do it right now please," Tank brushed past the uniformed officer and headed to the back of his Shogun.

He was met at the rear by his colleague Grace Farrington, who was of West Indian decent. Grace was currently one of only two female members of the Terrorist Task Force, and she was Tank's best agent. She looked concerned as he approached her. The black skin on her forehead was creased into a frown. Her beauty still struck Tank whenever he saw her, even now after all the years that they had been fellow agents and lovers.

"What are you frowning at? You'll get wrinkles doing that," He pushed her gently as she stood on one leg whilst pulling on a white paper forensic suit. She nearly toppled over and punched him on his massive bicep.

"I'm looking at the state of the Porsche," she replied, nodding toward the mangled wreck.

"It's bent completely in half by the blast, an absolutely classic sign of an 'explosive formed device', I would hazard at a guess," Tank picked up another paper suit and sat on the tailgate while he pulled it on over his clothes.

"I haven't seen damage like that anywhere outside of Afghanistan, have you?" Grace asked.

"No, not even in Northern Ireland, it's definitely Iranian technology similar to the devices they're using in Iraq, only more powerful," Tank answered.

There was nothing new about roadside bombs, but there certainly was something new about devices that could take out an armoured battle tank. Iranian militias had developed the formed devices, and then passed on the technology to Iraqi insurgents and the Afghanistan Taliban fighters.

"What are your first thoughts?" she asked, zipping up the front of her suit and pulling up the hood.

"If we can identify who the target was, then we have a good chance of identifying the bombers," Tank said. He reached into the trunk and grabbed two mag-lights, handing one to Grace.

"Let's go and see what we're dealing with then."

They approached the wreckage, which was now screened off from the public's view by canvas screens. The spotlights cast a stark light illuminating the crumpled vehicle and forming eerie shadows beyond it. Graham Libby, the head forensic advisor for the taskforce saw them coming and walked to meet them on the periphery of the crime scene.

"What do you know so far?" Grace asked, looking at the Porsche with an expert eye, searching for clues all the time they spoke.

"There's a stainless steel base plate in those bushes there," Graham Libby pointed beyond the wreck.

"I noticed the bushes are burnt," Tank added.

"Yes they are, and the plate is buckled. There is what appears to be the remnant of a welded exhaust pipe attached to it, and a remote detonator manufactured from a garage door activator," he explained.

"How do you know it's from a garage door?" Grace asked.

"It's still intact, with the manufacturer's name on it. They are made predominantly to activate up and over garage doors for the domestic market," the scientist enjoyed putting the puzzle together.

"What's the range of the remote then?" Tank mused, looking around for a convenient place to detonate the bomb from.

"Probably a few hundred yards or more," he answered.

"That gives us a wide search area," Grace said.

"I think they could have been in a vehicle, parked on the car park, detonated the device and then left quickly, no witnesses and no residual evidence. All we have is the device itself and the target vehicle," Graham Libby explained.

"What information do we have on the target?" Tank asked.

"It's a leased vehicle registered to a notorious financial institution, which has dominated the news headlines of late," the scientist explained smiling at his cryptic description.

"Rashid Ahmed?" Tank didn't seem too surprised by the news.

"You don't seem surprised," Libby noted.

"We interviewed him a few weeks back about allegations of arms dealing, but there wasn't enough to make anything stick at the time. We investigated him and I remember one of his properties was in this area, so I guessed that he could have something to do with it," Tank approached the mangled wreck and shone his mag-light inside, trying to find something that would confirm the victim's identity. There was nothing distinguishable left intact.

"There are two more crime scenes in the town centre, I'll have to move on to them when we have finished here," Graham Libby played his trump information card.

"What?" it had the desired effect, as Tank looked puzzled, and so did Grace.

"An estate car was used to transport gas canisters and other firebomb making paraphernalia into the town centre, and then it was rigged to explode simultaneously with the head office of a certain bank," the scientist explained.

"Rashid Ahmed's Blackstallion finance?" Grace was intrigued.

"Exactly, I'm thinking that it was a decoy to get Rashid into his car at night when the service road was deserted," Graham Libby held out his hands like a magician ending a card trick.

"Now that would take some planning," Tank looked at Grace, almost impressed by the complexity of the plot.

"It also indicates a bomber with a conscience," Grace added.

"I don't follow that," the scientist said.

"What Grace means is that to go to those lengths to ensure that the target vehicle was the only one on the road, indicates that our bomber didn't want to risk any collateral damage," Tank filled in the gaps.

"Our bomber must have wanted Rashid dead, desperately to risk an operation this complex," Grace speculated.

"This could have been carried out simply by one man, providing the preparation was immaculate," Tank said. He knew that a plan like this would take the training and knowhow that only a handful of Special Forces trained operatives possessed.

"I think we are looking at a Special Ops unit," Graham Libby speculated.

"What, operating in the United Kingdom? Absolutely no

chance," Tank snorted in a derisory fashion. The thought had occurred to him, but he had dismissed it just as quickly.

"Why not? It wouldn't be the first time a foreign national has been assassinated on our soil," Graham Libby came back strong, remembering that it was only twelve months since a Russian exile had been poisoned with a radioactive substance in his cup of tea.

"No it isn't, but look at the planning here. Whoever set this operation up was making sure that no one else got injured in the blast," Tank countered.

"Tank is right, a foreign Special Ops team wouldn't give a monkey's who got injured. They would have taken him out and been out of the country before we found him, but this was set up to draw him out of his home, after dark, when no one else was around," Grace joined in, agreeing with Tank.

"So that only leaves us with a few million people with the motive to kill him," Graham Libby said, referring to the adverse news coverage that Rashid's bank had received.

"Well if you play with fire," Grace said.

"Then you get burned," Tank finished it off.

"It'll take us a couple of days to confirm who your victim is, but it seems to be clear that this isn't a random attack. It is a well planned, well executed, targeted attack carried out with military precision and there-in lies the conundrum ladies and gentlemen," Graham Libby said.

# CHAPTER 19

# WARRINGTON POLICE STATION/ TERRY NICK

Terry Nick sat in a stinking cell in Warrington's Victorian built police station. The cell was twelve feet long by six feet wide, fitted with a stone cot bed and a stainless steel toilet pan. The cot had a thin rubber coated mattress on it, which stank of urine. The smell in the cell was almost overwhelming when he had first walked into it, but its noxious effect was wearing off now. He had been sat in the cell for nearly six hours now, without so much as a drink of water being brought to him. The explosion at Westbrook had taken all the on duty police officers out of the station, leaving only a skeleton staff to guard the prisoners that were already occupying cells in the custody unit. Of course none of the current prisoners knew what was going on across town.

Terry had spent more nights in these cells than he cared to remember, usually as a result of assault charges following trouble in one club or another. Few of the charges had stuck over the years, but the inconvenience of being held in custody for twenty four hours was still irritating. He looked at his watch, and then realised that the police had taken it from him when they booked him in. A flash of frustrated anger shot through his troubled mind and he stood up and kicked the heavy metal door. The pain in his toes screamed up his leg and he grabbed for the injured digits. The police had also taken his boots from him, kicking a metal door with just bare socks as protection was not clever. He hopped back to the cot and cursed under his breath, while he rubbed his injured toes. There were footsteps coming toward his cell door, and he stopped and listened for a moment. The metal hatch clunked open and a face that he didn't recognise appeared.

"Any chance of a brew?" Terry shouted.

The hatch clunked shut again, and the footsteps walked away from his cell door, disappointment set in.

The only positive thing that he could take from the experience was the fact that he hadn't been at liberty to organise a premature retaliatory hit on the Somali Yardies, or whoever they were. He had plenty of time to think things over while he sweated in his cell. Two of the Brigade men had been put under surveillance and then targeted in a hideous attack, designed to send a message to their organisation that the Manchester gang meant business. They wanted to take over the Brigade's door contracts in Manchester city centre, which equated to less than five percent of their financial income. Although the Brigade fronted an extreme right wing politically active organisation, it was the business side of the organisation which allowed it to function. The contracts in Iraq and Afghanistan wouldn't last forever. The Americans and the British couldn't wait to get their troops out of there, which meant that the domestic security business had to be protected at all costs. The Brigade relied on its hardcore membership for its existence, and their hardcore members relied on being employed by Brigade Security Ltd. If the organisation ever had to rely solely on the subs paid by affiliates and fringe members, then they would cease to exist.

Terry Nick had time to stop being angry, and to think like a businessman in charge of a multi-million pound company, which essentially he was. All their door contracts were legally binding rolling twelve month agreements. The only get out clause for the customer was if the Brigade acted in a manner which brought the premises into disrepute, or if they lost their licence to operate as a security guard agency. The clubs that the Brigade monitored were trouble free, and their customers overlooked their political agenda because they were guaranteed to remain so. Brigade security didn't allow anyone to peddle drugs of any description, except the dealers who paid them a hefty tax to ply their trade. This system was highly illegal however if drug supplies were not controlled and restricted then it became a free for all, so it was tolerated by the club owners, and ignored by the police drug squads, in exchange for information from time to time.

In the cold light of day, sat in his cell there was no crisis. Brigade Security Ltd had been transformed from an established and somewhat respected doormen agency, which outperformed any of their opposition, into a private mercenary army supplying well trained soldiers to allied governments, including their own. Responding to the horror of the previous evening's events with violence would ultimately result in the Brigade losing men and their core business interests, which he couldn't allow. The gang that had attacked them were ruthless, and there was no doubt in his mind that they wouldn't just walk away and leave them alone. No small drug ring had tried to move into the city centre with such audacity in the three decades that Terry Nick had worked on the doors, which meant that something had changed to affect the equilibrium.

Six hours sweating in a urine stinking cell had cleared his mind and allowed him to think clearly and rationally. The difference had to be that a new ambitious leader had established himself as the new boss in Moss Side, a ruthless killer that was now looking to expand his drug business. Terry Nick was going to offer the police as much information as he could dig up from his wide circle of informants, as a public display of cooperation. Behind the scenes he was going to behead the snake that had bitten them, and redress the balance of things. At least that was his plan.

# CHAPTER 20
# JAY/ CANAL ST. MANCHESTER

Jay looked at his watch when he heard the first siren in the distance. Six minutes had passed by since he'd called the emergency services. He smiled and walked into the Phallic Palace. Danny Holley and Brendon were lurking by the front doors, still on edge about the kidnapped Yardie in their van. Brendon was making exaggerated chewing actions, as if he had a golf ball in his mouth instead of gum. He was glaring around the busy dance floor almost daring someone to step out of line. Jay chuckled to himself at Brendon's attitude. It reminded him of his younger self.

"Brendon have you still got your lockup in Warrington?" Jay asked, thinking that he had better get the Somali moved before the police swamped the area, but not wanting to panic the younger Brigade men into making a mistake.

"Yes, I keep my motorbike in there," Brendon perked up, as he loved to talk about his motorbike.

"I'll cover you here, get that van tucked away in your lockup, and make sure the Yardie can't escape, we'll sort him out later," Jay grabbed his arm firmly and guided him toward the back of the club.

"What's all the panic about Jay? He's not going anywhere," Brendon hated being ordered about, and he didn't want to miss out on the action.

"The police are on their way Brendon, now get that fucking van out away from the city centre, and do it now," Jay glared down at Brendon and saw the flicker of anger in the younger man's eyes, but he also saw fear.

Brendon thought better of antagonising a Brigade General and snatched his arm away from Jay's grip. He stormed off toward the fire doors at the back of the club. Jay breathed out a sigh of relief and looked around the club. Danny Holley sidled up to him, not wanting to be left out of the action.

"Where's Brendon going?" he asked annoyingly over the sound of the blaring music.

"He's moving the van," Jay turned toward him.

"Why, what's the rush?" Danny looked put out that he hadn't been consulted before one of his men was sent home.

"Shut up Danny," Jay said.

"Don't tell me to shut up," Danny puffed out his chest and sucked in his beer belly, but Jay wasn't paying any attention to him, he was looking around the busy bar area.

"Shut up Danny, who is dealing in here?" Jay glared at him.

"Tom Welsh, he's over there," Danny flushed red with anger and pointed to a fat man standing next to the gents toilets.

Jay walked through the crowd quickly toward the dealer. The dealer wasn't familiar with him as Jay usually handled the dealers in Liverpool. The dealer saw the massive skinhead making his way in a bee line for him, and expected the worst.

"Hello mate I'm Tom, Danny knows that I'm working here," he said as soon as Jay was within hearing distance.

"Good for you, now I need you to do something for me, and we'll forget tonight's rent," Jay grabbed his arm in a vice like grip and pushed him toward the front door.

"Okay mate, there's no need to drag me, what do you need me to do?" the fat drug dealer complained as he was practically carried through the crowd.

"Stand near the footbridge, and when the police arrive tell them that you saw the bouncers from Marley's bar dragging a black bloke down the alleyway," Jay said and pushed him out of the door.

"You're fucking joking aren't you, I'm a dealer," the fat man shook his arm free and faced Jay.

"I'll make sure that you never deal again anywhere my fat friend, now do as you're told and stand by the bridge," Jay pushed the unwilling man away from the club as the first police cars screamed down the canal banks on both sides.

The policemen were members of an armed response team,

and the only unit that could enter a potential gun crime scene, until it had been declared safe for their fellow officers to attend. Two vehicles screeched to a halt and one of the officers barked a series of orders to the others. Three officers approached the baffled doormen outside Marley's reggae bar with their guns drawn.

Jay couldn't hear what was being said across the canal, but within seconds the two burly black bouncers were pinned up against the wall being frisked. Two more police cars arrived and uniformed officers entered the reggae bar, within minutes the music had been turned off and their customers were being processed outside. There were three uniformed policemen taking names and addresses, checking ID's and asking questions.

Jay watched with interest as two of the armed response team made a quick search of the bouncer's alcove. Voices were raised and several more officers ran to the alcove when the Berretta was discovered underneath the stack of magazines. The black doormen began to protest that they knew nothing about any guns, but they were already handcuffed against the wall. Jay couldn't hear the words but he could see them becoming agitated. One of them panicked and tried to run. He only succeeded in making it three yards before a swarm of uniformed officers were on him, batons drawn. Jay grimaced as the baton blows rained down on the bouncer's arms and legs, beating him into submission. He could hear the black man shouting for them to stop but the beating went on about sixty seconds longer than was necessary, especially since the man was already cuffed. A blue custody van arrived on the scene and the two doormen were manhandled into the back by half a dozen over eager policemen.

"What's going on Jay?" Danny Holley was on his shoulder again.

"I'm not sure mate to be honest, looks like something has gone off at Marley's bar," Jay lied, the less said the better.

"I'm not fucking stupid Jay, what's happening?"

"Well if you're not stupid mate, then you can tell me what is going on, because I haven't got a Scooby doo," Jay walked away toward the front door and nudged it open with his knee.

Police cars were manoeuvring around the side of the Phallic Palace, forming a metal barrier between the nosey public and the entrance to the alleyway. There were three officers huddled together discussing their next move when another one of their colleagues approached them, leading Tom Welsh, the fat drug dealer with him.

The drug dealer pointed to the alleyway as he explained what he had allegedly witnessed. The policemen took his details and made a fuss of thanking him.

"What is Tom Welsh doing talking to the dibbles?" Danny asked Jay. Jay ignored him.

One of the officers organised a search team consisting of six uniformed policemen, and they set off down the alleyway using long metal torches to illuminate their progress. Jay lit a cigarette and waited for the inevitable gruesome discovery, and sure enough before he had smoked it halfway down the body of a black man had been discovered in a skip with a bullet through his brain.

# CHAPTER 21
# TERRY NICK/ ALAN WILLIAMS

Tank was sat behind a mirrored glass window watching Terry Nick talking to his legal representative. He recognised the Brigade leader. The Terrorist Task Force had the Brigade under permanent watch, as did the security services, MI5 and MI6. Right wing groups like the Brigade were becoming more and more prevalent across the British Isles as the country's education and health services buckled under the weight of immigrant numbers. Integration was becoming a myth as religious and ethnic ghettos appeared and began to fester in every major town and city. Racism was becoming an everyday fact of life as resentment grew, and organisations like the Brigade fed on the hatred. Racist attacks were on the increase, and were becoming better orchestrated every day. There had been discoveries of weapons grade explosives made, uncovered by covert agents who had infiltrated right wing groups. Tank feared that it was only a matter of time before material of this type fell into the wrong hands undetected.

The door to the interview room opened and two plain clothed detectives entered. They both looked dishevelled, collars unbuttoned and ties hanging loosely down at odd angles. The officers were unshaven and red eyed, obviously well past the end of one shift, and a considerable way through the next. They didn't speak as one of them ripped the cellophane wrapper from an interview cassette, and slotted it into a recording machine. The detective pressed play and record.

"This is the recording of an interview with Terrence Nickolas, present in the room are detectives Bill Smith, and John Jones, and legal brief," the detective nodded to the lawyer, indicating that he had to confirm his presence.

"Alan Williams," the lawyer said, running his hand through his thinning hair.

"Terry, I can call you Terry can't I?" the detective began, trying to build a rapport.

Terry didn't respond to the detective's feeble attempt to break the ice. He stared at the policemen.

"We have spoken to the doctors at the hospital, and your friends are both in intensive care. One of them is undergoing reconstructive surgery to reattach his hand," Jones tried to make a connection.

"What can you tell us about the men that attacked them?" Smith asked.

Terry looked to his brief, and he nodded for him to answer the question.

"There were two cars, both two door hatchbacks, both customised with big bore exhausts and boom box stereos," Terry began to explain the evening's events.

"What about the men?"

"They were all tall, all skinny and all black, probably Somali," Terry said.

"What makes you think that they were Somali?" Jones interrupted.

"I travelled to Kenya on holiday a few years back, all the security guards were from Somali because they're tall I think. They have distinctive facial features," he explained.

"Anything else?"

"The gunman had gold teeth," Terry added.

"It's all a bit vague Terry," Smith said.

"What do you mean vague?" Terry snarled. "It was dark and the headlights hid them from view, all we could see was silhouettes, and the next thing there was a fucking Mach-10 blasting bricks off the building. What should I have been doing, taking notes?"

"Calm down Terry. We're trying to catch the men that killed Mandy Bates, and hurt your friends," Jones interrupted trying to calm things down.

Terry looked at detective Jones and sat back in his chair. His lawyer placed a hand on his arm trying to settle him.

"You were close to Mandy weren't you?" Smith enquired.

Terry sat bolt upright again and glared at the detective. His lawyer put his hand on his arm again, but he was coiled like spring.

"What's that supposed to mean?" Terry asked, taken aback by the inference.

"Just exactly what I said, people have told us you two were close," the detective shrugged indifferently. He was probing for a reaction, looking for Terry's weak spots.

"No comment," Terry fastened down the hatches.

"Do you think she was shot to get at you personally?" Jones pushed.

"No comment," Terry was finished with cooperating, before they had even got started.

Detective Smith realised that the interview was going nowhere. Everyone was tired and tetchy, so he began to change tack.

"Look Terry, we're trying to get to the bottom of why anyone would attack you and your men, killing Mandy Bates in the process," the detective coaxed.

"In my business you make a lot of enemies, as you well know, and you know who most of them are without me telling you," Terry said wearily.

"Fair enough that's true, but why this tonight? Why so brutal Terry, there must have been some reason?" the detective asked, opening another button on his shirt. He rolled up his sleeves.

"It's a brutal world detective, someone wants to move in on our business interests," Terry explained.

"Okay, I want to turn your attention to another issue," the detective placed two photographs in front of Terry Nick. His lawyer slid them closer and studied them intently.

Terry sat back and folded his arms, raising the barriers again.

"Do you recognise these places?"

"No comment," Terry didn't recognise them, but they seemed familiar somehow.

"This is the Blackstallion bank in the town centre," Smith pointed to a picture of the remains of an entrance doorway, reduced to a gaping black maw. The mangled remnants of a double metal doorframe lay on the pavement twenty yards away from its previous home.

Terry chewed a nail on his little finger ignoring the detective.

The policeman pushed the picture closer to Terry angrily. Alan Williams spoke for the first time during the interview.

"My client has no knowledge of this and we will not answer any questions relating to it, on the grounds that he may incriminate himself," the lawyer quoted the law book verbatim.

"What about this?" Jones pointed to a picture of a twisted car wreck.

"No comment," Terry said without looking at the photograph.

"This vehicle belonged to the owner of this bank," Jones pointed to both photographs in turn.

"No comment."

"We think that someone firebombed the bank in the knowledge that the owner would be contacted, and then blew his car to bits," Detective Smith made wide circles in the air with his hands, depicting an explosion.

"No comment."

"Are you actually going to ask my client a question?" the lawyer interjected.

"We are investigating an act of terrorism against a Muslim businessman Mr Williams and we are giving your client the opportunity to divulge any information that he may be in possession of," the detective pressed the point, never taking his eyes from the Brigade leader, looking for the tell tale signs of guilt.

"No comment."

"We think that the perpetrator has a military background, and probably belongs to a racist organisation like the 18th Brigade," Smith continued.

"That is not a question detective," the lawyer made a note on his file.

"We will need a list of all your active members Terry," Jones jumped into the fray.

"That information is protected by the data protection act," Alan Williams didn't even look up from his note making as he spoke.

"Not if the information protected is, or becomes, part of an investigation which could lead to the apprehension of terrorists Mr Williams," the detective countered.

"My client is not a terrorist detective, and the fact that he is here helping with your enquiries reinforces the irrefutable fact that he was elsewhere when these incidents occurred," the lawyer looked straight into the detective's tired eyes. They were getting nowhere. The police were on a fishing trip, but nothing was biting.

"We have not accused your client of anything other than being in possession of information which could benefit a murder inquiry," the detective spat back, slamming his pen down on the table.

"I think the detective is getting pissed off now," Terry turned to his lawyer sarcastically.

"I think so too, you don't have answer any more questions unless they charge you with something," the lawyer picked up his papers and started to pack them away. The police detectives looked to each other for inspiration but none was forthcoming. Their silence said everything that Alan Williams needed to hear.

"Then if there's nothing further then I must insist that you release my client immediately," the lawyer tried for checkmate.

"Your client is going nowhere until we get some answers," The detective slammed his hand on the desk.

"Oops! Calm down now officer, you'll do yourself a mischief if you're not careful," Terry sniggered at him.

The policeman stood up quickly, his chair scraped noisily across the floor. Terry Nick jumped up to meet him and the two men glared at each other across the table. Alan Williams placed his arm on Terry's shoulder and whispered into his ear.

"Don't give them any excuse to hold you."

The door opened and in walked a heavily decorated police chief. Terry didn't recognise his rank, but he looked important. The two detectives blushed red and looked perturbed at the senior officer's interruption,

"Do you have anything to charge Mr Nicolas with?" he asked curtly, showing no emotion at all.

"Chief Constable, sir we are interviewing Mr Nicolas as a key witness to a violent murder late last night."

"I asked you if you were going to charge Mr Nicolas with anything detective," the chief flushed angrily, his hands shaking slightly.

"Not at this stage sir."

"Your client is free to leave," the chief spoke to Alan Williams, completely ignoring the Brigade leader. Terry smirked across the table at the silent detectives.

"But sir, we haven't finished questioning the witness."

"Are you deaf detective?"

"No sir."

"Then see Mr Nickolas out of the station and do it now," the chief nodded at the solicitor and slammed the interview room door behind him.

Tank watched the scene from behind the two-way glass and turned to Major Timms.

"What just happened there then?" he said confused and amused at the same time. He hadn't expected anything much to be gleaned from the interview in the first place. The Brigade seemed to be a tight run ship nowadays.

"I think someone further up the pecking order has applied some pressure, don't you?"

"They must be very high in the pecking order because that was the Chief Constable of Cheshire," Tank remarked.

"Do you think he was withholding anything?"

"What about the roadside bomb?"

"Yes, and the bank," the Major added.

"No, I don't think he knew anything about it. His face didn't even flinch when they showed him the pictures," Tank answered rubbing his shaved head with a big hand.

They watched slightly bemused as the Brigade leader left the room with his solicitor, followed by two angry detectives.

# CHAPTER 22

# LEWIS

Lewis woke up in a very distressed state. His mouth was so dry that he couldn't swallow, and when he tried he was gagging on something that had been stuffed into his mouth. His head was foggy with alcohol, and it took him several minutes to realise that he'd been bound and gagged. The sound of a diesel engine and the sensation of moving at speed indicated that he was in a vehicle, but he couldn't understand why anyone would tie him up and kidnap him. He swallowed hard and gagged again almost choking. There was the distinct taste of white spirit on the material that was in his mouth, and it was making him nauseous.

He tried to recall what had happened prior to waking up in this nightmare, but it was a drunken blur. He remembered being in a gay bar on Canal Street, because the Yardie gang that he belonged to weren't welcome in the clubs frequented by mostly black customers. They had made too many enemies within the Afro-Caribbean communities of Moss Side, especially since the arrival of Omar to the gang. It was dangerous going out into the city centre anyway, but with just two of them they daren't risk Marley's bar or the other reggae clubs. In hind sight it was a mistake going to town, full-stop. The gang members had been warned that there was something big going down, and to take precautions, but the call of women and beer had been too tempting to resist.

Lewis had been born in the coastal town of Marka, one hundred miles south of Mogadishu, Somalia. He had been brought up as strict Muslim by poverty stricken parents, who struggled daily to feed their eight children. At ten years of age he had been taken to the capital city, Mogadishu by his father, and sold to a militia for three bags of rice and some powdered milk. The militias were always on the lookout for new recruits. In return for pledging allegiance to the militia the young recruits were fed daily and given an endless supply of drug weeds, which they chewed every day giving them a cocaine type high. It was here that he'd first encountered Omar.

Omar was older than Lewis and already had a reputation as a cold blooded assassin. He feared no man, which is a valuable attribute in a cauldron of violence like Mogadishu. As time went by more and more rival militias had a price on Omar's head. His notoriety was becoming a liability to the entire militia, which wasn't the strongest outfit in the city by a long chalk. Eventually the militia leaders realised that Omar was worth more dead than he was alive and they betrayed him by setting him up to be taken by a neighbouring gang. If captured he would have been tortured to death as an example to others. Lewis caught wind of the plot to betray his older comrade, and he warned him of the conspiracy. They both left the city under the cover of darkness and headed for their new life in Britain. Lewis looked forward to a new life, a life of peace. He couldn't have been further from the truth. Omar had ambitious plans and a driving desire to achieve his goals regardless of how they affected anyone else. Lewis was dragged along in his wake.

Once in the country they headed for the Somali community in Moss Side, and soon joined their ranks. Lewis was mesmerised by the city centre and its night life. He had never seen white women in the flesh and he became obsessed by them, partying at every opportunity. While Lewis was becoming a social animal, Omar was becoming an animal of different type. The two men drifted apart as they established their relative positions within the gang, Omar as the new ruthless leader, and Lewis as a fringe member, rarely given anything important to do.

Lewis realised with a jolt that Michael had been winding up the skinhead doormen all night. He had joined in himself although he wasn't sure why. There was a foggy memory of going outside to answer his phone, and then he recalled a concussive blow to the back of the neck. Now he was trussed up like a prize pig, and he had no idea where he was being taken, or by whom. There was one thing that he had learned from his experiences in Mogadishu, and that was when someone was kidnapped and tied up, it rarely had a happy ending.

# CHAPTER 23
# TERRY NICK/ JAY

The sun had been up a few hours when Jay eventually woke up. He was still tired. The police found the Yardie's dead body in a skip down the alleyway and had shutdown everything on Canal Street. Jay had slipped through the back doors of the club and headed for his motorbike, leaving Danny Holley to coordinate their men in Manchester. Everywhere had been quiet, and there were no other sightings of any of the Somali gang members.

There was a loud banging on the front door, which dragged him from a deep slumber. He stood up and wiped sleep from his eyes. In front of him there was a wide mirror fixed to the wall and he caught his reflection in the glass. Thick heavily muscled shoulders and arms, covered in tattoos supported his massive neck and shaved head. He slapped his belly and breathed in, any desire to own a six pack had been beaten down by age and a taste for beer. The loud knocking at the door began again.

He walked down the stairs stealthily, stepping lightly on the carpet with bare feet, suddenly feeling vulnerable in just his boxer shorts. Heavy bangs on the door again made him jump. There was a baseball bat positioned next to the front door, leaning against the frame in case of emergencies. It would take a brave crew to come looking for Jay, but it was not unheard of, and the audacity of the Yardies had taken everyone by surprise. He picked up the bat and held it behind his back, hidden from view by his legs. Then he slid the security chain into place. It wouldn't stop a sustained attack, but it might hold an attacker long enough for him to make a quick getaway. He took a deep breath and opened the door.

"Open the door dickhead," Terry Nick barked through the narrow gap between the frame and the door.

"Fucking hell Terry! What are you doing here?" Jay complained as he unfastened the chain and opened the door.

"I need a word in your ear," Terry growled as he pushed past him into the house.

Brendon followed Terry like a mini-me into the house, grinning like a Cheshire cat.

"Alright fatty," he sneered and patted Jay on the belly as he walked by him. Jay breathed in instinctively.

"Don't push your luck Brendon, it's too early in the morning," Jay scolded the younger man.

Jay followed Terry Nick and Brendon into the kitchen, feeling like his personal space had been invaded. Terry was filling the kettle with cold water from the tap in silence. Jay was worried as to the reason for this uninvited incursion into his home. Terry plugged the kettle in and switched it on. He opened a cupboard door and rummaged around for teabags and a sugar bowl, which he placed on the worktop next to the kettle. Then he reached in again and came out with a packet of Hobnobs. He took the first three from the top of the packet and stuffed the first one into his mouth, and then passed the biscuits to Brendon. He followed suit eating hungrily from the packet.

"Just help yourself why don't you?" Jay snatched the biscuits from Brendon and put them back into the cupboard, slamming the door shut. Brendon burst out laughing, and sprayed the kitchen with half chewed Hobnobs.

"We need to talk Jay, but we are tired, and hungry, been awake all night in the cells," Terry Nick said.

"That's fine Terry, but I'm not having this little toe-rag walking into my home and taking the piss out of me," Jay stepped toward Brendon and stabbed a chunky finger in his chest.

Brendon fronted up, but he stood a long way short of the big general, and a good three stones lighter. He would definitely have come off second best against Jay. Jay glared down at the younger skinhead, and Brendon backed down and broke his gaze, thinking better of annoying him.

"Brendon tells me that we have a surprise package in his lockup," Terry said ignoring the standoff next to him, and pouring boiling hot water into three mugs.

"That's right," Jay said, turning away from Brendon and opening the refrigerator to remove a bottle of milk.

He smelled the white liquid to confirm that it was still fresh, and then passed the bottle to the Brigade leader. As he turned toward Terry Nick, Brendon was standing directly behind him, holding his index finger to his lips and pointing through the kitchen window. Jay was confused and looked at Terry, who nodded slowly and placed his finger to his lips, in a shushing action. Brendon grabbed a post-it-note pad from the fridge, which had a small plastic pen attached to it by a coiled plastic extendable spring. He scrawled one word on the pad.

'Police! '

"I'll have two sugars in mine," Jay said looking out of the window, but he couldn't see anything untoward.

"I was questioned for three hours by detectives this morning," Terry said, adding milk to the steaming brews, as if he was talking about the weather.

"About the shooting at the Turf?" Jay played along with the charade.

Terry Nick passed out the hot tea to each of them, and slurped a mouthful of his own before replying.

"Well, they obviously wanted our witness statements, but they spent more time quizzing me about a firebomb attack at that bank in town," Terry moved his hands in a circular motion indicating that they should draw out this particular conversation.

He put down his tea and picked up the note pad and pen, and he started to scribble something that Jay couldn't see from where he was standing, so he moved closer to him, sipping his tea as he went.

"Why would they be asking you about that then?" Jay waffled.

"They seem to think that is was a racially motivated attack, and that we might know who did it," Terry continued to scribble.

'I think we were followed by a surveillance team, don't say anything about the Somalis' the note read.

"Why would they think it was us?" Brendon piped up, trying to join in the pretence, but not quite having the intelligence to carry it off.

Jay and Terry looked at each other in disbelief, shaking their heads.

"Have you had a look in the mirror lately you stupid twat?" Jay answered him. Brendon flushed bright red realising how stupid he had sounded. His hand went to touch the swastika tattoo under his right ear almost unconsciously, confirming that he looked every inch the racist thug that he was, as did all his colleagues.

"I wish we had done it," Terry nudged Jay and pointed to the notepad, "Whoever it was did a blinding job of it. They firebombed the bank and wacked the owner when he was called out to the fire. Now that is classy, well impressed I am." Terry finished writing and passed the note to Jay.

Jay read the note, nodded and started to scribble the answer to Terry's written question, while keeping up the staged conversation for the benefit of the police surveillance team.

"That would take an awful lot of planning. I don't think any of our boys could have pulled that off without someone knowing about it, do you?" Jay said.

"No way, I think they are barking up the wrong tree, but we'll have to investigate just in case, we'll need all the rotas for the last week or so, and then we can see if anyone has been absent without leave," Terry took a long gulp of tea, and read what Jay was writing.

Brendon looked on a little bored of the game now that he'd realised that it was better if he kept quiet. He picked his nose and pulled out a meaty piece of snot, which he studied closely before wiping it on the side of Jay's refrigerator.

'I have a CD of our last meeting. I'll put it on then you two fuck off out of the back door the Somali boss is called Omar, his missus lives on the fourth floor, number 43 Salford Towers, off Cross Lane. I'll meet you at the lockup in a few hours' Jay's scruffy handwriting was barely legible.

Terry nodded in the affirmative, and finished his tea with one huge gulp, and he folded the note into his jean's pocket. He patted his huge general on the back, a gesture of praise and gratitude. Jay went into his living room and flicked through some CD cases until he found the one he wanted. He looked at the label and then thought for a moment. The one underneath was more suitable. It was an interview with a reporter from the Liverpool Echo newspaper, who wanted to talk about the increase numbers of disgruntled people joining up to right wing organisations like the 18<sup>th</sup> Brigade. It was mostly himself and Terry waffling on with well prepared answers, which they had since edited for use elsewhere. He slotted it into the stereo and pressed play. Terry's voice filled the room mid sentence, explaining that the Brigade was ultimately a legitimate limited company, often maligned and blamed for any racist attacks that occurred in the north of England. Jay turned it down a touch and then went back into the kitchen. He pressed play on a cassette recorder that lived on top of the fridge. The right wing skinhead band Screwdriver burst into song, adding to the sound of the recorded interview.

Terry passed Jay his car keys, shook his hand, gave him a bear hug and slipped out of the back door. Brendon passed Jay, thought about bear hugging him, and then thought better of it. He jogged through the back yard catching up to the Brigade leader, and gave Jay thumbs up sign as he entered the alleyway at the rear. Jay closed the back door deftly and headed upstairs. He was going to get an hour's sleep while the police listened to no one. It would take at least an hour before they realised that the recording was on a repeat setting, by which time Terry would be free from surveillance, and a team would be well on the way to Salford Towers.

Omar would wish he'd stayed in Somalia.

# CHAPTER 24

# THE ARSENAL

Dano had been released from the cells in Warrington an hour before Terry Nick. He'd made a few calls and arranged for one of the Brigade members to pick him up from outside the police station. His junior colleague turned up in a dark blue Jeep Cherokee, the old model with the square bonnet. Dano opened the door and climbed into the passenger seat, rocking the vehicle as he did so with his considerable weight.

"I thought you might be hungry," his junior handed him a brown paper carryout bag from McDonalds, two Big Macs, large fries and a fried apple pie, washed down with a chocolate shake.

"You are a fucking superstar," Dano said stuffing the salty fries into his mouth with one hand, and ripping open the first Big Mac box with the other. He didn't speak for a few minutes while he chomped his way through most of the food. Quick service restaurants had become the staple diet for doormen across the country, as the burger giants started to open their doors twenty four hours a day.

"One of our informer friends in the police station called me and said that you were being released. He also said they're questioning Terry about the firebomb in town earlier on, and that a surveillance team had been sanctioned to watch us." The Brigade men had informers within the ranks of the uniformed police.

The Brigade welcomed ex-service men into their ranks, as did the police force. Many ex-army personnel shared the anti immigration ideals of the Brigade, and organisations like them. The sympathetic police officers were a constant stream of information which kept the Brigade one step ahead of the law. There were many officers disillusioned by the rising crime rates following the deluge of foreign immigrants. Political correctness gone mad had left the police handicapped when they were dealing with foreigners and the race card was played at every opportunity. Nine times out of ten suspects walked without being charged, leaving the police snowed under with useless paperwork to complete upon their release.

"They'll follow Terry, not us," Dano said with a mouthful of burger and fries.

"That's what I thought," the junior said.

"Have you heard anything from the hospital?" Dano asked.

"Yes, they're still trying to reattach Norman's hand, and Dithering is out of surgery but still in intensive care."

"I think we need to break out the weapons, before the police start tailing us," Dano crammed the last piece of Big Mac into his mouth and reached for the apple pie box.

"I agree, we'll head over there now if you want to," the younger man selected first gear and the Cherokee pulled away from the kerb, heading down the deserted street.

Dano bit into the hot apple pie and the thick sticky interior burnt his lip. It didn't deter him from taking a second bite as he removed his mobile phone from his breast pocket. He punched in two numbers, using a speed dial and then waited for the quartermaster to answer. The quartermaster was an old soldier, once a proud member of the Red Berets, 2nd Parachute Regiment. They were an elite fighting force if ever there was one. His father had seen action in the killing fields of Normandy toward the end of the Second World War, when they had been part of the biggest parachute drop of all time, dramatised in the movie 'A Bridge too Far'. The military tradition continued when he followed his father into the service, and joined his father's regiment, and then his son also followed him, and gained the prestigious Red Beret too.

The quartermaster held a large stock of the Brigade's automatic weapons in his cellar, where he lovingly stripped, cleaned, and serviced the machineguns, keeping them in excellent condition. Although he was well into his seventy third year he was still as spritely as many men twenty years his junior. His son had been part of the Brigade in its formative years, before leaving home to join the parachute regiment.

Old Jim, as he was called, kept in touch with his son's friends when he left to join the paras, and he attended some of their meetings and became involved in the organisation eventually offering a safe haven for their weapons, and a free maintenance service to boot. The Brigade kept a reasonably small arsenal in his cellar, which was used only in emergencies or for training exercises. Their training was done covertly because of Britain's strict gun laws. Old Jim shared the Brigade's racist ideals and was only too happy to help, especially because it meant he could still be around guns. Jim would be a soldier till the day he died.

He was woken from a troubled slumber by the telephone, and he recognised the caller from the illuminated display.

"Hello Dano, is there trouble, it's the middle of the night?" the quartermaster said sleepily, rubbing his tired eyes and searching for his glasses. He put them on and reached for his alarm clock to verify the time.

"Hello Jim, sorry it's so late, or early, but we need some gear"

"I gathered that, what do you need?"

"Half a dozen Uzis, five hundred rounds, and a dozen fragmentation grenades should do it Jim."

"Fucking hell Dano! Are you starting world war three or something?"

"Yes, something like that, but we didn't start it."

"Does Terry Nick know your taking the gear?" the old soldier was a stickler for protocol, and he made sure authorisation from a senior Brigade man was given before he'd hand over any of the arsenal.

"He's banged up, but he'll know as soon as he gets out Jim, we'll be thirty minutes," Dano clicked off the phone, avoiding any further argument from the old soldier. He liked Jim, and had once been good friends with his son, but he could be a real pain in the arse when anyone needed a weapon.

Jim struggled to swing his weary body out of bed, while his joints remained stiff from slumber. He pulled on a pair of loose tracksuit pants and padded into the bathroom. He sighed as he relieved himself, dark urine filling the pan, an indication that his kidneys were not working as well as they used to. Jim lifted the lid off the cistern and removed a sealed plastic bag which contained the keys to his cellar. He headed downstairs treading slowly, allowing his knees to loosen up as he descended. There was a doorway beneath the stairs which he opened to reveal a small cupboard containing his gas meter and a few carrier bags full of old books. Jim moved the carrier bags and placed them behind him in the kitchen. He rolled the frayed carpet back and exposed a brass ring pull, which he tugged, lifting up a concealed trapdoor.

The trapdoor hid a steep set of wooden stairs which descended into the gloom of a large cellar area. Jim walked down the first three steps and then felt for a light pull that was hanging from the ceiling. He pulled it, illuminating an awesome display of automatic weapons attached to the wall and laid out on the work benches. The cellar had the aroma of old wood and gun oil, mixed with polish and white spirit. The atmosphere was dry and warm, ideal for storing mechanical weaponry and avoiding dust and rust, which had cost many a soldier his life. A jammed weapon is no more use than a club in a battle zone.

Jim approached a workbench and placed a large suitcase on it. He removed an Uzi machinegun from its holding bracket on the wall, and handled it fondly as if it were a much loved pet, or a fragile antique vase rather than a lethal killing machine. He took an oil cloth and wiped the cold dull metal lovingly, wondering at its deadly beauty. The weapon slotted into a moulded inner, inside the suitcase, alongside two similar weapons. Jim repeated the process with three more machineguns, and then added a box of nine millimetre slugs, before locking the cases shut.

Jim carried the heavy cases up the cellar stairs one at a time and put them near the back kitchen door. He returned to the arsenal and used a thick moulded plastic toolbox to store a dozen fragmentation grenades. The grenades were stored beneath the workbench, kept inside a cool storage box which was designed for picnics and camping. He noted that the lid on the box next to it was on the wrong way around.

Jim looked at the box for long moments trying to remember if he had checked the contents recently, he hadn't. He was fastidious about his arsenal, and where everything was kept. None of the Brigade men came down into the cellar. When weapons were needed Jim packed them and then left them in a left luggage locker at the bus station. That way if the Brigade were ever caught in possession of illegal firearms the weapons dump would still be a secret. Years ago the Brigade lost all their firepower in one foul swoop, which taught them a harsh lesson not to put all their eggs in one basket.

Jim lifted the lid from the cool box and panic set in. He caught his breath in his chest and looked in disbelief. The Brigade had acquired six kilos of military weapons grade explosive, just a month ago. Jim had been very uncomfortable storing the material, but after some research on the internet, and some monetary persuasion he'd conceded. As he trawled through his mind for an explanation he picked up the empty box and stared into it, as if six kilos of explosive were hidden in the corner somewhere.

He shook his head searching for an explanation, but there wasn't one. Only a handful of the Brigade knew that there was cache of weapons. There were rumours about an underground arsenal, but none of them knew where it was, or about the trapdoor, or where he kept the keys. Jim sat down on a stool and continued to look open mouthed into the empty cool box, shaking his head in disbelief.

He hadn't moved it.

He hadn't mislaid it.

Someone had gained access to his house, located the keys and the hidden trapdoor, removed the explosive and returned everything to its rightful place without leaving any evidence of the incursion.

As his mind raced realisation hit home. He couldn't tell Terry Nick that the explosive was missing, presumed stolen. No one would believe his story. They would assume that he had panicked about storing it, lost his bottle and dumped it or worse still, sold it for a profit. Either way he wouldn't see another birthday, and that was a fact. The telephone rang again.

"Jim it's Dano," he had lost track of the time while he had been traumatised.

"Hello mate."

"Never mind hello mate, where the fuck are you?"

"I'll be ten minutes, I'm leaving now."

"There isn't a problem is there?"

"No.......no problem, I was stuck on the loo that's all, bad guts, you know how it is at my age," Jim tried to control his nerves.

"Yes you silly old fart, hurry up," Dano hung up impatiently.

"I am a silly old fart, you have no idea exactly what a silly old fart I really am," Jim said down the phone to no one but himself. He had that twisted sick feeling in his stomach, the one you get when you are really scared.

The only person that knew where the arsenal was, had come back from Afghanistan a year ago, and he was so badly injured that he hadn't left hospital yet.

# CHAPTER 25
# SALFORD TOWERS

Lewis felt the van come to a halt and he hoped that they would kill him quickly. The white spirit soaked rag that gagged him had caused painful blisters in his mouth, and he couldn't swallow properly. The plastic bag ties that bound his arms and legs were digging deep into his flesh, and the more he struggled the deeper they cut. He'd heard voices surrounding the van shortly before, and then the engine had been started. He felt the vibration of two passengers climbing in beside the driver before the doors were slammed shut. The journey was a mystery to him as the occupants in the front of the vehicle remained silent for the duration of the trip.

The backdoors opened and he sensed daylight entering the back of the van through his blindfold. Strong hands grabbed at his legs, dragging him out roughly. He felt fingers fumbling with his blindfold and then there was a blinding pain as his eyes tried to become adjusted to the sudden rush of light. Lewis squeezed his eyes tight, and then opened them squinting and blinking to become adjusted. He saw six men stood over him, hooded and dressed in dark clothing. They were all carrying machine pistols, which he recognised as Israeli Uzi nine millimetre weapons. As his eyes began to focus one of the men removed the stinking gag from his mouth, and he heaved, bending double and vomiting stale alcohol onto the floor, splattering six pairs of shiny combat boots.

"Dirty twat," Brendon jumped back out of vomit range.

"Shut up Brendon," Jay said through his balaclava

"I'm getting sick of you lot telling me to shut up," Brendon responded being churlish.

Jay slapped him hard across the face with the palm of his big hand. Brendon's head was knocked sideways by the force. Jay was tired and his nerves were on edge. Terry had stayed at the Brigade headquarters. He'd been released from the cells only to be informed by his men that he was under surveillance. Only a flash of brilliance from his general, Jay, had thrown the police off his trail. He had then contacted Dano and arranged to meet up with a crack team of men, armed and ready for a retaliatory attack. Terry spent all day planning the attack, waiting for the sun to go down so that they could use the darkness as an ally. Two Brigade men had been sent to the tower block earlier to make sure that Omar hadn't already left the building. They couldn't risk their business interests with open gang warfare, so this would be a one off decisive attack, aimed at beheading the Somali gang, and sending them back to selling crack on the street corners of Moss Side. He could not jeopardise their international business by being implicated in criminal activity of any kind. He intended to come up with a plan of action, and then disappear from the scene.

"Now is not the time Brendon, so shut the fuck up," Jay leaned toward the smaller man as he spoke. Brendon remained silent, but he was tempted to use the machinegun that he held tightly in his hand.

Jay saw the glint of defiance in his junior's eyes, and he knew that this was the end of the line for his young colleague. He couldn't tolerate insubordination, but he couldn't allow anyone with as much inside knowledge as Brendon had to walk away either. It was a shame, but he had seen it coming for a while now. He turned back to the trussed up Somali, who appeared to be confused by the dispute between his hooded captors.

"What's your name," Jay grabbed the Somali by the jaw and lifted his head up at an obtuse angle.

"Lewis."

"Do you know where we are?"

"No," said Lewis trying to look around, but his head was locked into place by the Brigade leader's grip.

Jay rolled his captive's head right and left, allowing him to see the tower block behind him. There were only a handful of lights still burning, as the rest of the inhabitants slept unaware of the danger lurking below.

"Do you know where we are now?" Jay snarled into the

Somali's face.

"Salford Towers."

"We know where Omar's woman lives, fourth floor number forty two right?" Jay lied.

"That's right man," Lewis lied too.

"Good," Jay said nodding, "Is the door reinforced?"

"No way man," Lewis lied again.

Jay pointed to the back of the van, and Dano reached in and grabbed a sledgehammer.

"Ask him again Dano," Jay said stepping away from the lying Somali, allowing his much bigger colleague room to swing the hammer.

"What number does she live at, is it forty two?"

"Yes man, I told you it was forty two," Lewis stared into Dano's eyes trying not to show any fear or anxiousness.

"But your friend Michael told us it was forty three, just before my colleague shot him through the head."

"I'm confused then, I'm sure it is number forty two, init," fear crept into his voice as realisation that his friend was already dead set in.

Dano swung the sledgehammer in a high sweeping arc, bringing the seven pound metal head down on the Yardie's foot. Brendon smothered the man's scream with his hands and struggled to control him as his body jack knifed in pain. Lewis shook his head quickly pleading with Dano not to hit him again. His eyes widened and tears ran down his face as he watched in terror as the hammer swung again. The hammer struck the same foot again, crushing the few remaining bones to a pulp. It was only his shoe that kept the mangled flesh attached to him.

Lewis lost consciousness for a few brief moments, but was rudely awakened by a hard slap across the face.

"I truly hope that you're no longer confused Lewis," Dano said leaning on the handle of the sledgehammer like it were a walking stick.

Lewis shook his head and gasped for breath. The pain in his foot was unbearable. All feelings of loyalty to Omar had gone before the second blow had landed, sadly too late to save him from the terrible torment that he now suffered.

"What number does she live at?"

"Forty three, she lives at forty three," his words came out in short rasps.

"Is the door reinforced?"

"Yes, it has a metal door inside the front door, and there is a view hole cut into it."

Jay looked at Dano and nodded thoughtfully. Metal inner doors were par for the course wherever drug dealers were concerned. They were virtually impossible to smash down using tools. It would have to be opened from within or blown off its frame with explosives.

"He keeps a weapon behind the door, a sawn off shotgun," Lewis offered the information freely, pain was dulling his mind and his body was going into shock.

"What do you think Jay?" Dano turned to his boss.

"I'm wondering if our friend Omar will open the door for his man Lewis, especially if he thinks he's hurt," Jay mused.

"We've brought grenades," Brendon interrupted.

"We just want Omar, not to demolish the fucking building," Jay snapped.

"I'm thinking more of a two pronged attack. My brother told me about them from his army days, like the Iranian Embassy siege," Brendon continued, excited by the prospect of using hand grenades properly, as opposed to tossing them into a lake in the middle of nowhere, just to see what happens.

"What the fuck are you on about Brendon," Dano asked incredulously.

"You have to think outside the box in the military," Brendon repeated his brother's favourite saying.

"I think he's off his box, never mind outside it," Dano was becoming frustrated.

"Look, you're all stumped because the Yardie has told us that the door is reinforced. Do you think that would stop the SAS?"

"I'm going to shoot him in a minute," Jay said quietly.

"The front door is not the only way into the flat, but it is the only way, that they will expect you to come in.....you see?" Brendon became animated as he tried to explain.

"It's four floors up Brendon."

"So how do they wash the windows then smart arse?"

Jay was shocked and stunned, but also pleasantly surprised.

"What have you got in mind Brendon?" Dano was catching up with him slowly.

"There will be a window maintenance cradle on the roof, so you go to the front door, and draw their attention, while I toss a couple of grenades through the windows. Simple, you don't even have to go in," Brendon was giddy with excitement.

"I think I like this thinking outside the box idea," Jay said. He liked it a lot, as he could kill two birds with one stone, literally.

# CHAPTER 25

# 'TANK'

John Tankersley woke up and stretched his huge arms, trying to loosen his shoulder joints. He was incredibly muscular in build, which meant that he often woke up with cramp and dead arms, due to his weight squashing his limbs as he slept. The telephone was ringing on the bedside table next to him, and he knew that it must be work. He felt a sharp dig in the ribs, prompting him to answer the ringing phone.

"Answer it you lazy oaf," Grace Farrington always sounded husky when she awoke, and it turned him on. That and her well toned body too.

"Agent Tankersley," he said gruffly, sounding like he had just woken up.

"Morning John," Major Stanley Timms sounded as perky as only he could in the middle of the night. The Major was responsible for the Terrorist Task Force, and the only person that Tank answered to. He was an ex-Royal Marine, Green Beret officer with a war record that would make Rambo blush.

"Morning Major."

"I've had the results on the roadside bomb back from forensics."

"What do they tell us?" Tank yawned and stretched again.

"The victim was indeed a member of the Ahmed family, unfortunately it was Mrs Ahmed in the vehicle," the Major said matter of factly.

"So, someone has scored a miss," Tank said.

"That's what I thought, if they missed their target then they could be tempted to try again," explained the Major.

"Assuming that her husband was the target, does anyone know where he is?"

"He's not been traced yet, but we're pretty certain that he's in the country somewhere. We have to assume that he was the target," the Major answered.

"It doesn't help us to identify the bombers though does it?"

"No evidence at all on that front, the bomber was very thorough in removing incriminating DNA, so I suppose we are still faced with the usual suspects," the Major stated the obvious, as the operation had been too well planned to be tarnished by a simple mistake.

"I've been thinking about when we watched the interviews with the 18th Brigade men, including their leader Terry Nick," Tank said.

"What did you make of them?"

"They have come a long way from the last time we were involved with them, more sophisticated, far more intelligent and legally well protected. They're far better organised than they ever were, and exceptionally well funded, but...," Tank left the sentence unfinished.

"But what?"

"Their leader didn't seem to be hiding anything, although he made a no comment interview to most of the amateurish interrogation, I really don't think he knew anything about it. He almost seemed intrigued by the crime scene photographs and impressed by the operation logistically," Tank recounted his observations.

"We have had a very unusual directive from Westminster regarding the Brigade," the Major spoke cryptically.

Grace had been lying still and listening to one side of the conversation, but she needed to pee, and she climbed out of the bed and walked across the room naked toward the bathroom beyond. Tank wondered at the muscular curves of her body, accentuated by her black skin.

"Don't tell me we can shoot them all?"

"Unfortunately not, quite the opposite in actual fact," the Major skirted the details, drawing out the conversation.

"We have been instructed not to investigate the 18th Brigade unless we have irrefutable evidence that they have been involved in terrorist activities."

"I don't understand, why would anyone protect them?"

"Does Blackwater Worldwide mean anything to you?"

"Of course they do. I had to work with some of their cowboy security guards in Iraq. What have they got to do with it?"

"They are a little after my time really, what do you know about them?" Major Timms hadn't been operational for many years.

Grace walked back into the room with two steaming cups of coffee. The cups held a full pint, and were printed with the Disney character Grumpy, a reference to Tank's demeanour in the morning. She passed one to Tank and then scrambled back into her side of the bed. He looked across at her beautiful black body and remembered how they had become lovers.

Grace Farrington had beaten all the other female applicants during the selection trials and most of the men too. Whole rafts of men from a myriad of regiments were asked to apply to make the new Terrorist Task Force, along with a handful of women. She had finished third overall after the gruelling physical tests of strength and stamina. Her father had been the first ever black man to reach the rank of Regimental Sergeant Major in the British army, although he fought tooth and nail to prevent Grace from joining up, she stuck to her dream and was now at the ultimate peak for enlisted soldiers. She had become a key member of the elite taskforce, which consisted of the cream of Special Forces. Tank took a sip of his coffee and carried on talking to the major.

"To cut a long story short, they were formed by an American Navy seal called Erik Prince in the late nineties, initially as a security contractor. They are based in North Carolina where they now have the largest tactical military training facility in the world, training upwards of forty thousand men every year, military offensive training, defensive operations and close personnel protection techniques," Tank had learned a lot about Blackwater during his last tour of Iraq.

"Forty thousand men every year, almost a small army."

"That is exactly what they have become. At the last count they had hired and trained over one hundred thousand men, all ex-military or ex-security services. The American government has a multi-billion dollar contract with them to provide close personnel protection all over the world, especially in Iraq, the Middle East and Afghanistan," Tank explained.

There had been uproar amongst the allied soldiers on Tank's last posting when Blackwater troops began to arrive in Baghdad. They were earning three times the salary of a normal enlisted British soldier. They also operated with impunity, mercenaries allowed to run amok without consequence. The American government brought them in to relieve the stress on their conventional troops, initially as bodyguards, but as time progressed they were tasked with protecting embassies and government facilities.

On September 16th, 2007, Blackwater guards opened fire in Nisour Square, Baghdad, killing seventeen civilians. Witnesses said that the mercenaries attacked unprovoked and continued to fire on civilians as they tried to run away. An FBI investigation found that at least fourteen of the dead were killed unjustifiably, and there was no evidence found to corroborate claims that the civilians opened fire on the Blackwater mercenaries. Because of their impunity they could not be prosecuted by either Iraq or America.

"It would seem that our government is in negotiations with sixteen large security companies in the British Isles, looking for them to provide a similar role in active battle theatres, releasing our troops for the front line," the Major explained sounding very concerned.

"What, and the 18th Brigade are one of those companies?"

"They are not just one of them. The Brigade are being favoured because of their numbers and military style hierarchy. When that is combined with their apparent success at controlling violence they are on a short list. They have a surprisingly large number of ex-military personnel, policemen and security guards within their ranks," the Major said.

"I can't believe Westminster would want to build a mercenary army."

"It's just for personnel protection apparently."

"That's how Blackwater started, and now they protect facilities as far away as the Philippines and Indonesia. Did you know that they were the first troops to be sent to New Orleans after hurricane Katrina hit?"

"No, I didn't."

"Within twenty four hours they had shot three alleged looters," Tank recalled.

"All that aside do you think the 18th Brigade are involved in this roadside bomb attack?"

Tank remained silent while the thoughts bounced around inside his bald head. The rise of giant security firms and mercenary armies across the Western world was a frightening concept, but a very real one too.

"I don't think that the organisation planned and executed the attack, no," Tank admitted somewhat reluctantly.

"Then we leave them alone for now. I'll speak to you when you get into the office," the Major sounded reluctant too.

"I'll be in shortly Major."

"Oh, one more thing John."

"What's that?"

"Say good morning to Grace for me please," The Major rarely acknowledged that they were an item, it was against taskforce guidelines, but on the odd occasion he let it be known that he was aware of it.

"Yes Major, see you later," Tank smiled and hung up the telephone on its cradle.

"What did he say?" Grace asked.

"He said that I had to say good morning to you for him," He turned to her and pulled her lithe body close to him.

"How long have we got?" she whispered into his ear, her breath sending shivers down his spine.

"Long enough."

# CHAPTER 27
# SALFORD TOWERS

Brendon stepped out of the lift on the top floor of the tower block and knelt down in a military defensive position, pointing his Uzi one way, and then the other, down the silent corridor. He pulled his balaclava down over his face and ran toward the roof access door. There was a rusted padlock hanging from a clasp and bracket fitting. Brendon had a small eight inch wrecking bar on his utility belt. He'd stolen the belt from his soldier brother the last time he was home on leave, before he'd been released from active service on mental health grounds. His brother was his hero, and a decorated veteran of three tours of Iraq, but the final tour had taken a heavy toll on the mental health of his older sibling, resulting in him being sectioned for months at a time, as he slipped in and out of severe fits of depression.

Brendon had aspirations to follow his hero brother into the army, but a long list of minor criminal offences on his youth record had stopped him from joining up. The army refused to take young offenders into their ranks. He had dealt with the disappointment by joining the 18th Brigade, which was the closest thing to a military organisation that he could find, and they utilised his excessive penchant for violence to the full.

Brendon slipped the bar into the padlock and snapped it down quickly with limited noise, no louder than a door being closed. He paused and waited a moment, listening for the sound of anyone moving behind the closed doors, alerted by his lock breaking.

He couldn't hear anything untoward so he opened the heavy door and entered the narrow stairwell beyond it. He closed the door behind him, leaving the access shaft in almost total darkness.

There was a light switch next to him, but he was relishing his covert mission, and so he opted for a small penlight from the belt. That's what his brother would have done, never expose yourself until you're ready to be seen. As he switched the penlight on, a circle of light appeared on the stairs in front of him. There were six stone steps between him and the next door. He bounded up them in two strides, and then twisted the roof access door handle, which opened without complaint. There was no separate lock attached to it. The block management had assumed that if you had reached the roof door, then you must be an authorised key holder.

On the roof he immediately spotted the maintenance cradle to his right. He ran toward it and leaned over the lip of the roof wall, trying to coordinate his position with that of the target flat. The height was awe inspiring. He could see right over the entire city, a panoramic view of a million twinkling streetlights stretching to the horizon. He looked down over the edge of the high rise tower block, and the vehicles below him looked like fixtures in a model village. A torch blinked from the car park six hundred feet below him. Brendon waved his penlight in answer to them, letting them know that he was in position.

The torch light below moved across the car park and then climbed up the wall of the building, stopping above the window of flat number forty three, confirming its position to him. The cradle needed to be moved about seventy yards to the left, in order to be positioned directly above the fourth floor flat. The cradle was twelve feet long and hung from two U shaped bars, which were welded to a guide rail on the roof. The guide rail had a winding handle attached to it, and Brendon turned it quickly. The well oiled cog twisted silently, and the cradle moved without making a sound along the edge of the roof.

Brendon leaned over the wall and checked the position again. It was set directly over the target row of windows. He cocked his leg over the wall and stepped into the cradle. The cradle swayed gently and he grasped the edges and froze, frightened by the dizzying height, yet flushed with adrenalin and excitement. He checked his kit again, three hand grenades, a lump hammer and his Uzi, all present and correct. Brendon crept along the cradle slowly toward the electric pulley motor. There was a square metal control box attached to the cradle by a thick extendable flex. He put the penlight into his mouth and gripped it between his teeth while he studied the buttons, up, down, and stop. He grinned in the darkness and pressed the button marked down. The cradle rocked gently as the motor whirred into life and began to descend toward the unsuspecting targets below.

# CHAPTER 28

# LEWIS

Lewis regained consciousness with a jolt. He blinked and looked around, trying to get his bearings. The harsh reality of his situation came crashing down around him as he felt himself being dragged across a tiled floor. There were two sets of strong hands holding his arms in a vice like grip. He could see a trail of blood smeared across the beige tiles, which was leaking from his tennis shoe. The pain in his foot and ankle was mind numbing. It felt like it was on fire. The gag had been stuffed back into his mouth and he couldn't swallow. The back of his throat tasted of acidic vomit and white spirit. He tried to shout for help, a futile attempt to escape the horror of his desperate circumstances. A crushing blow to the bridge of his nose deterred him from making any more noise. Blood ran freely from both nostrils and the thick coppery taste of his own life force mingled with the others, making him queasy. He felt like he was going to vomit again, but he knew that to do so would choke him.

The surroundings changed as he was dragged into a lift. Stainless steel walls daubed with graffiti, and numerous bodily excretions, and the overwhelming stink of urine floated into his surreal world of pain. Lewis felt like his senses were being completely swamped, pain, panic, and fear mixed with a sickening myriad of tastes and smells. He knew that he was probably about to die, but he still couldn't embrace it. He wanted to fight it. All the years of war and violence that he had experienced in his native Somalia flashed before his eyes. He could have died a million times before this moment. He wondered if he had survived all that Somalia had thrown at him only to die with a stinking rag choking him to

122

death. The elevator doors opened and he was dragged out onto a wide landing area.

Each landing led to a small community of ten apartments, five to the left hand side, and five to the right. There were three two bedroom flats on each side, and two, three bedroom flats on the other, which balanced the use of the architectural living space. The even numbers were to the right, and the odd numbers were to the left. Lewis felt himself being dragged to the left of the landing. His injured foot snagged on the lift door as he was pulled through it, sending stabbing bolts of pain shooting through his body. He arched his back, every muscle in his body tensed to combat the pain. He screamed in agony but the gag muffled the sound to a garbled cry. There was another heavy blow to his already broken nose, rendering him useless. Unconsciousness dragged at his befuddled mind, mercifully dulling his senses. He heard voices whispering but they seemed very far away now, as his brain began to shut down, and he drifted toward the darkness.

"That's the door."

"Text a message to Jay with your mobile and tell him that we're here."

"Cut his hands free."

"Who's got the nail gun?"

"It's here, hurry up and cut him free."

The screen of the mobile phone glowed and it beeped as a return message arrived.

"Jay is at the fireman's switch. He's going to kill the power as soon as Brendon has reached the windows."

"Tell him to fucking hurry up, if someone comes out of their flat we're fucked.

"Shut up; nail him to the wall opposite the door, directly in front of the spy hole."

"Help me lift him he's out of the game, a dead weight."

"Hold his arm up there, I'll put it through the palm of his hand, and one through the wrist so that it doesn't rip out."

Lewis heard the whispering, but it was dream like. It didn't affect him anymore. Pain was a thing of the past, or that's what he believed for a few precious moments, until the first nail punctured his right hand, pinning it to the wall. He was shocked back into the land of the living just in time to feel a second nail punched through his wrist. He gagged, and his eyes widened, almost busting out of his head. Hot stinging tears ran like small rivers down his face and his body started to convulse as his left hand was nailed to the wall in similar fashion. The volume of his struggling cries was increasing despite the gag. A solid punch to the stomach knocked the wind from his lungs and his body sagged, supported by the cruel nails. Lewis was delirious with pain and agony, wanting death to come and release him from his torment. The overriding sensation of warm blood running down his outstretched arms, tickling his armpits was surreal. For one brief second he thought he had died, but he hadn't, it was just the lights going out as the power in the building had been turned off at the mains.

"Take the gag out."

"What?"

"Take the fucking gag out, we need him to make some noise."

A hooded Brigade man snatched the gag out of Lewis's mouth, and he gasped clean untainted air deep into his lungs. He took another deep lungful and then started screaming for Omar's help. The Brigade men skulked in the darkness of the corridor and waited for a reaction.

# CHAPTER 29

# OMAR

Omar stood in the bedroom looking through the window into the night. Across the road was the head office of McDonalds, the burger giants. A brown brick building built on the outskirts of the city, beneath the tower block, because the real estate value of the land was significantly lower outside of the city centre. The burger moguls had made doubly sure that their administration headquarters wasn't just a financial drain on the system by building a huge drive thru restaurant adjacent to it, generating a constant profit.

The Golden Arches glowed brightly, an icon of the Western World. Omar drew deeply on a joint, allowing the noxious fumes to fill his lungs and seep into his blood stream, spreading its narcotic effect through his body. He was adjusting to cannabis resin. The Somalis recruit young men and boys into militias by offering food and lodgings, plus as much Khat as they could use. Khat is a drug weed, unique to Somalia. It is distributed at lunch time in the form of blades, similar to long grass, and is chewed throughout the day. The cumulative effect of the drug is displayed by the gang members as the day wears on. Fear disappears, and aggression takes control, resulting in fierce battles between rival militias, most of which are instigated by the excessive use of Khat.

Omar yawned and moved away from the window. He was thirsty and needed to drink water. He still found the taste of clean cold running water from the tap heavenly. His girlfriend, Gemma, stirred in the double bed, reaching over to where he should have been lying. They had spent all day sharing drug fuelled sex, stopping only to roll another joint or sniff another line of cocaine. Gemma's pale skin seemed luminous in the darkness. She was strawberry blond, almost platinum sometimes and other times golden, depending on how the light caught her hair. She had highlights bleached into it which made it shine, and catch the eye. Omar stared at her body in the glow from the streetlights outside. She was built like a goddess, lean where she should be, curvy at the hips with a flat stomach and a narrow waist. He treated her body like a sexual theme park, his first white woman, his first blond, brilliant white teeth and the smile of an angel. She moved again and he smiled as he opened the bedroom door and headed toward the kitchen.

He poked his head around the doorway as he past the living room. There were two of his affiliates crashed out on the armchairs, one of them still holding a long black Colt 45 as he snored. The television was still on, casting shadows around the room as the scenes changed. There was an ashtray overflowing on the coffee table in-between the sleeping Somalis. Omar deduced that they had smoked at least half a pound of weed between them, little wonder they were sleeping. He walked over to the television and switched it off, plunging the living room into darkness. He chuckled to himself as he walked back toward the door, and then he stopped suddenly. Omar thought he'd heard something, scraping outside the window. Maybe it was intuition developed by years of living in fear for your life, or maybe it was the drugs making his hearing muddy. He looked toward the window and stared at the heavy drapes, trying to see through them with his mind's eye, piercing the curtain material and the glass beyond, searching the darkness outside for danger. He stepped toward the drapes and reached for the Colt, when suddenly the power was cut and the flat was plunged into darkness. It was only moments later when he heard the screaming start.

# CHAPTER 30

# BRENDON

The cradle swayed gently as it descended. The further away from the electric motors on the roof it travelled, the quieter the journey became. The height was frightening, and he held on tightly to his machinegun for comfort. There was a strong breeze blowing around the corner of the tower block, but as he neared the lower floors it seemed to ease substantially. Brendon took one of the fragmentation grenades from his jacket and turned it in his hand nervously. The cold dull metal felt heavy in his hand.

He had a fascination with grenades, brought on by watching war films as a young boy. When he'd played war games as a kid his friends would use sticks and run around making machinegun noises.

"Da-da-da-da-da-da-da-da-da-da." He could remember those long summer days like they were yesterday. Brendon always filled his pockets full of small stones, which he would bite to mimic removing the safety pin, and then throw at his friends.

"Ka-booooom!" he'd cry as his pretend grenades struck their target.

Now all these years on he was still playing war games, fighting rival gangs, but now the stakes were much higher and the grenades were very real. The machinegun in his hand was capable of firing nine hundred high velocity bullets every minute. He had only ever used his weapons at training camps in America, and once shooting rabbits in the wilds of Snowdonia, turning the fluffy bunnies into red mush instantaneously. Brendon had longed to be like his brother, fighting wars on foreign soil, killing with impunity, feeling the god like power of taking a life with a machinegun.

Here he was approaching the fourth floor of Salford Towers,

armed to the teeth. All of a sudden he felt very alone. The breeze whistled through the steel cables of the cradle, a desolate sound almost warning him to turn back. He shivered and steeled himself against the wind, pushing the doubts from his mind; after all it was his own plan, a good plan, a plan his soldier brother would have relished and been proud of. Brendon peered over the cradle as it reached the fourth floor. He put the gun down and grabbed the remote control box; he pressed the red button and stopped the platform level with the window ledge. The cradle juddered as it stopped moving, and it bumped the building making a scraping sound. He froze and instinctively ducked down below the ledge, holding his breath as he did so. He took his mobile out and texted just two letters, 'OK'. He stuffed the phone into his jacket pocket and reached for his gun, just as all the lights went out.

Brendon didn't move as screaming started from somewhere deep inside the flats. He heard a door slam beyond the window, and the shuffling sounds of movement inside. There were hushed voices coming from a room beyond, one deep and male, and the other softer and female. The screaming was further away, but it was becoming louder. He could hear movement coming from other flats now, bedroom doors opening and closing, angry voices calling for the racket to stop. Someone shouted that he was working the early shift in the morning, another called that he had only just gone to bed. The building was coming to life, woken by the screaming inside. He decided that the best thing to do was abort the mission, as the whole plan revolved around stealth.

He grabbed the control box and pressed the 'down' button, but nothing happened. He stabbed at the 'up' button with the same result. It suddenly dawned on him that all the lights had gone off simultaneously, and someone must have killed the power. Brendon was trapped in the cradle four floors up. Whatever was going to happen next the police would be called, and with Brendon's previous convictions if he was found in possession of an automatic weapon and grenades he would be going to prison for a very long time. He realised that whoever killed the power was hoping that he would have smashed the window with the hammer, and tossed the grenades into the flat, before trying to move the cradle away from the blast. At that point it would have been too late. He reached for the hammer and cocked the safety on the Uzi, he'd have to fight his way out.

# CHAPTER 31

# OMAR

Omar heard the screaming coming from the corridor and reacted instinctively. He had spent his life in Mogadishu hunting his enemies, or being hunted, and he had a heightened sense of survival. The man screaming outside the front door was calling out his name, and pleading for help, using English, but he also kept slipping into Somali and shouting a warning. There was an ambush outside the front door, and one of his men was being used as the bait. The man screamed in Somali again and Omar recognised Lewis's voice. Many weaker men would have wavered at the sound of an old friend screaming for help, but Omar was a different breed. He was made from stainless steel, tough and ice cold inside. Everything he did revolved around his own very selfish agenda. If there was nothing to be gained personally then there was no point in wasting time with it. Lewis being used as bait wasn't pleasant to listen to, but his obvious distress meant that Omar had been alerted to the danger outside, therefore it could be tolerated.

Omar ran into the living room and slapped his affiliates around the face. They moaned in protest at being disturbed from their narcotic slumber. He shushed them when they spoke and gritted his rotten gold teeth as he placed his index finger to his curled lips.

"Trouble man! Someone has Lewis outside, cover the front door," Omar whispered.

The Somalis sprang into action, confused and unsteady on their feet, and they wobbled into the hallway aiming their weapons at the front door. Omar headed back into the bedroom where his girlfriend was still drowsy from cannabis use. He shook Gemma's sleeping body.

"What's wrong babe? Come back to bed, I'm still horny," she mumbled, and reached for him.

"Shush," he whispered and held her pretty face between his hands. He stroked her blonde hair gently and tried to rouse her without causing her to panic. She was the closest thing to love that Omar had found. He wasn't sure why she loved him, but she did. He was in total awe of her beauty, when she walked into a room he could feel himself staring at her, open mouthed. From the first time he'd seen her until present day he had put her on a pedestal, a feminine goddess, a walking talking sexual fantasy come true, which he could only wonder at. She tensed suddenly as she woke properly and heard the tortured sound of a man screaming nearby.

"What's going on?"

"There's trouble babe, init, I need you to get dressed quickly."

"Omar, you promised me that there would never be any trouble here, not at my flat, this is my home Omar."

"I know that babe, but trouble has found me. We have to get out of here, now get dressed quickly."

"Just call the police Omar, because I'm frightened. I don't want to go out there."

"No police babe, init, they'll send me back to Somalia, and you know that. We have to get out, get dressed."

Gemma tutted and rolled off the bed, her curves were accentuated by the artificial light which seeped into the room. Despite the imminent danger he took a long look at her, and sighed, if only there was more time.

"Lock this door behind me, and don't open it for anyone except me," Omar slammed the door closed and headed for the hallway. He had left his bag in the shoe cupboard next to the kitchen door, which contained the Mach 10 machine pistol that he had used in Warrington.

"Have you looked through the spy hole yet?" Omar asked as he joined his men near the front door.

"No way man," I think that's Lewis out there man, heavy duty. I don't want to see him like that."

Omar shook his head; he just couldn't get the staff in this country. They were all squeamish compared to the war hardened veterans he ran with in Mogadishu. He opened a small electric meter cupboard which was behind the front door, inside was a twelve bore, sawn-off shotgun. Omar rattled the metal cage that reinforced the door, checking that it was fitted flush into its housing. It would take a bulldozer to knock it down. There was a three inch square sliding plate fitted to the cage. Omar slid the plate and peered through the spy hole at the dark corridor beyond. He swallowed hard as he looked into the dark landing area, and saw Lewis through the gloom crucified to the wall opposite him; his face was a bloody mess. There were shiny new nails piercing his deep black skin through his hands and wrists, and a pool of blood was spreading at his feet. Omar felt anger rising in his throat, but realised that was exactly what his tormentors wanted. They were trying to provoke a reaction.

Lewis wasn't struggling against the cruel nails anymore, and his cries were growing weaker and less frantic. Omar reckoned that his friend and companion had reached the end of his tether in this world, and he was already on his way to the next. He had to kill him, it was the only compassionate thing to do in Omar's warped mind. He had to help him to be free of the pain, and allow his friend's soul to move on.

He pushed the sawn-off shotgun through the letterbox flap and pulled both triggers together. The shotgun roared and buckshot hit Lewis on the right hand side of his head, ripping a huge piece of scalp and skull bone away, and splattering the pale walls with grey brain matter, which trickled down the walls mixing with fresh blood. Omar slammed the sliding plate closed as three Uzis opened fire at the door, blasting long splinters of wood across the hall way. Lewis's ruined body stopped twitching, free from the pain of torture at last.

Omar and his men moved away from the front door as hundreds of high velocity rounds smashed it to smithereens. The metal frame behind it was too thick to penetrate and the sound of bullets ricocheting around the landing area filled the air. Despite the lack of electricity the tower block was coming alive, woken from collective slumber by the sound of gunfire. Raised voices could be heard on every floor and the telecommunications networks were jammed with emergency calls.

The Uzis fell silent for a moment. Omar figured that they were either reloading or waiting for something else to happen, another part of the plan that was yet to be revealed. Years of civil war had given Omar a sixth sense. It was the only way that some of the young men of Somalia survived when so many of their compatriots perished beside them. He looked back down the hallway toward the living room, and remembered the scraping sound that he'd heard just before the lights went out. It suddenly occurred to him what the men in the corridor were waiting for. There was a flanking move yet to come.

Omar chambered a round into the Mach 10 and ran to the doorway of the living room. He stared into the gloom, trying to see beyond the heavy drapes. As he watched and waited he saw the slightest glimmer of movement, a darker shadow mingling with the gloom, and it seemed to be growing taller, as if someone where standing up outside the window. They were four floors up, but there was no denying what was in front of him, and his instincts were rarely wrong. He lifted the machinegun and was just about to fire when the windows shattered. A shrill wind blew into the room lifting the drapes away from the window, revealing the dark silhouette of a hooded man, pointing an Uzi directly at him.

# CHAPTER 32

# VIGILANTE

The television news was running a continuous loop focusing on the violence that had hit Warrington in the previous forty eight hours. There had been two fatalities and two critically injured, one of them was his kill, but the others were allegedly attacked by drug gangs. There was some speculation from reporters that the drug gang was of Somali persuasion, Muslims. He shifted in his chair uncomfortably, and his knees were burning in agony from their extended excursion the previous day. He was still nowhere near ready to walk around unaided for any real length of time. His prosthetic limbs irritated the stumps terribly if he used them for any length of time. The doctors had told him that it could be years before his legs would adapt. Although he had managed to become mobile well before anyone expected him to be, the pain he suffered after walking was quite simply intolerable.

The cameras panned to the Westbrook explosion and the subtitle at the bottom of the screen turned red. The title 'breaking news' scrolled across the screen.

"We have news just in from the Cheshire Constabulary that the victim of the road side bomb attack at Westbrook, a suburb of Warrington in Cheshire, was in fact Mrs Rashid Ahmed, the wife of the disgraced bank mogul Rashid Ahmed," the reporter said.

He rubbed his knee and the pain shot through him. It was strange that he always had an incredible itching sensation at the back of his calf, even though it had been blown off over a year ago. He winced, not sure whether it was the pain in his missing limb, or the news that he had killed the wrong member of the Ahmed family.

"It is believed that Mrs Rashid Ahmed had been called out by her alarm company to a firebomb attack at their Warrington branch, and her vehicle was targeted as she made her way to the incident. The police are connecting the two scenes as being part of an elaborate plot, which the police assume would have targeted Mr Rashid Ahmed, and at this point the police can only speculate as to who the perpetrators would be," the reporter continued.

"It has been a black forty eight hours for Warrington, however the police have ruled out any connection between the Westbrook incident, and the shootings at the Turf and Feather public house in Locking Stumps." The camera images changed to show the shattered windows of the public house, surrounded by flapping yellow crime scene tape.

He emptied his can of Stella Artois and hurled it at the television, bouncing it off the screen and spraying the wall behind with remnants of Belgian lager. It certainly wasn't the first time that he'd been involved in an operation that had killed the wrong target, and it probably wouldn't be the last, despite his condition. As long as he had a breath in his body he would fight against the invading hordes, who were not here to integrate, but were only here to bleed it dry while they plotted against the state. There was no way he was going to sit back and allow Islamic Jihad to be fuelled and supplied from within his own country, no way, not ever.

He reached underneath a small coffee table which was to the right of his chair, and removed a folder that he compiled over his long months in hospital. Inside were the details of suspect individuals and organisations that he had categorised as legitimate targets. He had researched the details of companies, and individuals that were accused of supporting Afghan Taliban fighters and Iraqi extremists. There was list as long as his arm of sympathisers of Kashmiri separatists in Pakistan, and Sri Lanka's Tamil Tigers, not to mention groups that ran charity shops raising money for the insurgents in Iraq. He fumbled through his files looking for the details which related to Rashid Ahmed. His files were organised into alphabetical order, and he flicked through searching for domiciles.

Rashid Ahmed had nearly a dozen properties in his portfolio, but only four were situated in the United Kingdom. He had to assume that the investigation into his arms dealing and financial donations to the Taliban rebels by the British government had resulted in his passport being confiscated. Rashid must therefore still be in one of his British properties, hiding from the media spotlight while his business interests were put under the microscope.

The first address was Ambleside, in the Lake District, which is a stunning tourist town set in the Windermere valley, at the north shore of the lake. The banks of the valley rise sharply to the east, and are spotted with beautiful slate built bungalows which all have a glorious view across the lake to the breathtaking mountains beyond. Rashid was a keen walker, and a lover of the mountain districts, probably a throw back to his years in Afghanistan. The address he had listed included a telephone number. He picked up the handset and punched in the prefix numbers 141, which withheld the caller's identity, and then dialled the number listed as belonging to Rashid's property. The line clicked into life as the number connected. He let it ring for nearly ten minutes before cutting the call off. There was no one at the Ambleside property.

Brighton was the second property on the list, a Victorian coastal resort on Britain's south shores, that had become the home of the rich and famous because of its close proximity to London. He repeated the process using the prefix to camouflage his call. The number rang out six times and then clicked straight to a voice mail facility, which declared that it was full and there was no room for any more messages. The media frenzy surrounding Rashid meant that the paparazzi were hunting him down twenty four hours a day, trying desperately to attain the first interview with him since his wife had been assassinated. He held the receiver to his head and thought about the situation. If he had found the details of his properties then the determined press would have reporters outside of every single one of them. The information was in the public domain, available to anyone that could be bothered to look at the land registry. Rashid Ahmed had spent decades in the arms business, ducking and diving, making an art form of concealing his actions as well as his whereabouts.

It occurred to him that it would be far too easy to find him at one of his holiday homes. There must be something else in his files that could indicate a less obvious refuge. He referred back to his files, and flicked from the domicile section to commercial properties. There was a four page list which contained the addresses and contact details of every bank and associated business that Rashid Ahmed owned. There were hundreds of properties listed. He grabbed a yellow highlighter pen from the coffee table next to him and studied the lists. Most of them were clearly identified as branches of Blackstallion bank, others appeared to be offices or administration centres connected to them. It wasn't until he reached properties which began with the letter 'N' that he noticed an unusual listing. It was listed as a storage facility called Montserrat, which was situated at a vaguely familiar place called North Stack, Holyhead, on the Island of Anglesey, which is situated off the North West coast of Wales. The facility had no company name attached to it, only the name of the building, which was usually unique to residential properties.

He was very familiar with the Welsh port, a frequent holiday destination from his childhood days, and the name North Stack echoed in his memory. It was a place he had heard of but never visited because of its remote location, therefore a place of mystery and intrigue to his young mind at the time. He gripped the arms of his chair and used his incredibly strong arms to lift himself over the side and plonked himself down in his wheelchair. When he was in the service he was renowned for his awesome prowess in the gymnasium, seventy dips in a minute was a walk in the park for him. His injuries hadn't detracted from his remarkable upper body strength.

He flicked off the brakes and pushed the chair across the sparsely furnished room to his computer. He typed in the web address for Google earth, and then entered the details of the property at North Stack. The computer programme displayed an aerial view of the port. The satellite picture zoomed into the area. Holyhead has a huge international deepwater harbour, servicing tankers from all over the world carrying aggregates used in the manufacture of aluminium at a foundry close by, on the edge of the town. The port spreads east to a manmade marina, which is protected by a mile and a half long seawall know as the 'breakwater', an ingenious piece of Victorian engineering.

From the marina the shore rises steeply and meets the craggy slopes of Holyhead Mountain. The mountain stands over a thousand feet tall, and the opposite side of the mountain runs into sheer cliffs, which drop precipitously into the Irish Sea. North Stack was situated on the edge of the cliffs to the north of the mountain, an uninhabited desolate place, which was high enough to look across Holyhead and the island of Anglesey, to the snow capped mountains of Snowdon beyond.

The picture showed one isolated property situated on the shoulders of the cliffs, overlooking the sea. He zoomed into the building to get a better look at it. There was a large white house with a slate roof, adjacent to three smaller outhouses; all surrounded be a low dry stonewall. Tall wooden telegraph poles carried power lines and communication cables from the port to the house, provided at huge expense by the original owner. A narrow path ran from the garden across fern covered headland, before it dropped sharply and twisted its way down the mountain to a disused quarry. There the ancient stone quarry's service roads joined the main coast road about a mile away.

There was no helicopter landing pad near the house, he guessed the winds up there were too perilous to risk that particular mode of transport. The path leading down the mountain side was far too steep and narrow to navigate, even for the most powerful four wheel drive vehicles. That meant that the occupants of the house either walked, or had another mechanised option. Perhaps scrambler bikes or all terrain cycles, maybe high powered quad bikes.

It was the ideal hideaway. He turned the wheelchair around and guided it back to his armchair. He picked up the handset and dialled direct enquiries services.

"Hello direct enquiries, how can I help you?"

"I'm looking for the number of Montserrat House, North Stack, Holyhead please."

"Do you have the name of the resident?"

"Try Rashid Ahmed."

"I'm sorry sir, that number is ex-directory."

"Fine, but is it listed to Rashid Ahmed?"

"I'm sorry sir but I can't give out that information."

"I realise that you have a protocol to follow but it is a matter of life and death."

"I see, I can't give you any information I'm afraid, but it isn't registered to that name."

"Oh dear, would it be registered as Blackstallion bank?"

"As I said earlier it is ex-directory, and it isn't registered to that name either, I'm very sorry."

He stabbed at the off button and ended the call, convinced that he had found Ahmed's bolthole. The chair span as he wheeled it quickly back to the computer. The terrain was difficult for a fully able bodied soldier, almost impossible for a man who walks on prosthetic legs, but where there's a will there's a way. He would have to plan thoroughly to take out Rashid Ahmed in his cliff top hideaway, but there was no going back now.

There was a short sharp knock on the door before it opened, and the nurse entered with his evening meal.

# CHAPTER 32
# SALFORD TOWERS

Omar dived forward as the windows exploded into a million deadly shards. The nine millimetre bullets from his Mach 10 machinegun had blown the windows out, at the same time as Brendon had smashed them in with his sledgehammer. Omar dived for cover as the Brigade man opened fire with his Uzi. Large chunks of plaster were scattered across the room as bullets peppered the walls. The maelstrom of bullets subsided momentarily, and Omar took the opportunity to retaliate. He rolled toward the settee and sprayed bullets toward the flapping curtains, long strips of material were ripped from drapes and floated down toward the car park in the darkness. Muzzle flashes lit the room, revealing the cables of the maintenance cradle outside the window. Omar grinned in the darkness as he emptied his machinegun, and his gold teeth twinkled, reflecting the flame from the barrel.

The Mach 10 clicked empty as the firing pin hit an empty chamber. Omar dived for the living room doorway, rolling over as he tried to escape the killing zone. He smashed into the doorframe, which stunned him for a second, pain shot through his shoulder and he dropped the Mach 10 on the floor. Suddenly there was a dull thumping sound, followed by something rolling across the room. Omar's eyes widened in realisation. He threw himself into the hallway slamming the door behind him.

"Grenade!" he shouted. The Somalis crouched behind the kitchen doorframe, and waited for the imminent explosion.

The noise of the explosion inside the flat prompted a new barrage of machinegun fire from the Brigade men on the landing outside. The front door disintegrated beneath the shattering force of the high velocity rounds. The metal gate now took the brunt of the gunfire, and the tower block echoed with sound of ricocheting bullets. Omar stood away from the living room door, anticipating the attacker's next move. High velocity bullets ripped through the flimsy interior door, and a pattern of bullets holes snaked up the wall as Brendon fired the Uzi from inside the room.

Years of guerrilla warfare had taught Omar that patience and restraint would always overcome blind force, and he waited calmly for the telltale clicking sound of his enemy's weapon running out of ammunition. He discarded his empty magazine, twisted it over and clicked a full clip into the Mach 10. A huge chunk of the door was blasted away by Brendon's Uzi, and then he heard it click empty. Omar crossed the hallway in a flash and pulled the trigger. He could see his enemy silhouetted through the gapping ragged hole in the door.

Brendon was struggling to reload his machinegun in the gloom, not a real soldier with years of experience like his brother. He was thinking back to his brother's tales of stripping down and reassembling weapons blindfolded. It had seemed like a pointless exercise at the time of listening, but now he understood the benefit of being able to reload a machinegun in the dark. He looked up and saw the momentary muzzle flash of a weapon in the dark hallway, but he didn't live long enough to hear the gunshot because the round hit him in the teeth ripping his tongue off, before drilling an upward spiral through the roof of his mouth into his brain, blowing the top of his head off as it exited. His knees buckled and he collapsed in a bloody heap on the living room floor, his brains spilled onto the carpet from the gaping rent in his skull.

Omar listened to the noises around him, and assessed the situation. The machineguns outside had stopped firing and were replaced by a cacophony of shouting and screaming from numerous floors in the tower block. In the distance he heard the wail of sirens. He ran to the shattered window frame and looked over the city, blue lights were heading this way, but they were still a few miles away. Omar knelt down next to the Brigade man's body and quickly patted him down. Two unused grenades were clipped to his belt. He took them and ran into the hallway.

"Get in here," Omar whispered to his two affiliates, and they moved swiftly from the kitchen into the wreckage of the living room, hesitating slightly at the sight of Brendon's brains pooling on the carpet.

"Cover him up," Omar instructed one of them, "get into that maintenance platform and see if it can be operated manually, there should be a winding handle somewhere."

The two Somalis sprang into action. The first ripped down the remaining pieces of tattered curtain, and threw them over the ruined head of the dead Brigade man. The second man vaulted the window ledge without fear or hesitation, and scrambled into the cradle searching for a winding mechanism, which would be fitted in case of emergencies. Omar returned to the reinforced metal gate and placed his ear to it, listening for signs of the enemy lurking outside. He heard harsh whispered orders, and panic was present in their voices. The combination of the residents of the tower block waking, and the approaching sirens was putting the Brigade men in a precarious position. They were running out of time. Omar decided to speed up their thought process. He pulled the pins from both grenades, and then slid open the metal plate in the gate, quickly dropping the explosive devices into the darkened landing beyond. Immediately machinegun bullets began to rake the door, but he was completely safe, and the gunfire had covered the noise of the grenades landing on the tiles.

Instinctively Omer kept low and ran down the hallway to the bedroom. He banged on the door.

"Gemma, open the door, it's me," he said.

The door opened just as the grenades exploded on the landing, causing a deafening blast, despite the armoured gate, and there was total silence for at least ten seconds, as the tower block residents were shocked into silence. Then there was a wall of sound as injured men began screaming outside the front door, and the population of Salford Towers became a hysterical.

"Oh my god, what was that?"

"Shut up and get into the living room." Omar moved quickly, and grabbed a fleece top and black baggy jeans, he pushed his bare feet into Nike training shoes.

"Where are we going?" she asked incredulously.

"Out of the window babe, init," he answered smiling at her widely and the streetlights made his gold teeth glint in the dark.

Jay had followed Brendon up to the roof after killing the power to the tower block. He sent the remaining two men to back up the guys on the fourth floor. Jay looked over the roof parapet into the darkness below just as the grenades exploded on the fourth floor.

"Shit! What's happening down there Dano?" he hissed into a two way coms unit, set up between him and Dano.

"That dipstick Brendon must have gone down. The Yardies have just tossed a couple of grenades through the door onto the landing."

"Any casualties?"

"We've got two down, but they're making a lot of noise so I think they're recoverable," Dano knew that it was the quiet casualties that you needed to worry about in a fire-fight, if they were screaming then they were alive.

"Fucking hell! Get them out of there Dano there's blue lights heading in our direction from all over the city," Jay hissed. He was still watching the cradle when he saw two men climbing into it from the apartment window.

"How long have we got," Dano asked.

"You've got long enough to get our lads out of here, and don't leave anything that can be traced back to the Brigade," Jay instructed him.

"Roger that, what about you?" Dano asked concerned about how Jay would get out of the building.

"Don't worry about me, I'll give the police something else to worry about. I'll see you back at the Turf."

Jay looked along the edge of the cradle wall and saw the power cable which ran from a petrol generator all the way down to the remote control box inside the platform. Omar was scrambling out of the window from the apartment, helping what looked like a half dressed blond after him. It was difficult to see exactly what was happening from that far away, but it was obvious that the Somalis had disabled Brendon and were using the cradle as an escape route.

"Oh no you don't my African friend," Jay muttered to himself and he cut through the remote control line, leaving the generator power line intact.

He laughed out loud as the men in the cradle started panicking because the remote box wouldn't start the cradle moving downward. The master control was bolted to the wall and Jay firmly pressed the 'up' button. The cradle jerked, and swayed before beginning the long slow journey back up the tower block. The petrol generator was housed in a long oblong shaped storage box. Jay could hear the motor chugging away under the strain of lifting the maintenance cradle plus four occupants up the towering building. He smashed a flimsy padlock from a rusted clasp and the door flew open. Jay shone his mag-light into the generator housing and saw what he was looking for. Just inside the door was a red plastic petrol canister, the type used for cars, full, and holding five gallons of unleaded fuel.

"Just what the doctor ordered," Jay said smiling in the darkness.

# CHAPTER 34

# TERRORIST TASK FORCE

John Tankersley stepped out of the lift onto the top floor of the divisional police headquarters, Canning Place, Liverpool, on the banks of the River Mersey. The police station was built in the late sixties and early seventies at the same time as the country's most advanced tunnel scientists were constructing three major traffic arteries beneath the river linking the city centre to the Wirral peninsula, a mile and half away. At that time nuclear conflict with the Soviet Union was almost a foregone conclusion, and the British government had a huge secret underground command bunker built beneath the city simultaneously with the road tunnels. The construction companies and their employees were all forced to sign the 'official secrets act', keeping the bunker and network of subterranean facilities covert.

The huge number of subterranean sites that were being built under the river at the same time meant that the general public were completely unaware that anything more than traffic tunnels were under construction beneath their feet. The government bunker was central to everything that the British intelligence services did, both domestically and internationally. The network of tunnels spread for miles, incorporating training facilities, storage hangars for emergency military vehicles, which would be used in the event of nuclear attack. It was also the most technically advanced listening post in Europe.

The key personnel of the taskforce had been summoned to a multi-agency meeting. Government ministers were becoming increasingly concerned about the level of violence being witnessed in Manchester and Warrington during the previous week or so, especially as it appeared there was a religious agenda as well as a criminal element involved. The country had been balanced on a knife edge since the extremist bombings of 9/11 and 7/7. The intelligence units of the British counter terrorist agencies were monitoring over two thousand suspected extremist cells at any one time. Every Muslim arrested drove the wedge deeper between ethnic communities; racism and racial prejudice were at an all time high. The inner cities were a religious time bomb waiting to explode. All it would need was a string of events similar to those recently encountered, combined with some insensitive scaremongering in the media, and public order would be lost.

Tank walked into his office and looked out of the window toward the city. The regeneration of Liverpool had changed the vista outside of his work place dramatically. There was a whole mile square of new precincts called 'Liverpool one', which ran from the Albert Docks deep into the city centre, creating a magnificent shopping area. From his window the people looked like ants swarming along the streets, and the St. John's tower stood like a sentinel above them.

"Morning," Major Stanley Timms disturbed his thoughts.

"Morning Major, what are we to expect at the meeting?"

"Every man and his dog are coming, there's a real concern about the involvement of the Brigade in this recent violence. It could cause embarrassment in Westminster."

"Why? Because of the private security contracts?"

"Yes, the last thing the government wants is to get into bed with something that is going to bite them on the arse further down the line."

"Well the American experience with Blackwater hasn't been a pleasant one. Surely they can learn a thing or two from them."

"The thing is Blackwater haven't lost a single asset under their control, and that's why the government tolerate them."

"They are still a million miles away from the Brigade. It's one thing providing bouncers and marshalling pop concerts, but another providing close personal protection in a theatre of war," Tank hated mercenaries of any description.

"Apparently not," the Major said cryptically, picking up his paper briefs for the upcoming meeting in the bunker below.

"I don't follow you Major," Tank quizzed him further.

"I think that this meeting is going to be a real eye opener. The

Chief constables for Cheshire, Merseyside and Greater Manchester are all attending, along with four senior aides from the Ministry of Defence. It's all a bit bizarre really, but we'll see what comes out in the wash. You know that the meeting has been elevated to grade one don't you?"

"No, I didn't know that," Tank flushed red, anger rising. A grade one meeting excluded all the taskforce members except himself and the Major, and it was usually a precursor to underhand political hamstringing.

"They sent e-mail confirmation of the change of status this morning, which makes me think that there is trouble afoot," the Major explained.

"We don't even know what we are investigating yet, the chances are that everything outside of the Westbrook incident is a police matter," Tank picked up his own brief and flicked through the paperwork looking for some indication as to why Westminster aides were so keen to take control of the situation, especially when the lines were still so blurred.

"There is obviously more to this than meets the eye, but one thing is very clear, they do not want the Terrorist Task Force investigating the 18th Brigade's security arm," the Major opened the door and indicated that Tank should walk with him.

Tank picked up a dark blue taskforce bomber jacket from a row of coat hangers outside of the office, and struggled into it, squeezing huge biceps into sleeves designed for much smaller men. Grace was across the office at her desk, and seeing the two of them heading toward the lift she stood up, and pulled on her own jacket. Tank held up his hand palm facing her, signalling like a traffic cop that she wasn't invited to the meeting downstairs. She shrugged her shoulders and pulled a disappointed expression, and then removed her jacket and sat back down at her desk. Their work was always of the upmost secrecy, always covert, and nine times out of ten the bulk of the team didn't find out what they were involved in until the last minute. Being excluded from a meeting was just par for the course for Grace.

The lift door opened and they stepped inside. The buzz of voices in the taskforce office faded as the doors slid closed, and there was a mild sensation of descending as the express elevators hurtled toward the secret bunker below.

# CHAPTER 35

# SALFORD TOWERS/ GEMMA

Gemma climbed out of the darkened apartment. The smell of cordite hung in the air, sticking to the back of her throat and stinging her nostrils. Her home was in tatters, a dead body lay stinking on her precious sheepskin rug. She remembered the day she bought that rug fondly, deciding to buy it despite having no spare funds to pay for it. Gemma used the electric bill money to buy it and then pulled double shifts all week to cover the money. The sheepskin was her pride and joy, her living room centre piece and her comfort blanket on the many nights she spent alone watching the television with a bottle of wine and a bar of chocolate. She loved the feel of the sheepskin against her skin when she lay on it, but now it was covered in bloody goo and from the smell of it, much worse.

Gemma stumbled into the cradle and gazed around in shocked disbelief. The twinkling lights of the city spread out before her almost seemed pretty despite their precarious situation. She really couldn't grasp how it had come to this. Her mind raced backwards in time to the day she had met Omar. Gemma had spent most of her teenage years and early twenties bouncing from one party to the next. Her work as a receptionist was well paid and it funded her shopping habits and her wild social life, but only just. She hopped from one handsome guy's bed straight into the next one, never truly finding a man that she could stay with, and when she did like someone they usually dumped her for the next easy blond that came along.

Omar had approached her in a club that she frequented. It was late in the evening and there wasn't much going on. Her best friend had left earlier with a gorgeous Italian bloke, leaving

Gemma on her own talking to a fat sales rep who had spent half an hour explaining that his wife didn't understand him. Omar oozed menace and confidence, and he stepped between Gemma and the fat man without a word to him, offering only his back to complain to. The man scurried off with his tail between his legs, annoyed that he had invested four expensive cocktails into Gemma only to be blown out. Within ten minutes Gemma realised that Omar was at the top of the cocaine tree, and she found his menacing persona exciting. She was at a loose end and craved excitement. She shared a few lines of top quality cocaine with him, and then had rough sex in a toilet cubicle. Within a week Omar was virtually living with her, his friends came around all the time to pick-up drugs and drop off money. Her front door was reinforced, as a precaution, and the flat was turned into a fortress, all before she had had time to draw breath.

Omar and his friends were arguing with each other. The cradle wouldn't move, and then suddenly it did, but the wrong way. It started going up rather than down.

"Press the other button man," Omar shouted at his confused friend.

"I have done Omar, nothing is happening, init," he passed the remote to his leader trying to placate him.

Omar thumped the red stop button half a dozen times but nothing happened. The cradle swayed gently as it climbed. The wind blew and it whistled around the corner of the building, an icy blast which brought Gemma back from her memories.

"What's going on Omar?" she asked, her voice quivering.

"Shush babe, everything is fine," he dismissed her trying to get a response from the metal box.

"Don't fucking tell me to shush!" Gemma lost her composure completely. She stood up rocking the platform violently.

"For god's sake get her sat down man," Omar's colleague shouted.

"Shut the fuck up!" Omar turned on him.

"Don't fucking tell me to shush, you just blew my flat up!" she screamed now starting to panic. The cradle tipped almost forty five degrees and the Somalis grabbed the edges of it clinging on for dear life.

"Gemma, sit down woman!" Omar grabbed her arm and tried

to pull her down, but she struggled away from him. The platform jerked again, tipping the other way, starting to rock from side to side like a huge pendulum.

The wind blew again freezing Gemma to the bone. The cradle rocked making her feel sick and dizzy at the same time, but still the cradle climbed.

"Calm down babe, just calm down, we're going up to the top of the building that's all, and then we're getting off it and away from the police," Omar soothed her gently, trying to stop the platform from swinging.

"You've destroyed my home. There are dead people on my rug," she started to bubble, and tears ran down her face reflecting the millions of streetlights in the dark. Omar held her tightly calming her completely, allowing her sobs to subside before lifting her face to kiss her gently.

"I'll buy you a new rug babe, don't worry for now. Everything will be alright," Omar whispered in her ear. He just had her settled when the first drops of petrol hit them.

The droplets became a deluge of stinging flammable liquid, soaking their hair and clothes. Omar looked up into the darkness and saw a small flicker of flame, a lighter or match striking. Then the flame grew larger, a burning rag or something similar. He looked down at the streets below them, contemplating their chances of survival if they jumped, zero.

"What's that on me?" Gemma whined and held him tighter, hiding from the nightmare around her.

"Don't worry babe," he held her tightly, and stroked her head.

One of the Somalis panicked and grabbed a passing window ledge, trying to gain purchase from it if he left the cradle. He leaned awkwardly almost tipping the platform over completely. Omar hooked one of the metal cables into the crook of his elbow, and then he kicked out hard at the man. His foot connected with the man's buttocks and flipped him over the edge. He clung momentarily to the window ledge, fingertips gripping just inches of aluminium frame, sliding toward the edge, and then he fell. The darkness swallowed him up long before he hit the ground. Still the cradle climbed steadily upward.

Omar shuffled to the left and looked over the edge again, his mind racing, searching for a way out. The fear of falling from a great height seemed to be more powerful than the fear of being set alight, and then they switched places, maybe jumping was preferable. He felt his foot nudge something on the floor. He looked down and the steel head of a claw hammer glinted in the dark. Omar glanced upward and saw the burning rag falling toward them. He grabbed Gemma's arm tightly and reached down for the hammer. She screamed as she realised that the fluid she was soaked with was petrol.

"Hold me tightly," he shouted at her. He turned toward the building and launched himself at a passing window. The hammer shattered the glass and Omar and Gemma tumbled from the cradle, through the apartment window, just a second before the burning rag landed on the petrol soaked platform. His colleague wasn't so lucky, frozen with fear he tried to follow his leader through the window a second too late. The cradle was climbing too fast and he succeeded only in crashing into the passing brickwork. The burning rag hit the platform and turned him into a human torch. He stumbled about desperate to escape the burning fluid but he was covered in it. He opened his mouth to scream and the flames frazzled the delicate tissue in his lungs. The pain was incredible and he tumbled from the ascending platform. It was a long painful journey to the pavement hundreds of feet below.

# CHAPTER 36

# RASHID AHMED

Rashid Ahmed stood in the living room of his Anglesey holiday retreat. The property had been built by an American actor who once played the evil nemesis Lex Luther, opposite Christopher Reeves's superman character. It was the absolute celebrity bolthole. The building had once been a remote hill farm, becoming nothing more than a derelict pile of bricks in the sixties. The lack of running water and electricity, combined with its mountainous position, made it very unattractive to potential buyers. The actor had spent a small fortune connecting it to the main power grid, piping fresh water up the mountain and constructing a building which could withstand the elements at such an altitude. The only thing that couldn't be fixed was the access road. There simply was no solution, except to use all terrain vehicles or quad bikes to reach the residence.

The American actor had built the house upside down. The living room was situated on the upper floor, and connected to an open plan dining room and kitchen, while the bedrooms and bathrooms were downstairs. The upper floor was built facing due north, floor to ceiling windows offered a breathtaking view of the cliffs, and the tall isolated rocky stack which rose from the rough seas and towered a hundred feet above the crashing waves. It was a natural rock tower, a portion of the massive cliff face which had withstood the power of tidal erosion. It gave this part of the mountain its name, North Stack. From the kitchen at the rear of the upper floor the vista looked over the huge stone breakwater at the base of the mountain slopes several miles below. There was a clear view of the marina and the deepwater harbour port beyond, and across the island to the snow capped peaks of Snowdonia in the distance.

Rashid was frightened and alone. His legal advisors had told him to stay low until the media storm surrounding the death of his young wife had subsided. The furore which had followed his alleged arm supplies to Afghan Taliban rebels during the week prior to her death seemed to be forgotten for the moment. There had been shock initially, followed by page after page of his life story, and a myriad of different speculative versions of who had attacked his vehicle, killing his wife by mistake. The last few days all the articles had been full of speculation as to his whereabouts. He had been in hiding since the arms deals hit the press, and he hadn't left his mountain hideaway since. The chest freezers were running low on supplies, as was his supply of powdered milk. Rashid had broken protocol once already this week by calling his handler, but desperate situations called for desperate measures. He looked out over the Irish Sea and watched huge foaming breakers crashing into the base of the North Stack, while he dialled. The mobile he'd dialled clicked straight onto voice mail, which informed him that its owner was in a meeting, and advised him to leave a message. He turned sharply and tossed the handset across a low coffee table, which was stood on a thick goat's skin rug near the panoramic windows. He had been told that help would be on its way, and that he would be protected no matter what the press said. The longer nothing happened the more vulnerable he felt, but he was trapped. The government had his passport and he was now so well recognised as an international arms dealer that there were no friendly countries left for him to hide in.

The fact that his wife had been murdered hadn't properly sunk in yet. She was twenty years his junior, the daughter of an Afghan warlord who had offered her hand and arranged the marriage as a gift to his arms supplier. Rashid had accepted the offer of marriage to keep the fiery Afghan chief sweet as much as anything; although only fourteen she had been stunning as a teenager. Their marriage had been little more than a charade. She didn't enjoy sex, and he found nothing in common with her, after all she was uneducated, little travelled and had no ambition beyond bearing children. Within a year or two it became obvious that there was a medical hurdle stopping them from conceiving, and Rashid grew fond of her as a companion. She in turn became nothing more than his housekeeper, cooking and cleaning, washing and ironing.

Despite the lack of real romance they enjoyed their relationship and complemented each other. He cared for her wellbeing in a paternal way, and he now felt like he had lost a daughter, guilt plagued his dreams, and the violent manner of her death haunted his waking moments.

Rashid had spent virtually all his life dealing in death. Selling state of the art weapons had made him a billionaire, as well as advancing the global Jihad that he'd once embraced unquestionably. In recent years he had seen the death and destruction created by the weapons he sold in a different light. The countries of Islam were still stuck in the dark ages, despite the billions of pounds in oil revenue that had been generated by crude oil production. The phenomenal wealth that had been gleaned was being corralled by the ruling elite of the countries, and nothing was changing at grass roots. The majority of practicing Muslims were still not seeing the benefits of decades of oil production. The masses were easier to control when they were hungry and impoverished.

Rashid could see no significant improvement in the quality of life for millions of his kin, until the pointless wars and ancient tribal conflicts were put to bed for good. His weapons were being used by Muslims to kill other Muslims. Doubts had begun to rattle his soul, challenging his beliefs and torturing his soul. He set up his financial institution as a means to leave the arms business behind him, but he soon realised that if he retired someone else would set up in his place. There would be no end to the wars in Iraq and Afghanistan unless the key protagonists were removed from the equation.

Rashid knew them all. He didn't just know them; he knew where they operated, where they lived, who supplied them with food, and more importantly where their militias hid. It wasn't a huge leap of faith to progress from where his conscience was at, to arrive where he'd ended up. He walked into the kitchenette and looked across the harbour in the distance, and as his thoughts floated around his mind the telephone rang. He almost fell over as he stumbled toward the coffee table, and the goatskin slid on the wooden flooring.

"Hello," he said breathlessly, hoping that the caller had some news for him.

"Rashid?" the caller asked.

"Yes, who is this?"

"You were told not to call this number Rashid."

"Yes, I know, and I'm very sorry but no one has been in touch. I was getting worried. I need to bury my wife, and I need protection," Rashid rambled. Just hearing another human voice was a comfort.

"Your handler is dealing with everything, you are being watched, and protection is on the way, but you will not necessarily know that they are there Mr Ahmed, you'll be contacted later today, do not use this number again Rashid, is that clear?"

"Yes, sorry, what about my wife?"

The telephone connection was cut and static filled the line. Rashid shook his fist at the silent handset and gritted his teeth with anger. He cursed the caller and his family, and then redialled the number that he had been told not to call. The number switched directly to the voice mail box again, and again it declared itself full.

"You fucking bastard!" he shouted at the telephone and thought about hurling the handset across the room, just to teach it a lesson, but he realised that it was his only means of communication with the outside world. There was no mobile signal this far up the mountain, and nor was there any internet or broadband.

He thought about what the caller had said.

"I might not know that they are here," he whispered to himself as he crossed to the window.

Rashid looked across the fern covered headlands. There was thick knee high foliage for as far as the eye could see, broken only by the odd rocky knoll or giant grey boulder. There were plenty of hiding places for trained operatives to conceal themselves, but he would much rather see his protectors if they were really there. There was nothing obvious.

He thought about how protection would have arrived, when no one knew that he was here. If they did know, then how did they know where he was? Paranoia gripped him. Rashid had spent a life time trying to be invisible, and thinking that he was good at it too. Surveillance techniques had progressed at a frightening rate of knots over the past decade. Cameras and microphones could be planted at will, and they were almost undetectable to the untrained eye. He ran to the kitchen window. The outhouses looked locked and all appeared normal. There were two quad bikes parked inside the lean-to garage, just as usual. Low clouds were rolling in over the mountain top, moving imperceptibly down the slopes toward the house. Fog and sea mist descended quickly on the Welsh mountains claiming the lives of thousands of unprepared climbers who became unable to navigate, and suddenly the perilous cliffs and ravines were death traps. Rashid swore under his breath, knowing that the descending fog would make him a captive in his own home, until it drifted off again.

Rashid stood under the light fitting in the kitchen and studied it carefully, looking for evidence of hidden fibre optics, but there was nothing untoward. He repeated the process with every light on the upper floor to no avail. Every picture on the walls, every vase, and every pug socket could potentially be a spy in his hideout. Rashid didn't know why it bothered him if he was being watched by them covertly, but it did. He rushed around the upper floor searching behind every photograph and beneath every ornament, and perspiration began to form on his forehead as he dashed about like a human whirlwind hunting for covert devices.

If he was under surveillance then he could see no evidence of that. When he walked back into the living room there were two men standing at the top of the stairs. They both had shaved heads and were wearing black combat trousers, and dark bomber jackets. One of the men had a clear plastic earpiece, with a coiled communication cable which ran behind his ear, and down into his collar. Both men had telltale bulges in their jackets, indicating that they were carrying concealed weapons in shoulder holsters. They stood rigid and expressionless staring at him. His mind raced looking for answers.

'How did they get in? '

'How did they know that he was here? '

'Were they here to kill him or protect him? '

Rashid froze, frightened for his life like a rabbit caught in the headlights of an oncoming articulated lorry. There was a small logo emblazoned on the right arm of each man's jacket, 'Brigade Security'.

# CHAPTER 37

# THE BUNKER

The atmosphere outside the meeting room was frosty to say the least. Tank looked around the room and mentally made notes on who was familiar and who he didn't recognise. There appeared to be a very unusual mix of conventional law enforcement officers, and intelligence service personnel. Usually the two didn't meet, as public order units and civil law enforcement rarely had dealings with covert operations and counter terrorist units. He couldn't remember seeing so many senior uniformed officers in the same place as MI5 and MI6 directors.

The two key intelligence agencies rarely communicated with the Terrorist Task Force, until they had expended all their other options. The taskforce wasn't in the public domain. Tank and his team were usually the final violent solution to an unsolvable problem. The waiting area looked like a modern hotel foyer, white walls and lots of chrome and glass. Access to the waiting area was gained via a bank of three lifts which descended from various ports in the city above. The elevators beeped the arrival of new guests every couple of minutes, some familiar and some not so familiar. At the far end of the room was a thick plate glass wall, which had a revolving door set in its centre. The door led to a wide road cut through the sandstone bedrock deep beneath the city centre. The tunnel's stone walls were red and grained with a kaleidoscope of colour formed by the minerals that were embedded deep into the sedimentary rocks.

The tunnel branched off in three different directions, heading to the listening posts, and military facilities situated in the subterranean command centre. Army jeeps pulled up several times dropping of senior military brass, most of them were well known to Tank, but there was one American general that he didn't recognise. His thoughts were interrupted by a loud buzzer, signalling that the meeting was about to begin. He ambled through the entrance door and skirted the edge of the room avoiding unnecessary conversation with anyone. There was a folded tent card with his name written on it by hand, 'Tankersley' had been spelt incorrectly, and both he and the Major had been accredited wrongly with belonging to military counter terrorist units. This meeting was all wrong, and he knew that he wasn't going to enjoy it one little bit.

"Good afternoon everyone, we have called a meeting of the joint emergency agencies, which is the first of its kind, and it will be chaired by the Mister of Defence, Janet Walsh," a government aide introduced the meeting's chairperson.

"Thank you. We are here today because we are facing a very complicated situation, one which involves every single agency in the room," Janet Wash began in a no nonsense manner.

She had worked her way through the political jungle, firstly as a junior back bencher, a minister's private secretary. She eventually attained the role of cabinet member in her own right. Eighteen successful months in the education department, cleaning house financially, and cutting deficits had earned her the very senior post of Minister of Defence.

"I want to call your attention to the recent events that occurred in Warrington, and I want the Chief Constable of the Cheshire police force to take us through the facts as we understand them. Please keep a very open mind and listen to the details carefully, we'll keep all questions until the end."

A tall slim police chief stood up and cleared his throat with a gentle cough, his hand in front of his mouth as he did so. Tank thought that he looked nervous. His uniform was pristine, and his chest was adorned with a rainbow of commendation ribbons. He picked up a remote and a curved digital screen sprang to life. The screen turned deep blue and then a picture appeared with a subtitled description beneath it.

"This is a set of crime scene photographs taken at a public house in Locking Stumps, a suburb of Warrington, where two men were attacked and tortured, one of them losing a hand. During the aftermath a young woman employed at the pub was shot and killed by stray bullets," the chief explained. The pictures flashed by; there was a narrow path which ran between houses. It was lined with high bushes. The picture changed again to the image of the pub itself cordoned off by yellow crime scene tape. The crime scene pictures were followed by shots of the injuries inflicted, almost as an afterthought.

"Our investigation so far indicate clearly that this was a well planned, unprovoked attack on the 18th Brigade security company," the police chief seemed to be uncomfortable with his own explanation somehow. He coughed again as if the words had stuck in his throat, and he blushed.

"At the same time approximately four miles away a fire bomb was planted at the town centre branch of Blackstallion bank," he changed the images on the screen to illustrate his commentary. Pictures of the burnt out Volkswagen, and the smouldering ruins of the bank flicked onto the screen.

"We have deduced that the firebomb was a rouse to activate the bank's alarm, and draw the owner of the business, Rashid Ahmed into the path of a improvised roadside device."

A mug shot of Rashid appeared followed by a picture of the buckled Porsche. Thankfully there were no shots of his wife in the vehicle, or from the autopsy. He continued his presentation.

"At this moment in time all we know about the roadside bomb is that it was made by a munitions expert, but we don't have any suspects, and we are ruling out any link between the Brigade incident, and the bomb," he lowered his gaze as he spoke, so as not to make eye contact with anyone. Tank was certain that he had been primed about what he could say and gagged about what he couldn't. The faces around the table concurred with his instincts. The room was full of people that could spot a liar from one hundred yards away.

The police chief took his seat and handed the remote to a second uniformed officer. Tank recognised him as the uniformed chief from the Manchester division. He stood and mumbled a brief introduction.

"Following the incidents in Warrington we have investigated a shooting in an area of Canal Street, were a Somali immigrant was found shot through the head, and dumped in a skip behind a bar which is protected by Brigade security. We have no evidence of Brigade involvement, and there are two suspects in custody at present who are not linked to their organisation."

There were several confused glances exchanged across the table. There didn't seem to be any consistent thread running through the meeting so far, except how little evidence there was that the Brigade was involved in anything. Tank could smell a rat already.

"Twenty four hours after the attack at the Turf and Feather there was a gun battle at the Salford Towers. We can only speculate about the incident. All of the information that we have gleaned is from eye witnesses fleeing the building in darkness. We know that one black man was involved possibly a Somali gang member, but we don't know which gang. He was crucified to a wall outside of a drug den. One white male was shot and killed by a weapon that we can't find. There was no identification on the dead man and at present we cannot identify any of them because the whole building went up in flames." He shuffled his feet and looked as uncomfortable as his companion had before him.

"The dead Somali men found outside were known to the police, but the white man is not. The 18th Brigade is denying that they he was either a member of their organisation, or employed by them. The flat had been fortified to prevent easy access, and we think this was part of a local drug conflict," he flushed bright red.

The room remained completely silent as the police chief took his seat next to his well decorated colleague, who was still looking down and avoiding eye contact. Tank wondered what all the fuss was about. This wasn't the first cover up that he had witnessed, however it was one of the most glaringly obvious. The Minister shuffled her papers and looked a little disappointed with proceedings so far.

"So gentlemen, you all want to know why you are here," she began, "well there are several very important reasons."

She stood up and walked to the plate glass wall, keeping her back to the audience, all eyes were following her.

"Forensics found a small amount of the explosive Semtex in the remnants of the roadside bomb at Westbrook. It had been used purely as a detonator, but it matches samples belonging to a stolen batch which we think was about six kilos in weight," she explained. The military men in the room appeared to be aware of the missing explosives as Tank could see that there was no surprise in their eyes.

"The explosives were stolen from the Pirbright training facility six months ago, and we are informed by our colleagues in the intelligence services that the explosives found their way into the hands of extremist right wing organisations, however there has been no evidence of that until now," she turned and addressed the meeting face on. The men from MI5 nodded in agreement, silently supporting her information.

"The amount of explosive found was trace only, meaning that there is still around six kilos of military grade material on the streets, obviously now in the hands of an expert, willing to use it to kill."

"Is there any indication whom is behind the explosion," asked the Major, annoyed that the taskforce hadn't been supplied with the forensic information already.

"Only supposition, a military veteran certainly," the Cheshire police chief spoke.

"The 18th Brigade is full of army veterans," the American spoke for the first time, attracting a hardened glare from Janet Walsh.

"There is no evidence to suggest that the Brigade is involved in any criminal activity," she snapped. The room fell back into a confused silence.

"We must assume that whoever attacked Rashid Ahmed attacked him because of the allegations that he is dealing arms to the Taliban," Tank interjected, "which would suggest that they are either veterans or still in service."

"You're assuming too much," the Minister sniped. Tank didn't understand her reluctance to implicate the right wing extremist group.

"We should open a full investigation into the 18th Brigade and their activities, and we should stop them operating their business until we have done so," the Cheshire police chief seemed to gain his voice from somewhere. The minister stared at him angrily and shuffled uncomfortably.

"Is there a problem here that we don't know about?" Major Timms said, sensing the tension between the police chiefs and the government aides.

"Yes there is," the policeman blurted. "It's been a whitewash from the start. We are being gagged and I for one need to know why or you can have my badge right now."

"A little dramatic Chief Constable," Janet Walsh shot across the table.

"Can someone answer the question please, is there any evidence that the Brigade are involved in the death of Rashid Ahmed's wife?" Tank tried to steer the meeting back on track.

"There is no evidence at all that they are involved in any criminal activity," the Minister repeated herself slowly.

"So if we accept that as a fact then why are we here?" the Major asked.

"We need to find that missing Semtex for a start," she answered.

There were confused glances passed around the table. The subject of the meeting was still not crystal clear.

"Then that is a military issue," the police chief piped in.

"Not if the explosive is now in the hands of civilians," the American officer countered.

"Why do you think it is in the hands of civilians?" Tank asked.

"Because some of it was used to build that roadside bomb," he answered.

"Which we all agree was built and detonated by someone with extensive military knowledge," the police chief added, becoming frustrated again.

"That takes us back to the 18th Brigade again," Tank teased the insinuation into the meeting, fishing for more information.

"There is absolutely no evidence that they are involved in this attack," the Minister reiterated the point.

"This is bullshit! If we don't clear the air here then I'm going public on the issue," the American officer stood up and stared across the table at the politician.

Janet Walsh stared back at him for a long moment, and then dropped her pen onto the table annoyed at his outburst.

"We have a standoff gentlemen, and I'm afraid that we are being held over a barrel," she began.

"Oh spit it out woman!" the police chief was purple in the face. Tank thought that the policeman was going to have a heart attack if he didn't calm down.

"It is a matter of national security, and I must remind everyone of you that what we are about to discuss is strictly secret and highly confidential information," she said, ignoring the policeman.

She engaged everyone individually with her eyes, cleared her throat and continued.

"At the moment our armed forces are at breaking point, as are our allies. The Americans have one hundred and eighty thousand combat troops in Iraq, and a further six thousand in Afghanistan. The pressure being applied by Iraqi insurgents means that every embassy, control centre, hospital, power station, oil field and every member of staff that work in them, have to be protected night and day."

"Our troops are all committed to fighting the insurgents in the north of the country, and chasing down Iranian insurgents crossing the borders to resupply the militias," the American added.

"Our American allies have introduced the use of private security companies into the theatre of war in Iraq and Afghanistan, predominantly as close personal protection teams," she explained.

"Mercenaries," the Major interrupted.

"We prefer the term, private security companies," the American replied.

"Well you would, wouldn't you, but they are still mercenaries," the Major replied politely.

"That is public knowledge, so what is the point?" Tank asked.

"It is not exactly public knowledge," the Minister said coyly.

"What is the point?" Tank repeated his question growing frustrated with the way she was skirting around the issue.

"It is the number of private security company employees which is causing us a problem," the American said.

"The General is correct. There are now more private security company men than regular soldiers, and every one of them is absolutely essential to the war effort," the Minister added.

"Could you please tell us why we are all here," the police chief was growing increasingly annoyed every minute. Tank smiled at him but his face remained stony.

"The contracts that were first introduced by the American State Department held both impunity and an immunity clause in them, and they have never been changed since," the American General explained a little further. "The behaviour of some of their employees has been somewhat reckless which led to an FBI investigation into the events surrounding Nisour Square last year."

"For those of you not familiar with the incident seventeen innocent unarmed Iraqis were slaughtered by four armoured vehicles packing 7.62 millimetre machineguns, which are anti-aircraft weapons by the way," Tank hated mercenaries, but these guys were something else.

"Yes quite, thank you for that," the General coughed embarrassed and continued. "We identified six individuals within the Blackwater patrol that had used their weapons unlawfully, and they were incarcerated ready for deportation. Blackwater invoked their impunity clauses and then informed the Whitehouse that they were withdrawing their troops from Iraq with immediate effect." The General left the words hanging in the air.

"How many troops do they have there?" Tank asked.

"At that point there were one hundred and eighty thousand in Baghdad alone."

It was obvious to everyone in the meeting that had Blackwater removed their troops from Iraq there would be a huge void left behind. The role of close personal protection required immense manpower which the regular armed forces didn't have to spare.

"Okay so they blackmailed the government into submission, and telegraphed the strength of their immunity clauses to every mercenary soldier employed there," the Major summarised.

"Correct Major, except it has not just been telegraphed to every private security employee employed there," the Minister swallowed hard before she spoke again. "The contracts apply to all their contracted employees."

"What? Even when they are in their country of origin?" the policeman asked flabbergasted.

"Technically no, but we still have this huge threat of the withdrawal of troops. The company directors cannot take on any employees without the clause in place, or no one would do it. Who would fight a war if there was a threat of being jailed in a foreign prison? It is a very complicated situation," the General tried to clarify the position.

"All this is very interesting, but what has it got to do with us?" the Chief Constable of Greater Manchester asked, breaking his silence.

"We have mercenaries over there already," Tank answered his question without really knowing the answer, but it made sense. The British government had entered into immunity contracts with a mercenary company from within the British Isles.

"That's correct," the Minister said curtly.

"Surely the government hasn't hired the people we are discussing, not 18th Brigade employees, please?" Tank said.

"Yes, we do have some of them deployed in Iraq, but they are working as subcontractors the American Blackwater troops as well as a number of other trial companies," she replied.

The room was stunned into silence. The ramifications of this kind of information hitting the press were mind boggling. If the regular armed forces personnel demanded the same protection from prosecution then the defence of the realm could go into meltdown.

"How many 18th Brigade men have you employed?" Tank pressed.

"That's confidential," the Minister battened down the hatches.

"Roughly," he probed.

"Several hundred."

"So, this meeting is to tell us that we can't investigate any 18th Brigade employees, and if we do we are wasting our time because we can't prosecute them?" the Major said.

"Partly," the Minister answered.

"Good god, you mean that there is more?" the police chief quipped and sniggered.

"Yes, we must discuss Rashid Ahmed," she answered, staring directly at him.

Tank sat forward in his chair. He knew there was a reason why the Minister was so adamant that the Brigade weren't connected with the attack on Ahmed. A picture of Rashid Ahmed appeared on the screen. He was much younger and he was holding a Kalashnikov rifle, surrounded by men wearing Afghan robes and sporting Islamic beards. The director of MI5 stood up and walked toward the screen.

"Rashid Ahmed has been working with us for the last three years. He has been using his well established contacts to help us to supply the Taliban rebels with arms and munitions. The arms caches have all been supplied by our own intelligence agencies. Every single rifle and pistol that has been sold in the last three years is tagged electronically, and can be tracked by satellites. This operation has led to the discovery and disposal of several high ranking officials of al-Qaeda," the director looked very pleased with himself and a little too smug for Tank's liking.

"We spent three weeks investigating him when his arms dealing activities hit the press," the Major complained.

"That's unfortunate for you, but it adds to his credibility abroad I'm afraid, all part of his cover," the director dismissed the comment.

"Who leaked the information to the press?" Tank asked, annoyed.

"We don't know actually, but once it had been reported the situation was managed as well as it could be under the circumstances," his smugness was making Tank nauseous.

"Are we to assume that he's now in protective custody?" the Major asked.

"I'm afraid that's confidential," the director replied, enjoying the attention.

"Then why are you telling us this if you refuse to expand, there is no relevance to anything?" the police chief asked, incredulous.

"Because the press attention around Rashid Ahmed may have been sparked by a leak," the Minister interrupted. "If there is a leak then the attack on Rashid Ahmed may have been carried out by Islamic extremists, alerted to the fact that he is working with British intelligence agencies against the Taliban. It would make him a target for sure, and the report carried out on the explosion by the Terrorist Task Force, identifies the device as being similar to those used by insurgents in Iraq and Afghanistan, if I'm not mistaken," she explained and stared at Tank for a response.

"The device was similar, but the use of Semtex as a catalyst explosive is not consistent with an Afghan type device. The use of a catalyst explosive such as Semtex is a Special Forces technique, definitely a Western built device," Tank answered, he didn't buy into her theory at all.

"You're still leaning toward it being a Brigade operation, despite the lack of incriminating evidence aren't you Agent Tankersley?" she asked.

"And you are adamant that they're not involved, and I think that there is a reason behind that Minister, something that you haven't yet divulged," Tank countered.

"Rashid Ahmed has had close personal protection since the press coverage first began, but he may not have been aware of it," the Minister replied partially.

"Obviously the public's perception is that he is supplying arms to the Taliban illegally, and therefore we can't be seen to be protecting him," the MI5 director interjected.

"He isn't being protected by the 18th Brigade surely," Tank smiled, already knowing what the answer was.

"Yes he is, but that isn't the problem," the Minister interrupted. She asked for the remote to be used to move the images on a few places.

The picture on the screen was a confusing one, but shocking none the less. In the centre of the digital image was a burnt out truck, which looked similar to something you would see in a 'Raiders of the Lost Ark' type movie. A driver's cab, with a long wide flatbed cargo space behind it, once covered by a canvas tarpaulin. The canvas cover had been destroyed by fire leaving only a metal skeleton behind. The rubber tyres had been consumed by the inferno, and the body was a blackened hulk.

At the foreground of the picture was a knee high pile of what looked like transistor parts, untouched by the fire, left as a message to someone. Behind the pile of electronics was a row of wooden spikes, each one topped with a freshly severed head. The scene looked like a macabre coconut shy from a fairground in hell.

"This is the aftermath of an ambush, which took place in the Helmand Province of Afghanistan a week ago. The ambush was carried out by Taliban fighters, who were collecting a large cache of AK-47 rifles and RPG-3 grenade launchers," Janet Walsh spoke with a gravity which matched the dreadful scene behind her.

"We think that there was a leak," the MI5 director chipped in, pointing to the pile of electronics. "This is what's left of the electronic tags that were attached to the weapons. They were detected and removed, and then left to tell us that they are aware of what we were doing. Since this incident we have lost the signals from all of our trackers, bar an isolated few."

"The problem is that we have another large shipment on the

ground, eight hundred miles north of this spot. We don't know if the Taliban in this area are aware of what has been happening further south. They have no radio communications because they would give away their positions. So we have no way of knowing if they know the weapons are tagged or not," the Minister of Defence glanced at Tank momentarily.

"Who delivered the ambushed cache?" Major Stanley Timms asked, sensing there was more to this issue. He was thinking along the same lines as Tank.

Tank knew where this was going, and he flushed red angrily. He had the feeling that the Terrorist Task Force was about to be deployed as bait in a deadly game of chess.

"A troop of Afghan Special Forces," the MI5 director answered.

"Afghan Special Forces," Tank repeated, "they would hardly be my first choice option to deliver weapons that will be used to kill our own troops."

"That is why the issue is so sensitive Agent Tankersley, virtually all the new weaponry owned by the Taliban has been sold to them by Rashid Ahmed, with our blessing," the Minister explained solemnly. "We have been able to track them everywhere they moved for the last three years, but now they are completely lost. We also have the issue of the next arms deal, do we go ahead and risk more Afghan troops, or do we pull the weapons out totally and scrap the whole project?"

"Well you need to isolate the leak first and foremost," Tank said.

Janet Walsh nodded in agreement, and walked back to the horrific image on the screen.

"We cannot afford this to become public knowledge, it's far too complicated," she continued.

"Complicated? That's an understatement," said the police chief sarcastically.

"Who knew that the weapons were tagged?" Tank asked.

Janet Walsh looked to the intelligence director to reply. He shuffled back to his feet, obviously uncomfortable at being scrutinised now that the truth was out.

"At first only we did, but we think that Rashid Ahmed may have realised what was going on. He began to be a little less cooperative about a year ago, spouting on about betrayal. No one else knew what was going on, not even the electricians that fitted the tags. We couldn't afford the public finding out that we were putting weapons into that theatre, especially when the body count was rising on a daily basis," the director said.

"So the Afghan forces had no idea what they were delivering, or why?" Major Timms asked.

"No, none at all. They were under the impression that the weapons were deactivated, and that we were completing the handovers purely to identify possible al-Qaeda operatives amongst the Taliban.

"Where do you think the leak came from then?" Major Timms pressed.

The director looked toward Janet Walsh for confirmation that he could answer the question, and she nodded in his direction.

"We can only assume that Rashid Ahmed has turned against us," the director said.

"Your agency leaked the news about Rashid dealing arms to the Taliban didn't they?" Tank accused the director. He had a feeling that MI5 had lost control of its informer and had punished him for the betrayal by literally destroying him in the press, which in turn led to the collapse of his bank.

"There may have been a leak in our department, but it is purely speculation," he answered Tank's question with his head down, all his earlier bravado had now gone.

"Who deployed the Brigade to protect him?" Major Timms asked, enjoying seeing his opposite number on the rack.

"We did," the director replied.

"Why wasn't his wife given the same protection?" Tank asked.

The director looked to the Minister of Defence but she looked away failing to meet his gaze. Tank spotted that there was the chink in the bullshit armour, their united front had a weak spot and he aimed to capitalise on it in order to get to the absolute truth. Tank hated bureaucracy, especially when the taskforce was about to become involved. His agents would walk into any situation that he asked them to, but he wanted the real situation exposed before he could even begin to come up with a realistic action plan. The director remained silent, ignoring his question.

"Why wasn't Rashid Ahmed's wife offered the same protection

as he was, it's standard procedure surely?" Tank repeated.

The director coughed into his fist and blushed.

"It was an oversight I'm afraid," he mumbled.

"Bullshit, you left her exposed as a lesson to Rashid Ahmed for leaking information about the arms deals didn't you?" Tank laughed sourly. He hated the intelligence services and their underhand methods. Tank called a spade a spade, an arms dealer was always an arms dealer, and a liar was always a liar.

"I'm afraid the details of the incident are still a little sketchy, too much so for me to comment any further," the director bumbled on.

"You think Rashid Ahmed betrayed the intelligence services, so you exposed his past, destroying his financial institution, and left his wife exposed as a lesson to him," Tank clapped his hands in applause.

The uniformed policemen were aghast at what was being said. The world of domestic crime fighting is a very different one to the cynical world of espionage and covert operations, where people were erased and disposed of like refuse, as if they never existed. Angry glances and expressions of disbelief were shared across the table.

"We could not know that she would be targeted," the director replied angrily.

"She wasn't, Rashid Ahmed was the target, because you hung him out to dry in every national newspaper in the country. You invited someone to have a crack at him, trying to force him back into service," Tank answered him with the same amount of venom.

"Rashid Ahmed is an international arms dealer with a history of peddling death and destruction stretching back thirty years or more," the director snapped back.

"Exactly, not the type of man I would trust, especially to arm our enemies with weapons that will ultimately be used to kill our own troops. Someone has displayed a dreadful lack of judgement when they chose to ally with this man, and he in turn has paid a terrible price for his betrayal," Major Timms said.

"I'm guessing that if he wasn't being protected by a private security firm, then he wouldn't be alive right now," Tank stared at the Minister of Defence. She broke his stare and looked down at the table.

"That's ridiculous and downright libellous," the director replied, anger was making his voice shake.

"It's the truth. If he was under MI5 protection when the suspected leak occurred then Rashid Ahmed would have been erased," Tank continued despite the worried expressions on the faces of the regular law enforcement officers.

"I think that now would be a good time for a break," the Minister of Defence stood up to signal an end to proceedings, but no one moved for a long time.

# CHAPTER 38

# NORTH STACK

Rashid Ahmed sat in a huge leather armchair and watched the waves crashing against the North Stack hundreds of feet below the cliffs. The rise and fall of the waves seemed to calm his shattered nerves slightly. He held the telephone tightly in his sweaty hand as he waited for it to ring. The sudden appearance of two huge bodyguards, almost out of thin air had rattled him badly. He thought that they had come to kill him. The telephone conversation that he'd had earlier with his contact in the British intelligence agency had prompted the close personal protection agents to reveal themselves. The agency thought that it would give him some piece of mind. The Brigade had been protecting him covertly for nearly a month, and from the brief and curt exchange of words he'd had with them, they were annoyed that they'd had to reveal their presence.

"What's the point in you protecting me if they found it so easy to kill my wife?" Rashid blurted out at the Brigade men, frustrated that the intelligence agent tasked with looking after him still refused to answer his phone.

The 18th Brigade men looked at each other blankly, sharing a feeling of contempt for their charge.

"No one was protecting your wife Mr Ahmed, and more to the point you're still alive aren't you?"

"I was told by my contact that my family would be protected. His promises are worthless," Rashid quivered as he spoke, sadness overwhelmed him. The death of his beautiful young wife was beginning to eat into him. His eyes became misty with tears and he turned away from the bodyguards so that they couldn't see him weeping.

"You were being protected Mr Rashid, but you chose to hide and leave your wife behind to run your affairs. She was always going to be vulnerable on her own."

"Why wasn't she protected too if she was in danger?" Rashid whimpered.

"The government are only paying for one protection team, and they are paid to shadow you," a Brigade man answered him clinically.

"What do you mean 'paid for'? I'm supposed to be under government protection," Rashid turned to face the man angrily.

"We are contracted by the government Mr Rashid, but there are financial restrictions to our service. We do what we are paid for and we make recommendations to the government if more protection is required. Then it is down to them to respond," the big guard shrugged his shoulders.

"Did you recommend that my wife required extra protection?" Rashid asked wiping his running nose with his sleeve. He sniffled noisily waiting for an answer.

"We recommended it on day one of the contract. Unless you and your wife were permanently joined at the hip, then she was always in need of her own close protection team, always," the Brigade man explained.

"Are you telling me that she was not protected to save money," Rashid's sadness was replaced by anger.

"I'm saying that we are contracted to protect you, and so far we have a one hundred percent record, we also recommended that your wife needed her own personal protection squad. I have no idea why the government chose not to employ another team."

"I need to bury my wife, when will they be coming for me?"

"When will who, be coming for you?"

"The government men, the ones that are looking after me," Rashid snapped angrily.

"We have no direct contact with our employer Mr Rashid, we just keep you alive until we are told not to, and on the flip side of things, we haven't lost a contract primary yet, so you are safe for now," he sneered.

Rashid walked to the wide window and watched the sea again. There was a puffin flying near to the edge of the cliff. The wind was blowing so strong that it was hovering stationary in mid air despite flapping its wings rapidly. The wind dropped slightly and it soared off into the mountain mist toward the sea.

"You are mercenaries, nothing more. What use are two men against these people. It will not take them long to find me, and then what will two mercenaries do?"

"Who said there were two men?" the Brigade man smiled brightly.

Rashid looked out of the window again and studied the thick foliage, but he couldn't detect any more guards out there. He looked into the Brigade man's eyes for a flicker of untruth, but again he could see nothing to indicate that he was lying.

"Let's get down to business. The plans for this place show a panic room built beneath the staircase. We'll need to see that, and we also need to see the visibility across the headland from the downstairs windows. Are all the storm shutters in full working order?"

The Brigade man looked hard into Rashid's eyes, taking full charge of the situation with his assertive manner. Rashid could see why this man was a bodyguard. His eyes were like those of a shark, alive but ice cold. Rashid could tell that killing someone would not be a problem to this man. All the begging and pleading in the world would not bring a flicker of compassion into those eyes. It should have made Rashid feel safer, but it didn't.

"How do you know about the panic room?" Rashid was intrigued. Only Rashid and the architect, and the builders he employed should have known about that. It had been part of the construction contract that the interior modifications were kept a secret. The plans submitted to the council and the fire department didn't show the special additions, and because of its remote location, no one had ever been to the house to verify them.

"It's our job to know everything Mr Rashid, that's what we get paid for, and we are the best at what we do. As I told you earlier we haven't lost a primary yet."

"I don't like that," Rashid said regaining some of his composure.

"You don't like what exactly?"

"Being a 'primary'," Rashid said, "It makes me sound like a cancer."

The Brigade man looked to his colleague who smirked. There

were many in the 18<sup>th</sup> Brigade that would have agreed with his analogy. Most of the Brigade men that had seen active service had completed several tours of Iraq and Afghanistan. Islamic extremism had been the enemy for all of them, and it left most of them carrying a burning hatred of anything Muslim. The analogy of extremism spreading across the planet like a cancer was easy for them to imagine. Rashid saw the silent communication between his protectors and it worried him further still.

"Primary is just the word we use for our charges, or the people we protect, it's not an insult," the Brigade man brushed the comment aside and got back to business in a professional manner.

"Yes, I understand, come this way and I'll show you the strong room," Rashid resigned himself to be compliant with the two guards. At least he wasn't alone anymore, although he almost wished that he was.

"Tell me about the storm shutters, I couldn't get a definitive layout from the plans. Where they added later on?"

"Yes," Rashid paused at the top of the stairs which led down to the bedrooms on the ground floor. "They were fitted to protect the glass wall in the first floor living room."

"What about the ground floor?"

"No, there was no need to protect them because the headland plants act as a windbreak. They are only fitted to the first floor windows."

Rashid answered the big bodyguard's questions politely, but his mind wasn't really on the job in hand. He was worried about burying his wife. He didn't really see how he could do it in safety with any dignity left intact for her or her family. If he buried her normally the press would turn it into a circus. If he handed her body back to her family for burial then they would probably never tell him where she was buried. Rashid couldn't bear the thought of not being at her internment, it wasn't right.

"Where is the entrance to the panic room?" the bodyguard interrupted his tortured thoughts.

"What?" he muttered.

"I asked you where the panic room entrance is," the Brigade man repeated the question slowly, as if Rashid were stupid.

They had reached the bottom of the wide staircase which brought them to a 'U' shaped corridor. Bedrooms led off the walls furthest away from the stairs. The staircase was positioned in the centre of the 'U'. The Brigade man walked around the staircase looking for the panic room entrance, first down one corridor and then back down the other. He tapped the walls searching for the entrance, and then looked at Rashid confused.

"Where is the entrance?" he asked.

"It is very well hidden isn't it?" Rashid enjoyed feeling in control for the moment.

"There are no obvious breaks in the walls, no fake broom cupboard underneath, it's probably the best one I've seen so far, I can't identify the entrance, which means that I wouldn't know that there was a panic room unless I'd seen the plans," the Brigade man admitted.

Rashid walked to the foot of the stairs and kneeled down at the base of the first step. He slipped his fingers beneath the carpet on the first riser, and there was an audible click. The first four stairs lifted like the trunk of a car, hinged further up the staircase, revealing a dark narrow passage beneath. Rashid waved his arm like a maitre de showing an important customer to their table in an expensive restaurant.

"I'm impressed," said the Brigade man peering into the darkness.

"I hope that I never need to use it. I built it to hide from the British intelligence services, in case they discovered my occupation," Rashid said resignedly, as if he was talking about another life.

"Let's hope that you don't have to use it. How long can you remain in there?" the Brigade man knew that there would be a tungsten steel capsule buried somewhere in the dank passageway. Breaking in without a laser cutting torch was impossible, blowing it up was not an option, it was indestructible. Air would be pumped in by a solar powered generator which would be hidden somewhere far away from the building. The only time restraint on survival inside the pod was the amount of food and water that was stored in there.

"Six weeks, so I'm told," Rashid answered. It was like asking most normal people how fast does your car go, few have actually taken them to the absolute limit.

"Six weeks, I wouldn't fancy the smell in there after six weeks," the Brigade man recognised that Rashid was repeating the salesman's pitch verbatim. The amount of human waste generated over a six week period was not something that could easily be disguised in an enclosed space. His experience on covert missions told him that the timescale of human endurance in that environment would be less than half that period of time.

"Yes, I have to agree with you, apparently the waste disposal unit sits above a deep chamber drilled into the rock bed, but I'm sure the smell would soon become an issue shall we say," Rashid wittered on as if it were important, his mind was on darker things.

"Okay, I'm happy that even if our position were to be breached, that you could be made safe from harm in the panic room. If in the unlikely event there comes a time were you have to take refuge in there, then it is absolutely imperative that you remain in there until someone contacts you. I assume there is an, all clear, signal in there?" the Brigade man asked matter of factly.

"Yes, the activation button that I used cannot be used to open the pod once someone is inside, but it will alert the occupant to the fact that someone else is either in need of shelter, or is telling you that it is safe to come out," Rashid explained.

"For now only you, me, and your contact at the agency will be aware of that, you must trust no one else. Is that clear?" the Brigade man frightened Rashid with his manner. "The quarry access road and the mountain trail are set with motion sensors. If anything tries to climb up this mountain we will know about it. There is no need to worry Mr Ahmed, you're completely safe."

Rashid felt a cold shiver down his spine, and despite the reassurances from one of the biggest, coldest men he'd ever encountered, he didn't feel safe at all.

# CHAPTER 39
# SALFORD TOWERS

Jay had watched the Somali falling from the platform burning like a human torch. He grimaced at the thought, and wondered if the man was praying for the imminent impact of the cold concrete to stop the terrible pain of being burned alive. Jay had seen more than his fair share of burn victims during his tours of Iraq and Afghanistan. American 'Hellfire' missiles were loaded with a toxic flammable gel which ignites on contact with the air. They are a thousand times more devastating than the biggest napalm bombs used in Vietnam. The American bombers had dropped over ten thousand Hellfire missiles on the mountain cave system hideaways of Afghanistan, known as the Tora Bora, trying to kill Osama bin-Laden and his affiliates. Jay had been part of a clean-up squad, part American Delta Force and part British Special Forces, who were sent in to search bombed areas looking for survivors, and evidence of confirmed kills. On many of his missions they had discovered bodies burned beyond all recognition, some of the unfortunate victims of the Hellfire missiles however were found alive, suffering dreadful burns and unbearable pain, begging to be shot and put out of their misery. The experience stayed with Jay, especially on the dark lonely nights when those terrible fleshless blackened faces haunted his dreams.

The eventual arrival of a convoy of police cars and ambulances had startled him back to reality. The platform was ablaze but he had only seen one body falling. It was still too far away to see exactly what had happened properly. He had then tossed the empty petrol canister toward the blaze, destroying any evidence that he may have left. The burning cradle was still climbing the building at a steady pace, but now it was setting fire to every window frame that it passed, six floors were already starting to burn. The smoke and flames were adding to the chaos inside the dark tower block. People were flooding into the stone stairwells, and the noise levels were reaching crescendo pitch. Jay didn't have any problem slipping away past the emergency services on the ground floor, their priority had been the safe evacuation of the residents.

Unfortunately Omar had shared the same luck and escape had been relatively simple for him too. He reached his car and bundled Gemma into the passenger seat. She was behaving like a zombie, shocked by the evening's events. The car started first time and Omar had to wait for a fire truck to pass by before pulling the car onto the main road. Crowds of half dressed people were gathering, some only wearing dressing gowns. The top section of the building had been well ablaze when he noticed a big man crossing the road about a hundred yards further down the road, beyond the crowds. He was heavily muscled, his head shaved, and there was a tattoo below his ear that Omar couldn't make out, but he looked like a member of the 18th Brigade. He was one of the men who had been sent here to behead the Somali Yardies, by killing Omar himself. They had failed. Omar decided to follow him.

Jay turned up the collar on his jacket, heading away from the burning tower block while talking into his mobile telephone. He was guiding one of their men to his position to pick him up. A black panel van pulled across two lanes in a u-turn manoeuvre, and stopped alongside him. Jay looked up and down the street checking for the presence of the police. Once he was sure that he wasn't being watched he opened the door and climbed into the van. He noticed a small two door customised car crawling close to the pavement a few hundred yards away. He couldn't see the occupants but his instincts told him that they were following him. Jay smiled and shut the door, looking at the vehicle in the wing mirror.

"Are you being followed?" the driver had asked.

"Yes, I think so, just head back toward Warrington, and take the motorway," Jay ordered.

"Do you want me to lose him?" the driver slowly pulled away from the kerb, watching the coupe behind them doing the same.

"Pull a u-turn here, see if he follows," Jay said. The driver swung the van back around heading in the opposite direction. As they past the suspect hatchback Jay got a very brief look at the driver. He was black, but he couldn't see any more than that.

Jay watched in the wing mirror as the car's brake lights lit up. It pulled into the kerb. The passenger door opened and the interior light came on. A blond woman stumbled out of the car and fell onto the pavement, as if she had been thrown out. The door was pulled shut from within the vehicle, and then the car mirrored their u-turn and followed at a distance.

"He's following us," the driver said.

"I know, let him, I've got a good idea where to take him," Jay said dialling the cell phone of the 18th Brigade leader, Terry Nick.

# CHAPTER 40

# VIGILANTE

Old Jim approached the nurses' station and smoothed his grey hair back with the palm of his hand. His hair felt sticky with Brylcream. Jim always used the famous man's hair product, which was first introduced in the fifties to help the Teddy Boys and rockers keep their quiffs in the perfect shape. Jim had once sported a fabulous quiff. He had to shave it off during his army days when they were forced to keep hair hidden by the famous regimental red beret. Whatever hair was beneath their beret was their own concern. When Jim was a young Para he would trawl the dance halls with his friends looking for pretty women.

Jim spotted a young nurse behind the reception desk and his male instinct made him preen his hair. He still kept it groomed even though it was grey and thinning. It barely covered his pink liver spotted scalp.

"Hello Jim," she said in a broad St. Helens accent, making it sound like 'elloh'. Jim thought that it was a shame that she had such a thick accent. She looked so perfect until she spoke, then the accent ruined the moment. He was familiar with the pretty nurse from previous visits.

"Hello Yvonne," he replied, smiling to reveal yellowed teeth. His smile had once wowed the women, but now it attracted their attention for all the wrong reasons.

"Is he expecting you today?" she asked.

"No, I just thought that I would call in as I was passing, how is he doing?"

"He's up and down. One day he's jolly and full of beans, the next he's barely capable of holding a conversation with you. His moods seem to be swinging lower and lower lately. He still manages to get to the cinema a couple of nights a week though, getting used to using his new legs too," she walked from behind the desk.

Jim noticed how the crisp material of her uniform hugged her hips, accentuating her buttocks. If he was twenty years younger, he thought. Better make that forty years, she wouldn't know what had hit her. He tried not to stare but she caught him in the act and he blushed a little. Jim looked away quickly and headed off down the pastel coloured corridor. There were rooms situated on both sides of the corridor which stretched as far as the eye could see. He was on the second floor of massive residential nursing facility, which had been built to accommodate wealthy elderly people in a fully serviced mini-community. The facility had a huge foyer surrounded by shops, which sold everything you could buy on the high street. The ground floor area incorporated a library, gymnasium, spa-centre, bar, and several clothes boutiques, a proper self contained micro-town. In recent years the government had purchased a dozen or so of the one bedroom apartments to house recovering war veterans. The project was designed to give them more independence than they would get in a conventional hospital, but still offer them round the clock medical care, and group therapy support.

Jim chuckled to himself as he passed the imitation front doors and windows. The architects had come up with the concept of making the corridors look like a narrow street lined with terraced houses. Mock windows were fixed to the walls in-between the front doors. Each fake window was fitted with mock curtains and mock flower vases. The idea was sound; it was supposed to give the residents a feeling of normality, and to dispel feelings of claustrophobia or being institutionalised. To Jim it just looked silly, but then he didn't have to live here for years on end.

He reached the room which he wanted. The front door was imitation Georgian, painted bright red, with a polished brass doorknocker fixed to the middle panel. Jim chuckled again and rattled the knocker to announce his arrival.

"Who goes there, friend or foe?" said the voice from within.

"Friend, Parachute Regiment, may we enter," Jim laughed as he opened the door. They went through the same comedy routine every time he visited.

"Hello son," Jim said saluting as he approached the figure of a man in a wheelchair.

"Hello dad, I wasn't expecting you today," his son, Ross, turned awkwardly in his chair to greet him.

Jim still choked every time he saw his son in the chair. He had been caught in a fire fight in Afghanistan two years earlier. His convoy had been hit by three coordinated roadside devices. The first two bombs took out the lead and rear vehicles, trapping the remaining armoured cars between them. Standard procedure under these circumstances was to deploy the infantry soldiers out of the vehicles immediately. They would then set up defensive positions and create a bridgehead. The Taliban were well versed in Western military procedure and waited until the Paras left the safety of their armoured vehicles before detonating the third and biggest device. The ploy was used many times with devastating effect. The devices were activated remotely from hundreds of yards away. Once the armoured vehicles were neutralised the Taliban followed up with an ambush catching the British troops in a deadly crossfire.

Ross had caught the full force of the third blast as he deployed from his Warrior jeep. The blast had sheered his body completely in half at thigh level and shattered his pelvis. The shrapnel that ripped his legs and genitals from his upper body was so hot that it cauterized the injury, preventing him from bleeding to death at the scene. Ross wished that he had bled to death. He was under constant suicide watch. He felt no hope when he looked to the future and no sense of pride or achievement when he looked back at his military career. He would never have children, never have sex again, he couldn't walk, he couldn't even go to the toilet anymore because everything went into a bag. Ross had been fitted with prosthetic limbs but would always need a chair and sticks. He was a cripple and he saw no joy in living as a cripple.

"I was passing so I thought I'd say hello, catch up on the news," Jim playfully punched his son's shoulder. Ross clenched his fists and made a boxers guard, joining in the pretend fight.

"What's going on?" Ross asked pointing to the television. The local news was on and an image of the Turf and Feather flashed onto the screen. Then the image changed to show Terry Nick walking out of Warrington police station through a crowd of photographers.

"There's been trouble at the Turf son," Jim explained. "Do you remember little Mandy?"

"Yes, little barmaid that never smiled," Ross answered.

"That's her, well she got caught in a crossfire, took two in the head I believe, poor girl, she was a bit miserable sometimes but she didn't deserve that," Jim said, nodding to the television as he spoke.

"Fucking hell that's a bit harsh, who was doing the shooting?"

"Some Yardie gang from Manchester I'm told, although they haven't got anyone for it yet. Two cars turned up at the Turf and started shooting with a Mach-10, then they dumped Headbutt Norman and Dithering Dave on the tarmac, all cut up," Jim carried on with the story.

"Those two old boys were no harm to anyone, are they alright?"

"Last thing that I heard they were still in intensive care, horrible facial scars I believe, but I don't know any more than that really," Jim said.

"I bet they were both pissed eh?" Ross joked.

"Oh, there's absolutely no doubt about that son," Jim laughed.

"Bet they didn't feel a thing, pissheads," Ross laughed again, enjoying male company. His dad made him forget his injuries, even if it was only for a short time.

"Yes, I bet they woke up in casualty and thought they had fallen down the stairs," Jim carried on the cruel, but funny scenario, enjoying seeing his son laugh.

"Can you imagine those two if they were in the next bed to each other, they'd be sneaking vodka into their orange juice every five minutes."

Jim stared at the news laughing when the picture changed to the remnants of a Porsche, which had been hit by a roadside bomb at Westbrook. Jim swallowed hard before starting his next sentence.

"Have you been keeping up with that?" Jim asked, changing the subject quickly. Ross stopped laughing and his face darkened.

Ross leaned over the side of his chair and picked up a bottle of Teacher's whisky. He turned the top off slowly, and poured himself a large measure into a glass tumbler. He offered the bottle silently to his father, but Jim waved his hand as a refusal.

"Too early for me son," Jim said trying to keep the mood light.

"It's not really an issue for me," Ross said sourly. His mood had changed dramatically in just seconds, and it was the television pictures from Westbrook that had changed him.

"What do you think about that mess at Westbrook?" Jim pressed on.

"The bloke is an extremist collaborator, worse still he was arming the bastards that put me in this chair, so he got what he deserved as far as I'm concerned," Ross took a long gulp of whisky and then filled up his glass again.

"Have you heard that it was his wife and not him that they got?"

"Pity they didn't get them both and their kids too, fuck them." Ross swallowed the whisky in two gulps and filled up the glass again.

"You're hitting that a bit hard aren't you son?" Jim said.

"Fuck off if you don't like it, no one asked you to come here did they?"

"Alright son, I'm not having a go. Just take it easy on that stuff, it takes you down into the dumps that's all I'm saying," Jim held up his hands to calm his son down. He was incredibly volatile, all part of his condition now, and there was nothing anyone could do to help him. It broke Jim's heart to see him like this, but he had to know if he had anything to do with the missing Semtex.

"Do you know the details of the device?" Jim asked seriously.

"I don't need to know, it's obvious. You don't get that type of damage from anything else but an Iranian design improvised formed device, nothing else it could be," Ross drained the glass again.

"That's got to be last thing you would expect to see in your home town Ross, but you don't seem too surprised," Jim tried to coax an answer from him.

Ross ignored him and filled his tumbler with whisky again. Half the bottle had gone in less than five minutes. His face was flushed with anger, and the veins at his temples throbbed visibly.

"They reckon that the device was ignited by using a small amount of Semtex as the catalyst," Jim pushed harder, giving him a little more information as bait.

"So what," Ross said, swallowing another large mouthful.

"So, it isn't easy to get hold of Semtex, you don't just go to the supermarket and buy it," Jim sat forward and looked hard at his son, trying to see inside his troubled mind.

"What the fuck are you implying dad?" Ross didn't even look at his father when he spoke.

"The Semtex that I told you about has gone missing Ross, someone has stolen it, bit of a coincidence don't you think," Jim pressed again.

Ross seemed to freeze when he heard that the explosives had gone missing. He looked confused as he drained the glass for the third time.

"What do you think dad? Do you think I whizzed out in my chair and nicked your fucking Semtex?"

"I'm not saying that, but whoever built that bomb had the same training that you did. They also used Semtex to build it. There are four people who know that the Brigade acquired a batch of explosives. So far the only two people that know it has been stolen are me and the person that stole it. You are one of the people that knew about it Ross," Jim explained his thoughts calmly and rationally.

Ross poured the bottle again, filling the tumbler to the rim once more. He took a long swig of the potent liquid. Jim knew that the combination of drink and his medication would be catching up with his son very shortly. He needed an answer desperately.

"Maybe you've told one of your pals in here when you've been pissed, maybe you didn't mean to tell them but it just came out because of the drink," Jim offered his son a way out by blaming the drink.

"Maybe you've lost it yourself you senile old twat," Ross emptied the glass, and then lost his grip on it. It tumbled into his lap and then rolled onto the floor in front of his wheelchair. His chin lolled onto his chest and his eyes seemed to roll back into his head. Drool ran from the corner of his mouth onto his jumper. Jim knew that he would get no sense from him today. The moment had past.

Jim stood up and picked up the empty bottle of scotch, placing into the waste paper bin next to the bed. He knew when the explosives had been stolen. Jim had identified the days when the explosives went missing by using his diary. He surmised that the thief needed him to be out of the house for at least an hour or so. He had narrowed it down it to just two possible days. One day he had gone to the pub to watch the football. He had returned three hours later worse for wear from the beer he had drunk during the match. The second day he had been at a rare visit to the doctor for a routine check up, which had taken him away from home most of the afternoon.

On the sideboard, opposite his son's bed were his medical notes. They had to be filled in every time someone entered the room. Even the cleaners had to fill in the journal when they came and went. Jim flicked through the pages to the dates which fitted. He ran his finger down each day's events, first one day and then the next. Jim sighed deeply and placed the notes back on the furniture. Ross had been in is room all day, both days. It couldn't have been him even if he had had help.

# CHAPTER 41

# VIGILANTE

Sergeant Mel Hickey picked up his sports bag and slung it over his shoulder. He looked around his small living quarters and smiled sourly, thinking that he probably wouldn't be back for a while, if at all. He opened the front door and looked out at a mocked up corridor, made to look like a street of terraced houses. Mel had always thought the idea was a terrible joke, not so bad if you were in the final throws of Parkinson's disease, or Alzheimer's, but not so convincing for those with all their mental facilities intact. He stepped out and closed the fake red front door behind him. The imitation brass knocker rattled as it closed, making him laugh.

"Hello Mel," a voice said behind him, making him jump. His legs buckled a little as he shifted his weight. When he had first started to use them his balance was an issue but he was learning to adjust to them now. As long as he administered his pain relief on time he could stay on them for days at a time. Walking was still painful but it was when he removed them that he suffered the most.

"Hello Jim, have you been to see your Ross then?" Mel replied shocked at the sudden appearance of old Jim in the corridor. Jim was the last person that he wanted to see.

"Yes, I called in on the off chance that he would be sober, not much chance of that though, how are the bionic legs doing?" Jim looked bleary eyed, either tired or emotional, Mel didn't much care. He needed to be away from old Jim rapidly.

"They take some getting used to, I'll never be winning any races. Has he been at the whisky again," Mel said cheerfully, trying to pass Jim in the corridor.

"Listen to me a minute Mel," Jim grabbed his arm surprisingly hard for an old fellow. He leaned close to Mel's ear.

"Has Ross said anything strange to any of you lads in here?"

"What do you mean Jim?" Mel pulled away from him, but the grip on his arm tightened.

"Has he mentioned anything about the Brigade having a weapons stash?" Jim was desperate. He was fishing for any sign of untruth in Mel's eyes, but there was only anger and surprise there.

"Get your hands off me Jim or I'll break your arm," Mel spoke calmly but with enough venom to make the old man realise that he had crossed the line. He might have been a Para once, but that was a very long time ago. Mel would destroy the old man in seconds, legs or no legs.

"Sorry Mel, I'm upset, I need to know if he's been talking to anyone about weapons and stuff belonging to the Brigade, has he said anything to you?" old Jim stepped back and tears welled in his watery eyes.

"Look Jim, everyone in here is fucked up, me included, Ross likes a whisky or two and when he drinks he talks shit, but I haven't heard anything about any weapons," Mel stared into the old man's eyes cool as a cucumber, not even a flicker of deceit in his gaze. The old man's body seemed to deflate, and he nodded his head as he turned and walked away.

"Jim," Sergeant Mel Hickey called after him.

"What," the old man said, half turned away.

"You take it easy Jim," Mel said, and he saluted the old Para.

"I will, you too," old Jim saluted back, and then walked off down the corridor staring at the carpet as he went.

Mel Hickey adjusted his weight and then walked in the opposite direction from Jim. The corridor stretched a hundred yards before he would reach a bank of elevators which would take him down to the reception. He had a hire car waiting for him in the car park. He'd blown up his last vehicle when he attacked the bank to draw Rashid Ahmed out of his home, and he hadn't had time to replace it. He had killed the wrong target that time, but that didn't matter now because he was about to redress the balance. He planned to use the six kilos of Semtex that he had stolen from the Brigade's arsenal. Ross was very drunk the night he'd told him that there was explosives in the cellar belonging to old Jim.

In 2007 when he had opened fire in Nisour Square Mel genuinely believed that the convoy was about to be attacked by a mobile car bomb, which had broken down. The truth of the matter was that the mercenaries used by the American and British forces were constantly in fear of suicide bombers and that made them twitchy. Everyone was a suspect, and every vehicle was a potential hazard. When constant fear was combined with the heat and the dust then tempers became taught, and nerves were perched on a knife edge. The events of Nisour Square were covered up and brushed over, all the mercenary immunity clauses were invoked and evidence was manufactured to muddy the waters of the FBI's investigation.

Sergeant Mel Hickey had been hauled in front of his superiors and identified as the instigator of the massacre. The Blackwater employees lost a huge cash bonus because of the incident. The bonus only applied if there was no loss of civilian life during their active term in Iraq. Although he was safe from prosecution he had caused his employers a huge amount of hassle, and they placed him on light duties. Mel was traumatised by the incident. The camaraderie that he had enjoyed in the British Army did not exist in the mercenary ranks, and he was routinely castigated by his peers, who had been penalised financially as a result of his actions. The fact that a dozen other mercenaries opened fire that afternoon seemed to be lost on everyone. All the fingers were pointing at Mel and the following days and weeks became almost unbearable.

Sergeant Mel Hickey was posted on sentry duty outside an Iraqi police recruiting station. The station was a primary target for insurgents. Over two hundred Iraqi policemen are either murdered or completely disappear every month, and even now it is the most dangerous profession in the nation. No one really knows how many are actually slaughtered, or how many run away for fear of being killed. Iraqi policemen are deemed as collaborators. They are trained by the Christian invaders and therefore their families become legitimate targets and are murdered wholesale every day.

Sentry duty was a laborious task, mainly because of the relentless heat. The desert sun beat down on them without mercy all day long. There were huge concrete blocks in the road, in front of the recruitment station, stopping suicide bombers from driving cars packed full of explosives into the compound itself. The compound was surrounded by a crooked brick wall which had been rendered with white plaster, as is the custom in the Middle East. The render has a two-fold effect, firstly it looks cleaner at first, and secondly it hides the shocking quality of the bricklayers' workmanship. Mel knew that a determined bomber could drive a vehicle straight through the fragile wall, in fact they often joked that they could ride a push bike through it. Another mercenary had quipped that they could be attacked by the first skateboard bomber in history, because the walls were so poorly constructed. The rendered walls were pockmarked with machinegun bullet holes from several drive-by shootings. There was a constant queue around the building, ambitious poor young men eager to feed their families, and progress up the social ladder by landing a responsible job as a policeman. They waited patiently for hours upon end for their turn to enlist. Standing in the recruitment line had cost over sixty men their lives already that year.

Two weeks into his posting local Iraqis had got wind that the men guarding the recruitment station were in some way connected to the massacre at Nisour Square. Mel was nearing the end of a twelve hour nightshift, which spanned midnight until midday. The queue of eager recruits was snaking around the compound as usual, despite the intense heat, which was creeping over a hundred degrees. Mel was incredibly fair skinned, almost an albino, and he suffered from the heat more than most. His hair, almost white, offered no protection to his sensitive pink scalp from the sun's rays.

He was tired and hungry when a young Iraqi child approached him and his men. They were grouped together taking in some fresh water. They had to complete the required paperwork before handing the shift over to the incoming Sergeant. The night shift commanders were en route with a fresh troop of mercenaries. There was less than thirty minutes remaining before they could get out of the sun, eat and then get some well earned sleep. Mel noticed that the child appeared to be distressed, but there was something else which struck him. There was something different about her face.

It was unusual to see girls out alone even when they were young. They were rarely seen in public unaccompanied. This young girl was upset, crying and alone, and then it clicked. She was a Down syndrome child. Mel felt a wave of sympathy as he watched the little girl crying and walking toward them. He smiled, trying to calm her, and walked toward her. He offered her his bottle of water but her confused face showed no signs of understanding anything further than the fact that she was lost. It was obvious, what else would she be doing here on her own.

Mel heard a raised voice from the line of waiting men and he turned to see what the noise was all about. Some of the waiting men had started to run away from the approaching child. Mel turned back to the child and noticed her loose fitting smock had angular bulges beneath it, as if something had been strapped around her waist and chest. He realised too late that she had been taken from an asylum by insurgents, wrapped in explosive belts and then told to walk toward the soldiers. Mel looked around for the perpetrators who had sent the poor helpless girl to a dreadful death, but he never had chance to locate them. The explosive belts were remotely detonated from just fifty yards away, ripping the poor girl into bloody shreds. Because of his close proximity to her he was catapulted upwards away from the deadly shrapnel. His legs were blown off and couldn't be recovered, but he'd survived the blast, unlike his entire troop who were shredded by a wave of ball bearings and nails.

Weeks turned into months, and then into years as his recovery went from one stage to the next. Now he was walking with the aid of Hi-Tec prosthetic legs. His upper body was powerfully built and his mind was as sharp as a razor. The war in Iraq was the reason for his injuries. His injuries and the resulting mental damage were the reasons why he had eventually lost his wife and children to another man. His anger and resentment at his plight had eventually driven his family away from him. The turmoil in Iraq and Afghanistan was being dragged out by the Muslim insurgents. The insurgents were his enemy, Rashid Ahmed had been sending arms to the Taliban, and now was the time to even things up a little. He slung his bag over his shoulder again and headed for the car park. It was a two and a half hour drive to Holyhead Mountain, and a long climb to North Stack. Chances were that the climb would be too much for him, and he would probably have to wait for Rashid to come down, but he could wait.

# CHAPTER 42
# THE BRIGADE

Jay checked the wing mirror again and saw the hatchback still following them. He reached for the cell phone in his pocket, and pressed the speed dial button.

"Jay, how did it go?" Terry Nick answered.

"I think they got the message, but I've picked up a tail," Jay looked in the mirror again.

"How many of them?" Terry asked.

"There is only one of them, but he's been on his mobile for the last fifteen minutes, probably drumming up some backup," Jay explained.

"Keep him away from town. We don't need any more hassle with the police. I've had London on the telephone giving me a polite warning that our public image could jeopardise our international contracts," Terry didn't want to court any more adverse publicity. The contracts in Iraq had been much more complicated than he had anticipated them to be. The events at Nisour Square had caused reverberations across the entire world. Deploying mercenary soldiers was lucrative, but people were always going to die, that's what they do for a living. You just had to hope that they only killed the bad guys.

The situation in Iraq seemed to be coming to an end. The American public wanted their troops out of there immediately, and a British troop withdrawal was already underway. The situation was precarious to say the least. Buying weaponry and equipment was expensive, and when you consider that most of it stays in situ when the conflict is over, planning your purchases as a conflict comes to an end is a risky business. Terry Nick knew that there would be other conflicts and other governments that would need the services of his mercenaries, but he had to protect his domestic business too. Without the door security business everything else would implode. It supplied the cash flow to fund Brigade ventures overseas. His relationship with the gargantuan American mercenary company, called Blackwater Worldwide, was still intact. They welcomed the influx of highly trained British veterans into the fold with open arms, because they were the best.

Relationships at home were less cordial, and it seemed that the intelligence services kept blowing hot and cold with the Brigade, but they still had key primaries to protect. Rashid Ahmed was the priority right now, and the fact that his men had been ordered to reveal themselves complicated matters further. He needed to go to the remote safe house himself to assess the situation first hand. It was obvious that 'persons unknown' had carried out a well planned attack on Ahmed, and people like that seldom go away unassisted. The Brigade couldn't afford for their reputation to be tarnished any further by losing a primary. Rashid's mountain residence could be a blessing in disguise because the remoteness of the area could offer the perfect location to dispose of his latest problem, Omar and the Yardies.

"I'm heading down to Holyhead, you should head there too and bring that tail with you, do you have enough fuel to make it there without stopping?" Terry asked. He didn't want to offer any opportunities for the Yardies to attack Jay before they reached the mountain.

"We've got a full tank, are you already on the way?" Jay replied leaning over and looking at the fuel gauge.

"If I leave now, I'll be thirty miles ahead of you, put your foot down and you'll catch me up before the Conwy tunnel. If we can play this right then we can arrange a nice little welcome party for your friends, just keep him behind you," Terry ordered. Most well trained military personnel were taught how to keep a tail close enough to entice them to keep following, but far enough away to stop them getting into striking distance. The FBI call it 'following a suspect from the front', they pretend that they don't know they're being followed, allowing the tail to grow in confidence while an ambush is organised.

# CHAPTER 43

# TANK

The meeting in the subterranean bunker had been brought to an abrupt end by the Minister of Defence. The conventional law enforcement agencies had left, some reluctantly, and others indifferently. Tank knew that the idea of bringing MI5, MI6, military counter terrorist units, uniformed police chiefs, CI5 and the Terrorist Task Force was flawed, to say the least. The two worlds of conventional law keepers and covert agencies could never marry. The uniformed divisions spent all their time hunting murderers, kidnappers and burglars, while the covert agencies committed all three serious crimes on a weekly basis, without fear of prosecution. The intelligence world is a dangerous and cynical place to live in, and few people have long careers there, fewer still collect their pension.

The Minister was talking in hushed tones to the intelligence directors, while Tank and Major Timms waited impatiently.

"They're obviously in disagreement about something," Major Timms pointed his pen toward the Minister, as she appeared to be animated about something.

"Do MI5 ever agree with anyone about anything," Tank laughed cynically.

"Rarely," the Major agreed.

"What do you think the problem is?" Tank mused.

"The outstanding arms deal," the Major speculated.

"That's exactly what I think," Tank agreed.

The Minister waved to them through the reinforced glass wall. The intelligence directors stood up and walked toward the glass; the door opened and they stormed between them without saying a word. Tank smiled and entered the room, twisting his huge shoulders slightly to fit through the doorframe. Although the bunker was state of the art, all the doors were very narrow and were designed to add strength to the overall structure of the excavation.

"We have a problem," the Minister said, crossing her legs as she spoke.

"We have several from what we've heard today," the Major replied.

"Quite," she replied curtly.

"What are you going to do with the arms deal?" Tank asked saving her anymore embarrassment than was really necessary.

She looked at him and eyed him coolly, realising suddenly how transparent the situation really was.

"We are stumped frankly, if we don't deliver the cache then the whole project with Rashid Ahmed is over, if we do deliver we're risking the lives of another dozen Afghan soldiers," she shrugged not finishing her analysis, and leaving the sentence open.

Tank and the Major remained silent, playing the game. She fidgeted uncomfortably before being forced to continue.

"We need the arms to go in but under your protection. Your taskforce is made up of the best people that we have," she said abruptly, but not totally convincing anyone that she meant it.

Tank smiled and looked at the Major, shaking his head.

"The taskforce is the best covert strike force in the country, and I repeat the word 'covert' Minister. Afghanistan is a war zone, and you need soldiers, SAS, SBS, commandoes. The list of assets that you can use is endless," Tank said still smiling.

"You don't know where the leak is coming from do you?" the Major asked.

"No, we don't, but I know that it cannot be the taskforce because you have had no involvement so far," she answered honestly.

"You're talking to the wrong people Minister," Tank said.

"What do you mean?"

"You need to ask Rashid Ahmed if he is still on side, or if he is leaking information to the Taliban," Tank answered.

"What? Do you think he's just going to tell us even if he is?" she asked incredulously.

"Yes, given the right incentive to do so," Tank nodded.

"I don't understand. If it was so easy why haven't MI5 done that?"

"Because they're always looking for the subtle way of doing things, like leaving his wife unprotected."

"I don't believe that was deliberate."

"Then you're a gullible fool and the intelligence agencies are hanging you out to dry Minister," the Major interrupted.

She snapped her head toward him angrily at the affront, but her eyes registered that he had made a valid point. She was protecting the agency without questioning their role in the whole scenario. Their behaviour had been questionable at best, evil at worst.

"With all due respect there have been eleven ministers in your role while we have served in the taskforce, politicians come and go, and the intelligence director has probably seen another half dozen more than we have. They will play the game with you Minister, but only up to the point where it all goes tits up, and then it was all your decision making that was to blame," Tank leaned against the desk and chewed the end of a pencil thoughtfully.

"Okay, I'll accept the fact that their loyalty to any government is limited, but surely their agenda is the same as ours," she asked.

Tank and the Major exchanged amused glances. The Minister had no idea of just how sinister the world of spooks and spies was.

"Do you recall your predecessor?" the Major asked innocently, Tank smiled recalling the man, and the scandal behind his departure.

"Of course I do, that was a terrible business. His suicide was most unexpected," she seemed to be genuinely moved by the subject.

"How long had you worked with him?" Tank asked.

"I'm not sure, ten years, maybe more," she replied.

"Did you know that he had a penchant for teenage boys?" the Major asked.

"What? Don't be ridiculous, he was married with three children. His wife is a very close friend of mine, still heartbroken the poor woman," Janet Walsh couldn't see what was coming, but she knew that something nasty was on its way.

"I'm afraid it's true, and more to the point he fell for the oldest trick in the book, just weeks into his first term as Defence Minister, after that he was literally their puppet," the Major said.

"I don't know what you're talking about Major," she seemed to sag visibly.

"He was caught in a honey trap Minister, lured into a seedy hotel room by two pretty young rent boys, where he proceeded to take cocaine and indulge in what can only be described as depraved sex with underage boys, and it was all on camera," Tank continued with the story.

"It was a set up from the beginning to the end, all paid for by your friends at the intelligence agency. Having the Minister of Defence, responsible for allocating huge budgets, in your pocket for a few years is a priceless asset, however your colleague obviously couldn't handle the thought of his wife and family one day finding out about his sordid pastime," the Major finished off the tale.

"Your current personal secretary has a liking for white powder products too, and one of her dealers is on the payroll, she is passing information from your cabinet meetings straight back to the agency. They know what you are going to do before you do," Tank added.

"What!!" the Minister put her face in her hands trying to hide from the shocking truth.

"The Prime Minister's private aide has also strayed across the line into rent boys and drugs, needless to say they have quite a file on him already," the Major added fuel to the flames.

"I don't believe all this, how would you know what they are up to in such detail?"

"It's our job to know," the Major answered.

"Not everyone in the agency is in total agreement with their methods, and so we have informers on the inside that keep us up to date with what's going on. We have to know who we can trust and who is leaking information, and that includes cabinet ministers," Tank said.

"My god, spies spying on other spies, who can I trust?" she said bemused by the whole thing. The Minister looked like she was going to be sick, and the colour drained from her cheeks.

"Don't trust anyone Minister, it's really that simple," Tank replied.

She seemed to gather her wits around her somewhat, and she breathed in deeply before she spoke.

"Okay, now that I know where I stand, how do we deal with this cache of arms?" she said confidently.

"The point is Minister that the agency and their mercenaries are guarding the only person that really knows if that arms cache is heading for another ambush or not, Rashid Ahmed," Tank sat down opposite her and stared into her eyes. She nodded in agreement.

"What do you suggest Major," the Minister steeled herself, regaining some of her composure.

"We need to bring him in immediately, and hold him under the counter terrorism legislation until we are happy that we know the truth. Rashid Ahmed wants to return to the Middle East immediately to bury his wife. We need him to think that his Muslim brothers are going to be made aware of his cooperation with the British government over the last few years. If we can rattle him then he might think twice about coming clean. We have to make him think that he is no longer being protected by Her Majesty's secret service," the Major said.

She nodded in agreement again, looking lost.

"I'll have the director call you with his location immediately, and have him handed over to you for interrogation," she swallowed hard trying to recover her air of authority, but she failed miserably.

"We know where he is Minister, and we have to take him from them," the Major said.

"I don't understand, how do you know where he is?" she looked out of her depth again.

"Like I said earlier, it's our job to know."

"Of course it is," she said smiling nervously.

"No one must know that we are going to take him Minister, except you of course," Tank said.

"We must consider the possibility that the leak has come from the agency itself. Therefore they must not know that we are taking him, it's the only way to be certain," the Major concurred with the scenario.

"I understand, what about the protection unit that he has, they'll be armed won't they?"

"We know that and we'll take Rashid with minimal casualties, that's the best we can say at this stage," Tank said.

"I'll set up a snatch unit straight away and pick him up," Tank continued heading for the door. He could smell trouble a mile away, and he sensed that there was plenty waiting for them.

# CHAPTER 44

# OMAR

Omar overtook a large Japanese four wheel drive vehicle, which was pulling a caravan along the North Wales coast road. His English was very good now but he was still not accustomed to the names of Japanese trucks, and they all looked the same to him. The carriageway was four lanes wide separated down the middle by a low reinforced metal barrier. His headlights illuminated the dual carriageway which climbed gradually into the distance as it cut through the granite mountains at the edge of the Snowdon range. To his right was an inky black void where the land fell away steeply down to the River Dee four miles away, and in the far distance on the horizon the lights of Liverpool twinkled yellow against the night sky.

"Where are you?" the voice on his cell phone asked.

"Passing Holywell, init," Omar answered glancing at the name of the town on a road sign as it flashed by in the darkness.

"We're approaching Chester, about fifteen minutes behind you," the voice said.

"Nice one man, how many soldiers you got with you?" Omar asked accelerating harder to keep the van he was following in sight. The brake lights brightened and disappeared around a bend in the distance.

"There are two cars, mine and another twenty minutes behind us."

"Nice one, they're cruising at sixty five, put your foot down and you'll catch up to me. I'll call if they change direction," Omar clicked the phone off and turned the stereo up.

The previous days flashed by in his mind as he concentrated

on following the distant rear lights of the Brigade vehicle. He shivered as he thought about his friend Lewis crucified to the wall in a tower block, thousands of miles from home. After everything they had been through in Mogadishu, it didn't seem right for him to die that way, and someone would pay for that. Omar had no concept of the fact that he was responsible for starting the conflict with the Brigade in the first place. His memory took him to the alleyway where he'd used his knife to cut up the Brigade men. He'd cut them to send a message to the 18$^{th}$ Brigade, an attempt to frighten them into handing over an area of the city to them, so that he could expand their drug business. It hadn't worked. He had stirred up a hornet's nest, woken a sleeping giant, and losing Lewis was the price he had to pay for his foray into the dangerous world of drugs and private security. Omar had underestimated the strength and depth of the gargantuan door security company, but it wasn't the first time he had bitten off more than he could chew.

Three years earlier in the sun baked streets of Mogadishu, where reputations were built and maintained by the death toll a man had caused, Omar had made a similar mistake. He had stumbled across a drug deal being made on the outskirts of his neighbourhood. Mogadishu is carved up into blocks controlled by violent militias. Each militia protects their turf vehemently, to the point where straying into rival territory is a mistake that would cost you your life. The roads between rival blocks are counted as grey areas, where business deals could be conducted with impunity. Drugs arms and munitions were valuable currency, and the more a militia had, the more credibility they carried.

That particular day Omar and Lewis watched as a large amount of drugs was exchanged for money, eight Kalashnikov rifles and a box of bullets to match. He didn't recognise the protagonists making the deal, and he wrongly assumed that there were only a few of them because they were from weak militias. The fact was they were from the two biggest militias in Somalia. The reason they had only a few soldiers with them was because no one with any sense would attack either of them. On impulse Omar killed six men with a burst of machinegun fire before they could even move. He stole the cache of weapons and all the drugs, but the repercussions were swift and violent. His militia was threatened with annihilation unless they handed him over. Omar and Lewis were forced to leave their homes and flee for their lives.

Three years later on he had once again repeated his mistake of underestimating his opposition. Omar had expected the Brigade to come looking for them in the pubs and clubs of Manchester, but not to come through the living room window of his woman's fourth floor apartment. They had completely shocked him by crucifying his childhood friend to a wall. He wasn't sure where the Brigade man he had seen leaving the tower block was headed, but he intended to follow him until he stopped, and then he would wish that he hadn't hurt Lewis.

# CHAPTER 45

# NORTH STACK

Rashid heard the dull drone of an all terrain cycle and he walked toward the kitchen window. He looked out and saw two sets of headlights, belonging to quads, coming over the horizon. Miles away below the mountain, in the distance he could see the streetlights of Holyhead glowing yellow, and the powerful intermittent revolving beam of the Breakwater lighthouse, a mile and half out to sea. The huge bodyguards didn't appear to be concerned about the approaching vehicles, and there had been some radio messages crackling earlier, which were almost inaudible to Rashid. Now he realised that they had been talking to whoever was now approaching his remote hideaway.

"Terry's here," the big Brigade man called down the stairs to his colleague.

"Good, ask him for a pay rise, I'm bored stupid up here," the reply came.

"Signal the others to come in. He wants us all here to bring everyone up to date, and issue new briefs. I think something is going on."

"I don't like it when you think, and you think too much."

"Roger that," came the reply. More static could be heard on a coms unit somewhere. Rashid couldn't see it but he could hear several voices acknowledging the message to rendezvous at the house. Rashid peered into the darkness, but he still couldn't see anyone moving. He cupped his hands over his eyes to stop the lights reflecting off the window, and he peered into the night again. To the left about a hundred yards away across the headland, the undergrowth seemed to grow and move. A previously undetectable figure emerged from the deep foliage. He couldn't distinguish the shape or form because the edges were blurred, but it turned and moved toward the house, carrying a rifle with a huge scope attached. Suddenly there was movement two hundred yards to the right, and another shadowy figure seemed to melt from the long heather, and then another directly in front of him, yet another far left, followed by two more to the right. Rashid was impressed. He felt much safer now having seen the extent of the firepower which had been deployed to protect him. It would have been impossible for an assassin to approach the house past all those snipers. Perhaps the intelligence agencies were taking his safety seriously at last; unfortunately it was too late for his young wife. His stomach seemed to clench as he thought about her terrible death. The pain inside him steeled him to the cause once more. He had to know what the agency was planning for him, but his contact was still not answering his calls.

The front door slammed shut disturbing his thoughts. He looked down into the courtyard and saw the Brigade men gathering in a rough circle. The snipers were draped in long green net ponchos, which had been weaved with ferns and heather foliage to make them invisible on the headland. Their faces were daubed black and green with camouflage face paints, only the whites of their eyes were visible, giving them an inhuman appearance. The two new arrivals seemed to be in charge of proceedings, one of them in particular was giving orders out whilst pointing to a map. The conversation was brief and professional from what Rashid could see. The map was folded into a pocket, and the snipers headed off across the headlands again. Rashid watched them fading into the darkness as they passed the outer range of the artificial lighting, where they were headed he didn't know, but he felt more secure knowing that they were out there somewhere in the darkness.

The front door opened again, and he heard two sets of footsteps coming up the stairs. Rashid walked from the kitchen to greet them.

"We have a problem," Terry Nick said.

"I'm sorry, who are you?" Rashid asked, trying to grasp some control over his situation. He was being treated like a valuable object rather than a person, and he didn't like it one bit.

"All you need to know is that I'm in charge, and if you do as you're told you'll live, if you don't then you won't survive until the morning," Terry brushed past him and looked out of the panoramic windows toward the cliffs and the ocean beyond.

"There is no access from the cliff face?" Terry quizzed the Brigade man.

"No, we've completed risk assessments three hundred and sixty degrees. There is a minimal risk from the south, across the mountain but the danger zone is at twelve o'clock, the path you used is the only feasible way to get up here."

"Good, I want you to stay here with the primary, keep the radio to hand and the first sign of any shenanigans put him in to the panic room," Terry Nick headed toward the stairs.

"Primary this, primary that, put him here, stick him there, I'm sick of being talked about as if I'm not here," Rashid Ahmed shouted after the Brigade leader as he disappeared down the stairs. The heavy footsteps stopped on the staircase and there was a creaking sound as he turned and climbed back up them. Terry Nick stomped back into the first floor space and approached Rashid with an evil scowl on his face. He encroached his personal space and stared deep into his eyes, his nose was inches away from Rashid's. He was so close that Rashid could smell cigarettes on his breath.

"Listen to me Mr Ahmed, and listen well. You gave up your right to be considered in anything the moment you asked for protection from the agency. Now they own your arse, and they pay me to keep it alive. If you are looking for sympathy, then look in the dictionary, it's in between 'Shit' and 'Syphilis'." The Brigade leader turned and headed for the stairs again. "If he gives you any problems cut his throat, we'll blame the Yardies later on," he said laughing as he stomped down the staircase.

Rashid walked back into the kitchen, his temper was reaching boiling point, but what else could he do. He was in mortal fear of his life. He couldn't leave, but he didn't want to stay either. He was beginning to think that he was as much in danger from the agency and its mercenary thugs as he was out in the general population. Despite the collapse of his financial institution Rashid had millions stashed. He could disappear if he needed to, but if he did that he would never be allowed to resurface. He would be assassinated for sure.

"I'm making some coffee, would you like some?" Rashid

shouted to the remaining Brigade man, as he picked up the stainless steel kettle and filled it from the tap.

The Brigade man poked his head around the corner of the kitchen area and grinned widely. He was stroking the saw edged blade of a wide steel knife on his sleeve. Rashid looked at the glinting blade and made his mind up there and then. He looked the grinning mercenary in the eye.

"I have sold over a million machineguns to dangerous men in more countries than you could name. I have met many frightening men in my time, some of them could have killed me in the blink of an eye, trust me my friend when I tell you that I don't frighten easily, so do you want some coffee or not," Rashid held the big man's gaze. The Brigade man seemed to be thinking about what Rashid had said, he could almost hear the cogs whirring in his brain.

"Coffee would be great thanks, any chance of a biscuit?" the huge soldier became human in an instant.

"Milk and sugar?" Rashid turned back to the kettle and switched it on. He walked across the marble tiles and reached up to open a cupboard door. He took the coffee jar down and grabbed a packet of digestives.

"Yes please, two sugars," the bodyguard said. He walked over to Rashid and took the packet of biscuits from him. He ripped open the packet and stuffed three digestives into his mouth at once. Rashid frowned as a flurry of biscuit crumbs showered his polished marble floor.

"Are you hungry?" Rashid asked sarcastically. He opened the refrigerator and took out a carton of milk.

"Bloody starving, I've not eaten since this morning," the Brigade man mumbled spraying more crumbs across the kitchen floor.

"Here, take your biscuits through to the lounge, and I'll bring some sandwiches with your coffee," Rashid took a loaf of bread from the breadbin and returned to the refrigerator. The Brigade man was starting to salivate at the thought of food coming. He was even more pleased when Rashid opened the massive Smeg refrigerator to reveal a veritable feast of cold meats, cheeses and smoked sausages. He took the biscuits into the living area and happily looked out across the dark headland to the crashing ocean hundreds of feet below. The white horses and foam seemed to glow in the darkness somehow reflecting what little light there was. He could hear Rashid opening and closing cupboards and the clinking of plates and cutlery. The smell of fresh coffee permeated into the room, adding to the anticipation of satiating his hunger. He had munched through half the digestives before Rashid appeared carrying a steaming cup of coffee and a plate piled high with sandwiches.

"Here you are, tuck in, if we're going to be stuck up here then we may as well be civilised to one another," Rashid said as he placed the plate on the low coffee table.

"Thanks, he was only joking about cutting your throat you know," the Brigade man said biting into a smoked sausage and cheese sandwich that was two inches thick. He chewed it greedily and then slurped the hot coffee to wash it down.

"Like I said earlier, I don't frighten easily," Rashid smiled warmly, nodding like a wise old sage, who knew the secrets of the universe. Of course he didn't know the secrets of the universe, but he did know that the Brigade man's coffee and sandwiches were laced with enough diazepam to drop an elephant.

# CHAPTER 46
# SERGEANT MEL HICKEY

Sergeant Hickey put his metal foot down and the Ford increased speed silently. The power in the engine was impressive for a small saloon car, and he indicated before moving into the outside lane, overtaking a long line of cars and caravans that were heading into the mountains of North Wales. A large Japanese four by four was struggling to pull its mobile domicile up a long steep gradient, and was causing a tailback behind it. He passed the caravan and looked left at group of three customised hatchbacks that were travelling convoy like in the slow lane. There were big bore exhausts fitted to each one. The rear vehicle was fully loaded with passengers all of them were black skinned. Mel thought that they were probably Africans at first glance.

The second vehicle was the same, and he could almost have been passing the same car twice, fully loaded, all black males. The driver was deep in conversation with a mobile phone pressed to his ear. The third vehicle had only a solitary male, also black African, and Mel instinctively knew that he was talking to the man in the car behind him. The driver glanced toward him as he passed by and Sergeant Hickey caught a glint of light from his face, gold teeth probably, very classy.

The dual carriageway levelled out for a half a mile or so before it turned gently to the left and then ran steeply down a mountain side, before following the natural path of a river valley which snaked sixty miles along the Welsh coastline toward the island of Anglesey.

He continued to overtake the slower vehicles and had almost forgotten the unusual convoy of hatchbacks, when he passed a panel van on the inside lane. The interior light was switched on and the passenger was reading a map and talking on his telephone. The driver was a large male, shaved head and he had a blue tattoo beneath his ear, probably a swastika. Mel looked again quickly before accelerating away from them. He recognised the passenger as an 18th Brigade General, who had been in Iraq when he first arrived for his tour with the mercenary outfit. The Brigade General had only stayed in Iraq for two weeks of Sergeant Hickey's first tour, before being recalled to the UK, where he now looked after the domestic security business in the Liverpool area. The driver wasn't familiar to him but he fitted the bill as a Brigade employee. Mel had heard from his neighbour Ross, via old Jim that the Brigade had been having trouble with the Somali drug gangs from Manchester. He also knew that they had been involved in some heavy duty personal protection business domestically.

Past experiences had taught Sergeant Hickey that coincidences rarely existed in the theatre of conflict and espionage. He had a saying, if it walks like a duck, and looks like a duck, then the chances are that it is a duck. If the Brigade were protecting Rashid Ahmed then that was an unfortunate coincidence, but fore warned is fore armed. The fact that the Brigade van had a convoy of black Africans neatly tucked behind them, shadowing them at a discreet distance could also be a coincidence, but Sergeant Hickey didn't think so. He was seventy miles away from the quarry at the foot of Holyhead Mountain, where the path led up to North Stack, and his target. He floored the accelerator with his prosthetic limb, if he pushed the Ford to its limit then he could arrive in time to study the quarry before any else arrived.

# CHAPTER 47

# THE QUARRY

Terry Nick shivered as a gust of icy wind travelling at sixty miles an hour blew across the exposed headland off the Irish Sea. He really didn't need to be here right now babysitting Rashid Ahmed, a Saudi arms dealer who had turned 'supergrass'. Although it was a very lucrative contract he had other problems to deal with. The Somali drug lords were following Jay along the Welsh coastline headed directly toward them. It was a stroke of luck that Rashid had a property in such a remote location. It could be just what they needed to be able to confront the Yardies and deal with them once and for all. A gun battle on the streets of Manchester would not go unnoticed, and the fallout could put the Brigade' security business under intense scrutiny and further threaten their core business interests. He could not allow that to happen.

The quad bike shuddered and slid precariously on the muddy headland, thick tyres spun freely in the mud spraying moss and fern into the air behind it. Terry shifted his considerable bulk into the skid and the quad righted itself onto the path again. The wind howled through his clothes, even the Kevlar vest he wore offered no protection from the icy blasts. To the left he could make out two inhuman shapes approaching the edge of the cliffs which encircled the quarry below them. His sharpshooters were taking up elevated positions overlooking the quarry and the path which led from it. Their camouflage ponchos made them look like bushes or boulders from a distance, even through binoculars they weren't distinguishable as human.

The path narrowed and twisted steeply following a man made ledge carved into the rock face, and then zigzagged in a series of hairpin bends until it reached the quarry floor two hundred feet below him. The quarry hadn't been active for nearly a hundred years. The rocks mined from the base of the mountain were used to build the one and a half miles of breakwater, which protected Holyhead's marina and deep water harbour from the frequent violent storms that developed in the Irish Sea. Once the massive marine structure had been completed the quarry went out of business and the miners moved on to other parts of Wales to work. About the same time as the breakwater was completed miners at Dolgellau hit a gold lode and many of the miners from Holyhead headed there fuelled by gold fever.

The quarry was two miles from the port town, accessed by one narrow road which was once a railway track used for shunting gigantic cubes of granite to the breakwater. The old rail track road was carved into the surrounding landscape, and was bridged every few hundred yards by a series of red brick bridges which were built to appease angry local farmers whose land had been dissected by the railway. The railway road reached the quarry and then crossed three deep man made chasms which Mother Nature had filled with water. When the miners left the pumps stopped extracting water from the excavations and soon treacherously deep ponds were formed. The chasms were so deep the water was always bitterly cold and had a black sheen to it, almost as if they were filled with crude oil.

The quarry yard opened up beyond the ponds and two buildings stood alone, one had a tall granite chimney built at one end of the gable. It was a renovated furnace, once the heart of the quarry but now a tourist information centre. The second building was a derelict roofless warehouse. It had been left dilapidated for the visitors to wonder at. One hundred yards beyond the buildings, a sheer rock face rose two hundred feet up to the mountain shoulder and the sloping headlands. The narrow manmade ledge which zigzagged up the cliff face was the only way from the quarry up to North Stack.

Terry approached the top of the rock trail and slowed the quad down as it dipped and started to descend. The wind dropped suddenly, as it was blocked by the huge quarry walls and Terry felt instantly better, warmer and more confident that things would work out for the better tonight. He had men positioned on the cliff tops, and more in the quarry yard. Once their visitors passed by the ponds there was no way out, they'd be trapped in a killing zone. All he had to do now was wait. In less than an hour the Manchester Yardies would be at the bottom of the quarry lakes too deep for even a technical diver to find their bodies, and then he could get back to running the Brigade business as usual.

# CHAPTER 48

# TANK

John Tankersley leaned forward on the bench seat to try and make himself heard. The enormous twin rotor blades of a military Chinook were starting to gyrate, preparing to take Tank and a snatch squad to RAF Valley, Anglesey. The airbase was six miles away from the bottom of Holyhead Mountain, and from there they would take trucks onto Holy Island. Tank had chosen to employ a six man team from 'The Regiment', better known as the SAS, to carry out the extraction. The plan was to transport the squad up the only drivable road, which would take them to the tourist area at South Stack Lighthouse. From there they would be at approximately the same altitude as Rashid Ahmed's residence, although they would have to traverse over miles of rocky slopes to circumnavigate the mountain peak, they would eventually approach the building from the blind spot to the south. No one would anticipate an approach from that direction.

"The close protection squad are mercenaries, but don't underestimate them. They will be covering this road here," Tank said pointing out the old railway line on a detailed map. Camouflage faces, smeared green and black looked on as he explained the finer details of the extraction.

"The road is an old railway track, it's flanked by steep banks and bridged by a series of cattle crossings."

The elite troops could see a death trap if ever they saw one. The opportunity to be ambushed at any point along the quarry road was an obvious one to anyone with a modicum of military savvy.

"Things don't get any better at the quarry yard. The entire area is almost completely encircled by the quarry walls, which are sheer cliff faces hundreds of feet high in places."

The Regiment soldiers exchanged glances as he explained how well protected the approach to the mountain path was. It was impossible to breach. A handful of sharpshooters could defend the position against a thousand troops, and still repel them.

"We are going to deploy here at South Stack and traverse across the shoulder of the mountain, and hit the residence from the south side here where they will least expect it," Tank pointed to the map and the Regiment men seemed to relax. The plan made perfect sense. The only way to attack a well defended position like this mountain location was from the direction the taskforce leader had highlighted.

"Piece of cake," the Regiment commander said sarcastically.

"That's why you're here, because it's too easy for us," Tank replied laughing.

"How come you're not sending your people in?" the SAS man asked, lowering his voice slightly.

"What, hiking across a mountain in the dark for miles, now that's got your name written all over it," Tank said. "Besides, some of your boys are looking a little sloppy, and a good walk will do them good," they laughed, sharing the sarcasm.

"Seriously though, my people will be here, at South Stack," he pointed to the map again to explain where the taskforce would be during the extraction. "I'll be here with a unit covering any attempt to bring him out down the quarry road," there was a derelict hotel perched on the end of the quarry road where it joined the breakwater service road, and also branched off to the town centre.

"If they see you coming somehow then my guess is they will have an escape plan, you'll have no way of pursuing them from the mountain, so we'll have to cut off this route here, it's the only way in and out," Tank sat back. The Regiment men followed suit as the huge flying machine lifted off the roof of the Canning Place police headquarters. The engine noise seemed to reach a new deafening level as it hovered over the River Mersey, and then lurched forward toward the Welsh Mountains.

Grace Farrington took the initiative realising that all further verbal communication was pointless until they arrived at the airbase. There would be a short briefing there, but they needed as much information between now and then as they could. She reached into a kit bag and handed out photocopies of the floor plans for Rashid's residence. The eager troops studied them with professional interest, knowing where every door and closet was could save their lives. The drawings were relatively accurate although some of the later alterations hadn't been added by the architect. The Chinook cleared the city's airspace and accelerated to its full speed.

# CHAPTER 49

# THE QUARRY

Sergeant Mel Hickey slowed the Ford down as he reached the bright lights of Holyhead town centre. His map showed a wide open grassy area which sloped down to the shore of the port's yacht marina. It had a wide promenade road dissecting it. He studied the map as he reached the Newry Beach. He could clearly see the flotilla of yachts anchored in the marina, protected by the breakwater which was hidden by the darkness across the harbour. A lighthouse at the end of the breakwater flashed in the darkness. The promenade road appeared to be a dead end, as the road signs marked it as a 'no through road', but the map told him differently.

The map depicted a narrow service road which ran through a copse of trees, before splitting into two veins, the one on the right led to the breakwater, and the other to the left was the quarry access road. At the junction was an entrance, overgrown with bushes and small trees. There were tall stone gateposts barely visible in the dense foliage, beyond them was the derelict husk of the old Soldier's Point Hotel. It was a castle like building with fortifications along its roof line. It had once been painted white and could be seen standing like a proud sentinel from the promenade. It was once the destination for the port's rich Victorian visitors who championed it because of its coastal location and stunning views of the mountain and the sea.

He drove slowly down the twisting lane and killed the headlights as he approached the ruined hotel. It took a while for his eyes to become accustomed to the darkness. He thought about leaving his vehicle there and heading to the quarry on foot, but his prosthetic legs were not designed for trekking that far, plus his stumps would be a swollen mess by the time he reached the quarry. There was little choice but to drive on toward the quarry and try to gauge the lay of the land from nearer to the mountain. If his assumptions were correct then the 18<sup>th</sup> Brigade were protecting Rashid Ahmed in a remote residence up the mountain, well beyond his reach. One of their Generals was behind him en route, being followed by Somali antagonists that they had been having a turf war with. Sergeant Mel Hickey had to assume that there would be some kind of violent engagement and his money was on the Brigade coming out of that as the victors. The imminent encounter would compromise the security at Rashid Ahmed's mountain residence. News would leak out sooner or later and then they would have to move him to a new safe house. When they moved him Sergeant Hickey would be waiting for them with a few surprises. He engaged first gear and took the Ford at a slow crawl onto the pitch dark quarry road.

# CHAPTER 50
# TERRY NICK

"A vehicle has just entered the quarry road, a new Ford, not what we were expecting," a static clad voice spoke over the coms unit.

"Roger that, Can you see the occupants?" Terry Nick replied as he walked across the quarry yard toward the last footbridge before the lakes. He had two snipers positioned on the first bridge which was out of sight in the darkness, and two more were hidden on the bridge that he was approaching. The radio crackled but remained silent.

"Negative he's too far away for the moment, it looks like there's a single occupant," the reply came.

The Brigade had the road well covered. There were men on every bridge and half a dozen snipers along the cliff tops overlooking the quarry. Their trap was set but the arrival of an unexpected vehicle was not part of the plan. It created a nuisance factor to say the very least. They needed the Somalis to follow Jay all the way down the narrow road into the yard for the plan to be foolproof. A rogue vehicle parked in the darkness could spook them at the last moment. The Brigade leader needed to get rid of the vehicle and its driver immediately.

"Terry. You're not going to believe this," the radio crackled to life.

"Don't use names you bloody fool, what's the matter with you, has the Welsh air made you forget basic procedures?" Terry Nick was becoming irritable. Ever since the Somalis poked their heads above the parapet of the drug world they had caused him nothing but headaches. He had to remove them as a threat and get on with business as usual.

"Sorry boss, I've just had a bit of a shock that's all," the voice on the coms unit said.

"Don't keep us in suspense, please feel free to tell us what you're talking about," the Brigade leader sniped.

"The driver of the Ford is a white male, albino hair, I'm not one hundred percent sure but it looked like Mel Hickey," the voice whispered over the coms unit.

Terry Nick thought about it for a few long seconds. Sergeant Hickey had fucked up in Nisour Square, causing an international incident of gargantuan proportions. There was talk of him being hung out to dry by the Iraqi government but before anyone could do anything he had been hit by insurgents who had used a child as a human bomb. The unit had been wiped out except for the unfortunate Sergeant. The Brigade leader had only seen him once since his return from Iraq, and that was once too often for his liking. The increase in international contracts supplying mercenaries to companies like Blackwater had seemed like a no brainer at the time, but casualties had been frequent. The money ex-service men could earn was phenomenal, but the hazards were becoming increasingly harder to avoid and the consequences were incredibly cruel. Few mercenaries wanted to return after completing one stint in Iraq. Most of them chose to work for the Brigade in the domestic security business instead.

The scenario of Sergeant Hickey being the mystery bomber began to take shape in the Brigade leader's mind. It would make perfect sense. Hickey was aggrieved by his injuries and to compound the issue he was aggrieved by the response of his government. He had lost his legs, his career and then his wife and children to top it all off. Terry knew that the sergeant was well capable of making a roadside bomb. Planning to deploy it would be second nature to him. The only thing that confused him was the recovery he had made. He must be mobile, prosthetic legs maybe. The question was though, why was he here?

"Are you sure?" the Brigade boss asked.

"No, but I'm ninety percent sure."

Terry realised that the sergeant had come to finish the job that he had started in Westbrook, he'd missed killing Ahmed and now he wanted to complete his mission and annihilate the target. The Brigade leader had no desire to kill Hickey; in fact he hadn't been to see him because he had empathy with his situation. What had happened to him in Nisour Square could have happened to anyone in a civilian area during an armed conflict. He had opened fire though fear and even the toughest soldiers felt fear in a combat zone. There was no way of telling who was a potential suicide bomber and who wasn't, in which case innocents died frequently.

"The driver is stopping the vehicle," the voice said on the coms unit.

"How far down the track is he?"

"The next bridge away from your position."

"Roger that, standby," Terry walked over to his snipers and kneeled down looking down the quarry road into the darkness. The snipers had night scopes attached to them. Two high powered 7.62mm rifles were zoned in on the new arrival. The driver of the Ford was completely unaware that he was under the skilful aim of four sharpshooters already.

"Can you identify him yet," Terry asked the snipers.

"Yes, he's right, it's Mel Hickey sir," the sniper said without taking his eye from the scope.

"I don't believe it, he's tougher than I thought," the Brigade leader whispered, almost impressed by the invalid veteran's persistence.

"Do you want me to drop him," the sniper turned the elevation dial above the scope, calibrating the shot.

"No, he's no problem on his own. Have you got a shocker?" Terry reached over and grabbed a Remington 12-gaugue shotgun from the snipers bag. The snipers smiled at one another in the dark. Terry crouched low and headed down the footbridge and made his way along the top of the old railway bank which formed a natural flank to the quarry road.

He waited in the darkness for the invalid sergeant. The Brigade leader heard him before he could see him. The footsteps were irregular and heavy, almost a shuffle. Suddenly out of the darkness he could see a shadow emerging from the pitch blackness. The white hair had been covered with a dark woollen hat, and a scarf covered the lower part of the face.

Terry Nick stood up and chambered an EREMP round into the Remington's breech chamber, the metal click carried in the darkness and the shuffling figure stopped.

# CHAPTER 51

# OMAR

Omar pressed his foot to the accelerator and the hatchback lurched forward, closing the gap between him and the Brigade van. The driver of the van had obviously realised the vehicle behind him was encroaching into the safety zone that he had mentally set for it. The van accelerated and re-established the gap, never allowing Omar to get any nearer to it. Omar had survived over two decades of violent civil war in Mogadishu, and no one achieved that life span without a heightened sense of awareness. Omar's sense of self protection sent tingles down his spine and he smiled in the darkness of the car, a glow from the instrument panel reflected from his gold teeth.

"You know that I'm behind you don't you," Omar said out loud as he picked up his cell phone. He checked that his men were behind him and then took his foot off the accelerator, slowing his impromptu convoy down and allowing the Brigade van to increase the distance between them. The Brigade men were drawing them into a trap; that had become obvious now. Omar had used the technique of drawing rival militias into hostile territory in Mogadishu several times before with devastating results. He wasn't about to drive straight into a trap.

The dual carriageway threaded through a series of road tunnels cut through the Welsh mountains, a hundred feet above the rough seas of the Menai Straits. The lights of a service stop glowed in the distance, petrol station, toilet facilities and a hideously expensive self service restaurant, which was affectionately known as the 'little thief' because of its prices. Omar dialled the emergency number, 999.

"Hello emergency, which service do you require?"

"Police please, quickly the man has a gun," Omar faked panic in his voice as he indicated to turn off the carriageway into the service station. The Brigade van carried on its way and its red tail lights faded into the distance.

"I'm putting you through to the police sir, please remain on the line until you're connected."

"Please hurry up, they're getting away," Omar cried, still smiling as he brought the hatchback to a stop on the 'little thief' car park.

"Hello, police emergency."

"Hello. I've seen two men with a gun, they've threatened a man at the service station near Abergele," Omar read the sign post and tried to pronounce the Welsh town as best as he could.

"Has anyone been shot sir?"

"They fired the gun, but missed the man, init."

"Did you see their vehicle sir?"

"Yes, it's a black panel van, unmarked, registration MP3 NNY, they're headed in the direction of Anglesey," Omar wound his window down and waved to his men as they pulled into the parking bays next to him. He pointed to the cafe and made a cup sign, indicating that he wanted some coffee. His men looked a little confused at the unscheduled stop, but knew better than to question their psychotic leader.

"How many men did you see sir?"

"There were two of them, both big built men with shaven heads, bald you know, and they had tattoos under their ears, please hurry, my battery is running out on my cell," Omar cut the police operator off the line and laughed out loud. His gold teeth glinted in the darkness and he opened the door and stepped out of the little hatchback.

"Hey Omar what's happening, init?" two of the Yardies were leaning against their vehicle, smoking a joint. Their boss swaggered toward them grinning from ear to ear.

"We're having a quick smoke break my friends, and then we're going to be picking up our new van," Omar laughed.

He looked across the dual carriageway into the darkness, and he could see the tips of white horses crashing onto the wide beach beyond it. The Menai Straits widens out into the Irish Sea at that point creating vicious riptides and swirling currents. Two miles across the dark stretch of sea the streetlights of a castle town on Anglesey, called Beaumaris, twinkled in the blackness. Omar liked the sea, it calmed him. There was a different feeling to world when he was stood by the sea, and his thoughts drifted to the bullet scared buildings of his home in Somalia. The entire city of Mogadishu is pockmarked with shell holes, and every wall is riddled with bullet holes. It's such a stark contrast to the golden sands that meet the Indian Ocean just a stone's throw away.

"Here boss man, hot coffee," the Yardies voice pierced his thoughts. He turned toward him and grinned as he took the cup from him.

"I like this place, I think I might buy somewhere here so that we can come here and chill out," Omar said in his exaggerated accent. The group laughed in unison, which was a wise thing to do when Omar was holding court.

"What are waiting for Omar, are we letting them get away?" one of the braver Somalis asked.

"Have faith in me my brother, have a little faith," Omar took a sip of his coffee.

The sound of two loud police sirens approaching stopped the conversation. Two armed response vehicles roared past the service station with blue lights spinning on their roofs. Omar nodded his head and lit a cigarette, smiling from ear to ear.

# CHAPTER 52

# JAY BLYTHE

Jay didn't wear the title General well at all, as it conjured up the image of a stuffy ex-public school boy with an ornamental moustache. Jay had been a true commissioned officer in the British Army for a short period. He had been a snotty nosed lieutenant when he'd left the regular army, sick and tired of the military institution and its prejudices. Promotion up the ranks was never achieved by talent alone. The candidate's hereditary blood line and place of graduation were far more important than natural leadership ability. He had been overlooked for promotion several times before he finally couldn't stomach anymore.

Jay went back to civilian life with a spring in his step, full of ambition and optimism for the future. He was genuinely excited about starting a real career, although he wasn't really sure what form that would take. It didn't take long to realise that life outside of the service wasn't much different to the army; prejudice, racism and corruption ran through every big institution. Jobs were hard to come by and once his army pension had been eaten away by bills he was soon forced to take a job as a bouncer working on the door of a night club in Liverpool. His sheer size made it a natural step, and the pay wasn't too bad.

Word soon reached the senior hierarchy of the Brigade that he once had been a commissioned officer in the British army. Terry Nick took him under his wing and offered him a six month tour of Iraq, taking charge of two units of Brigade men who were being subcontracted by the American mercenary giant, Blackwater. The money was too good to turn down and he was back in Iraq as a mercenary before he'd had time to think.

One tour was his swan song as far as Iraq was concerned. During his tour he had grown in stature within the 18th Brigade and the position of running the domestic business in his home city of Liverpool seemed to be the ideal role for him. He was happy within the Brigade structure, plus the money was three times what his army salary had been. The domestic business was seedy and sordid to say the least, taxing money from franchised drug dealers and pimps. They organised the hijack and disposal of dozens of articulated lorries and their precious cargos as they left the Liverpool docks.

While their activities seemed to be highly illegal, (mirroring the Italian Mafioso in America), careful planning and military style execution left the law enforcement agencies baffled as to who was responsible. The business with the Somalis was just another day in the office for Jay. They weren't the first small time crime gang to rattle the 18th Brigade, and they wouldn't be the last.

Jay was staring into the wing mirror trying to work out why the Somalis had pulled into the services.

"They must be out of fuel," Jay said to the driver wearily.

"I'll slow down a little, they'll catch up when they're done fuelling up, that's if they want to," the driver replied yawning.

"Don't make it too obvious," Jay warned him, yawning too. The day's events were beginning to catch up with them, tiredness was creeping up. Travelling as a passenger at night on a long journey always made him dead tired.

"I won't make it too obvious, but I'll have to slow down," the driver replied. "What's in store when we get to the quarry?"

Jay looked at the driver in the darkness, and the dashboard lights gave his face an eerie glow. He turned back to the windscreen in silence, and never answered the question. His eyelids were heavy and he couldn't be bothered to answer a stupid question. The Yardies were as good as dead, but they didn't know it yet. Sleep was starting to take hold of him when the blue lights of two speeding police interceptors lit up the interior of the van.

"Shit," the driver said, looking in the rear view mirror. The two approaching vehicles were travelling at high speed toward them.

"What is it?" Jay mumbled from his doze, trying to recover his composure. He looked in the wing mirror and saw two vehicles travelling full pelt behind them. They seemed to be in pursuit of someone. They pulled into the fast lane as if they were heading somewhere further down the expressway.

"They're going past," the driver said.

"I'm not so sure," Jay reached for his cell phone. If there was a problem then he had to alert the Brigade men on the island.

The first police car roared past them in the outside lane. Jay thought it was passing them because of the speed it was doing, but as the vehicle cleared the van it swerved violently in front of them and slammed on its brakes. The Brigade man stamped on the brake pedal in an attempt to avoid hitting the police car but he was travelling too fast. They were thrown forward like a pair of ragdolls as the tyres screeched and the van fishtailed along the carriageway. The police car was now stationary and the skilful driver had handbrake turned it across both lanes. The Brigade van driver snatched the wheel hard left to avoid the imminent collision, and the van skidded across the hard shoulder, onto the grass bank before stopping in a flurry of burnt rubber and flying grassy sods.

Jay hit the dashboard hard. He'd loosened the seatbelt slightly while he was in a doze, and the force of the impact had propelled him forward, cracking his head on the hard plastic dash. The driver had been bent double by the crash, hitting his head on the steering wheel, micro-seconds before the airbag was deployed breaking his nose. Jay groaned and tried to regain his senses, but everything was a blur. He looked toward the driver, who was comatose in his seat, his head was hanging backward at an awkward angle with his mouth wide open, and blood was running freely down his face.

The passenger door opened and the cold night air swept over him clearing his fuddled mind for a second. His head hurt. Jay fumbled about on the seat looking for his cell phone, as instinct told him he had to contact the Brigade.

"Armed police! Put your hands above your head or we will shoot you, do it now!" the policemen were surrounding the vehicle, one at each door and two pointing Glock-17 automatics through the windscreen. Jay tried to put his hands up in the air, but they wouldn't move. He was still facing the driver, although he knew that he needed to look at the policemen, he couldn't move his neck.

"Move and I'll spray your brains all over that windshield," the closest policeman snarled. He fastened a steel handcuff around

Jay's left wrist. Jay was too dizzy to resist. He felt a warm trickle of blood running from his forehead into his eyes.

"Get your hand over here," the policeman shouted and roughly shook Jay. Jay felt wobbly and nauseous. His body slid down slightly and his head rocked backward onto the headrest. He was now facing the windscreen and could see the armed policeman to his left out of the corner of his eye. The policeman stared at him and lowered his gun.

"Keep very still," the policeman said. Jay detected a change in the policeman's tone, but it didn't register why. He isn't shouting anymore, he thought.

His right hand was cuffed to the left one in front of him. They flopped in his lap when the policeman let go of them. Jay was aware of a warm wet sensation around his groin area as urine soaked into his trousers. He knew that he was pissing himself but couldn't do anything about it. Jay wanted to move his hands but he couldn't. The policemen pulled the driver from the van and held him face down in the grass. Jay could hear harsh directions being shouted to him as he was cuffed and then searched. The policeman next to Jay opened the glove box.

"There's a nine millimetre in the glove box serge," Jay heard the policeman shout. He tried to focus on the gun but his head felt strange.

"Keep still mate, don't try and move," the policeman said.

Jay was aware of several bodies being close by to him, coming and going. He thought he'd heard someone being sick, a distinct retching sound and then vomit splattering on the grass. The urine on his trousers was starting to cool, making him feel uncomfortable and cold. The Welsh mountain air had a bite to it. Jay wanted to turn the heater. He wanted the radio on too, but he was feeling concussed.

He wanted to speak but couldn't. Jay felt more blood soaking into his eyebrows, and it felt like something lumpy was sliding over his skin. Like rice pudding he thought, strange because the sensation made him feel hungry too.

"There's an ambulance on the way," a voice said. Jay wondered who was hurt, probably the driver.

"Better get one of our boys to give it an escort, he's in trouble," another voice said.

"There's identification in his wallet, his name is Jay Blythe, he's an officer in the 18<sup>th</sup> Brigade, a mercenary."

Jay knew his wallet had been in the front pocket of his trousers. He thought it was funny that he hadn't felt them take it out. A blob of something gooey plopped onto his cheek and he tried to look at it. His hands wouldn't move and he was straining his eyes to look at the greyish blob on his cheek.

"You better find out where that ambulance is," a voice close by said.

"Fucking hell, take it out," someone else said.

"Don't touch it, you'll kill him," another voice said anxiously.

Jay wondered who they were concerned about, and he wondered why they hadn't pulled him out of the van yet. The driver had been dragged away kicking and shouting. One of the police cars sped away from the scene with its lights flashing. The blue strobe light lit up the interior of the van momentarily. He thought it was odd when he saw his reflection in the glass. It looked like there was a man with a mobile phone stuck in his forehead. Grey brain matter oozed around the handset and dripped down his face. Poor man, Jay thought as he died.

# CHAPTER 53

# RAF VALLEY/ ANGLESEY

The Chinook bumped on to the helicopter landing pad at RAF Valley and the engine noise started to subside as the pilots slowed the rotors ready to stop. The airbase was the home of advanced flying instructors of 208-squadron, and tactical weapons experts in 19-squadron. It was also less than ten miles by road to both South Stack and the old quarry leading up to North Stack. The big doors slid open and the Regiment men stood to disembark. Waiting on the tarmac were the data analysts from the Terrorist Task Force, Chen, and their information guru, David Bell, affectionately known as the fat controller.

Brief greetings were exchanged as the crisis unit were ushered into a low roofed building close by. Inside the building was lit by harsh fluorescent tubes. There were two lines of plastic chairs set out into semi-circles, facing a tripod which held a large flipchart. The Regiment soldiers and Task Force members took their seats in silence, as everyone was feeling the pre-mission nerves which kick in before any big operation.

The fat controller walked to the flipchart and turned the first page. Beneath it was a blow up section of an ordinance survey map of the mountain. He was wearing his trademark suit and tie, which made him stick out like a sore thumb amongst all the combat clothing. His trousers were altered to fit his round figure, and they were pulled up well above his bellybutton in an attempt to appear slimmer. He took off his spectacles and polished the lenses with his tie before replacing them.

"I'll keep this brief as time is of the essence," he began. "Satellite information shows us that as of an hour ago there were two people in the target building." He pointed to Rashid Ahmed's mountain residence.

"There were five x-rays positioned along this cliff line, we're assuming that they're sharpshooters, and half a dozen or so x-rays below the cliffs on or around this access road."

"So there's no one monitoring an incursion across the mountain itself?" the SAS leader asked.

"As of an hour ago it was unguarded," the fat controller kept caution in his voice, an hour was a long time when you were surveying a possible target, and assumptions got people killed in this line of work.

"That's excellent, any joy with the acquisition of a Unimog?" Tank asked. The Unimog was a military vehicle that looked like a cross between a tractor, a dump truck and a troop carrier. The wheels are six feet tall and have tyres that look like they could climb up a building. The huge ground clearance beneath the truck meant that it was equally at home up mountains as it was crossing deserts or ploughing through jungles and rain forests. They also run almost silently, and are the state of the art vehicle for transporting Special Forces close to their targets when helicopters couldn't be used.

"Our friends in the Royal Air Force have donated us two of theirs, on the assumption that we return them undamaged of course," the fat controller joked.

"Of course, we wouldn't want to upset the Ruperts would we," Tank said laughing. Rupert was the not so flattering nickname used by soldiers for air force officers.

"Okay, that puts Grace Farrington and her team here at South Stack, covering the Regiment's withdrawal, should anyone be persuing you back across the mountain," the fat controller carried on the briefing in a light hearted vein, last minute nerves often materialised as humour.

"My team will be here covering the exit from the quarry, and that's where we will remain unless we see muzzle flashes coming from below the cliff line, in which case we'll presume that you are in trouble, and we'll move into the quarry flanking the railway embankments," Tank ran his finger down the old railway line. He didn't envisage having to move into the quarry. To do so would definitely result in the loss of life. It was clear that Brigade snipers were covering that area in order to protect their primary. It was a standard close protection technique to surround your primary with a ring of steel, or in this case a ring of 7.62 millimetre high velocity sniper rifles. The plan to extract Rashid Ahmed revolved around sneaking in the back door across the mountain and taking him from under their noses.

"Don't underestimate the Brigade men, they're no mugs, but I'm expecting to be in and out in no time, without alerting those snipers. It appears they're positioned to defend against an incursion up the mountain, not across it," Chen added pointing to the cliff line.

"That's it, any questions before we leave?" Tank asked. The room stayed silent and the soldiers stood in unison ready for action.

# CHAPTER 54

# OMAR

Constable Thomas shivered as a blast of wind came off the Menai Straits and chilled him to the bone. He swore under his breath as he carried a triangular traffic warning sign down the dual carriageway and placed it fifty yards behind the Brigade van. The van had been left on the grass verge where it stopped when the police interceptors forced it from the road. Constable Thomas arrived at the scene to coordinate the traffic, and was caught up in a maelstrom of different law enforcement agencies that were tripping over one another to take charge.

The armed response units were trying to maintain control because someone had been killed during their operation, and because weapons had been retrieved. Internal affairs were sniffing around because a civilian death had been caused by the armed response unit running a vehicle off the road, armed or not, a fatality was a potential media nightmare for the police force. The crime scene investigator on call that night had taken a quick look over the scene and decided that nothing could be done until first light. The traffic police were there to ensure that the coast road remained open, and no further accidents were caused by the police activity.

The chaotic scene that confronted him when he arrived had soon been transformed into an abandoned van, some flashing lights and one lowly police Constable left to oversee it until the morning.

"How the fucking hell did I get to draw this duty?" Constable Thomas asked himself. The wind blasted again freezing him to the core. He blew into his hands trying to warm them up, and rubbed them together vigorously.

"I'll tell you why you got this duty shall I, because you breathalysed the Mayor, that's why. You bloody idiot, you could have let him go, given him a lift home so that he wasn't a danger to anyone else, but oh no, not Constable Thomas, he knows best doesn't he. Let's nick the Mayor and see what happens to your career," he answered his own question and began to remonstrate himself out loud. There was a role of yellow crime scene tape stuffed into his pocket, and he removed it and began to tape off the area to prevent unwanted intruders contaminating it.

"The crime scene team will be there first thing in the morning officer Thomas, can't do anything in the dark can they, so you'll be responsible for the vehicle until they arrive Constable. Well thanks a fucking bunch sergeant sir, responsible for an abandoned van up on the coast road, in the middle of bloody nowhere, fucking marvellous," the policeman ranted at himself in the darkness, only the flashing warning lights offered any illumination.

He stuck a five yard length of yellow tape between two striped traffic cones, and then snapped the tape with his teeth. The headlights of a vehicle twinkled in the distance. It was heading in his direction. The incident with the Brigade van had closed the dual carriageway down to just one lane.

Constable Thomas had parked his police car behind the van, leaving the blue lights flashing as a warning to approaching traffic. The last thing he needed now was someone running up the arse of his vehicle in the dark. He was in enough trouble as it was since he had inadvertently arrested the local Mayor for drinking and driving. The Mayor was related by marriage to the Chief Constable, who had taken great pleasure in making sure that he got every shitty job that there was to do, and some.

The oncoming vehicle slowed as it approached. The driver and his passenger were swan necking the accident as they passed. They waved at the lonely Constable before speeding off into the darkness.

"Goodbye, had a fucking good look have you? Why don't you stop and take a fucking picture? Pity you weren't here earlier there was some poor bloke with a mobile phone stuck in his head, you could have had a good look at that couldn't you?" Constable Thomas shouted after the vehicle, knowing full well that they couldn't hear him anyway, but venting his anger made him feel better.

"I'm Constable Thomas by the way, once a fucking Constable always a fucking Constable, that's who I am. Responsible for this entire crime scene I am, instead of catching criminals I'm catching a fucking cold," he kicked the base of a traffic cone hard, only to find that it was full of heavy sandbags. He stubbed his toe painfully which led to another tirade of abuse being hurled across the dark lonely coast road. The constable hopped to his vehicle and opened the door. He needed to climb inside out of the piercing wind for a while. Headlights lit up the interior of his car as he slammed the door closed and reached for his cigarettes. The vehicles slowed as they approached, and one seemed to stop just for a moment. He lit his cigarette and drew in deeply on the comforting smoke. One of the vehicles passed at a crawl and two black males stared into his vehicle. One of them nodded and grinned at him. The constable grinned back bitterly and waved.

"Hello, and fuck off," he said still smiling. The hatchback indicated to move left and pulled over on to the hard shoulder twenty yards in front of the abandoned Brigade van.

"What are you playing at you silly fuckers?" he said under his breath as he reached for his hat. Now he was pissed off. He couldn't even finish a cigarette in peace and quiet. Constable Thomas opened the door of his police car and climbed out of the vehicle. He put on his hat and angrily tossed the burning cigarette away, red sparks flickered from the end of it as it landed on the dark tarmac and the wind hurtled it across the road. A second vehicle passed at a crawl, and the policeman noted the occupants were black too. He was about to become concerned when a crushing blow to the back of his head ended his torment.

# CHAPTER 55

# THE QUARRY

"Hello Sergeant," Terry Nick said as he cocked the Remington.

"Terry?" Mel Hickey said straining to see in the darkness.

"What brings you all the way down here Sergeant?" Terry asked sarcastically.

"Oh, I don't know, I've always liked the sea, and the mountains. I can't say I've come to stretch my legs now can I, because I lost them working for you. What about you Terry, are you here on business or pleasure?"

"I think you know why I'm here Melvin, and you left your legs in Iraq because you let your guard down didn't you Sergeant. You came home Melvin but your men didn't, so whatever it is you think you're going to achieve here you need to forget it, turn around and go home," Terry stepped closer to the white haired veteran, still pointing the shotgun at his chest.

"I don't know what you mean Terry, how could I be of any harm to anyone?" he tapped his metal legs.

"You did a lot of damage with your little stunt at Westbrook Sergeant, pity you killed his missus instead of him though. Just another Sergeant Hickey fuck up to add to all the others really, Nisour Square, and then losing all your men along with your legs, and to top it all you blew up the wrong person with an improvised roadside device, well done. You've caused me no end of trouble. Did you think you'd start a war on Islam all by yourself, a one man crime wave evening things up and settling a few scores?"

"Like I said before, I don't know what you mean. I wanted to see you about some compensation that's all," Mel said with an acid tone.

"Of course you did Sergeant. Well here is your compensation," Terry shook the shotgun for effect. "Now get back into your car and go back to the funny farm until you calm down. You have no idea what you're stepping into."

"What, after I've driven all this way, that's not very nice is it Sir?"

"Last chance Sergeant, leave now. I don't have the time to fuck about with you right now," Terry stepped closer still.

"I wouldn't come any closer to me if I were you, or you could end up with a pair of legs like mine if you're not careful," Mel took his hands from his pockets and revealed an electric key fob. A tiny red light glowed in the darkness.

Terry Nick stepped back instinctively, realising that Sergeant Mel Hickey had wired his vehicle up to explode at the press of a button. The snipers behind had been watching events closely and one of them tried to buy the Brigade leader a few seconds. He flashed a powerful laser sight directly into the albino Sergeant's very sensitive eyes. Mel Hickey cried out in pain and instinctively put his hands to his eyes to protect them from the piercing laser. At the same time Terry Nick pulled the trigger and the Remington roared. The EREMP round smashed into the sergeant's chest, knocking him clean off his prosthetic feet.

# CHAPTER 56
# CONSTABLE THOMAS

Constable Thomas thought about his estranged wife for the first time in years. He hated the bitch, or that's what he had convinced himself that he thought. The truth was very different. They had married when he was just a few years into the job, a young and enthusiastic policeman with great expectations. His ambition then was to become a sergeant in the uniformed division, earning his stripes and the respect of his peers through hard work and determination. The next step would be a secondment into the Criminal Investigation Department before becoming a full time plain clothes detective.

Unfortunately for Constable Thomas he was impatient. He also had a shallow nasty personality. He was always the first to shun teamwork and he was also prone to progressing his own career at the expense of someone else's. Thomas was two faced and reported his fellow officers for breaching procedure at every opportunity that he could, in a vain attempt to enhance his own reputation as a forthright law enforcement officer. All he achieved was to gain the deep mistrust of his fellow officers, and a reputation as a backstabbing trouble maker from his senior officers. The icing on the cake was stopping the local Mayor in his car just a mile from his home and breathalysing him. The unfortunate Mayor tested positive by the slimmest margin. Once again Constable Thomas put his own ambitions to the fore, and he took the Mayor into the police station to be charged, thinking this high profile collar would lead to his promotion. He couldn't have been more wrong. He soon realised that his career was dead in the water and he turned to a bottle of whisky at night for solace, his wife however turned to his younger brother for solace, amongst other things, and the marriage spiralled into a bitter divorce. His family was torn apart by the affair, most of them siding with his brother and ex-wife.

Now as he looked over the crash barrier into the deep dark waters of the Menai Straits he realised that he still loved her deeply. He still loved his younger brother too, and he couldn't really blame her for running off with him, after all he had behaved like a chauvinist pig. Thomas was naked and the bitter wind was mind numbingly cold. His recollection of what happened after he had been hit over the head was hazy at best, but it was coming back to him in flashes. Blood was rushing to his head and his face felt like it would explode if he didn't get himself upright soon.

Constable Thomas remembered a sickening blow to the back of his head, and then the sensation of being dragged across the rough tarmac naked, and being handcuffed. Somewhere in between he had been stripped of his uniform and his hands had been cuffed behind his back. He heard men laughing and remembered seeing a black man dressed in his police uniform, parading around the Brigade van with the hat tilted at a silly angle. There was another burst of laughter when black ski masks were found in the Brigade van. The policeman could vaguely remember two men coming over to him with the ski masks pulled over their faces. The first one had spat in his face, and then the second man kicked him hard in the testicles.

Constable Thomas had keeled over and vomited on the grass, sickened by the pain which spread from his groin to his abdomen. There was more laughter from the men as he writhed in agony on the floor. He remembered hearing the Brigade van being started, and thinking that they must have hotwired the vehicle. Then they started his police car and switched the sirens on and off, only stopping when an approaching vehicle slowed down as it drove by. The men hid behind the van until the vehicle was well out of sight, and its brake lights had faded into the darkness. The men seemed to be organising themselves into pairs, so the van and police car could be driven away with the three hatchbacks. The talking and laughing stopped when they discussed what they should do with Constable Thomas. He realised that his life was in mortal danger, and that was when he started to think about his wife, and the love that he had lost.

The black men had dragged him across four lanes of the carriageway and then picked him up. They tried to toss him over the coast road barriers into the sea, but he'd become entangled in the wire mesh that prevented the cliffs from being eroded by the elements and stopped landslides. Now he was hanging upside down from the cliff top. Seventy feet below him the sea was pounding the rocks, white foam sprayed high into the air as each wave crashed over the last one. His head was becoming increasingly more painful as the blood flowed to it, and gravity prevented it from leaving. His body was numb with the cold. The muscles and tendons in his legs and ankles were at snapping point as they struggled to support his weight. He could feel the heel of his right foot being sliced by a thin filament of the wire cage that encased the exposed mountain slopes. The pain was becoming unbearable to the point where he was desperate to free the injured foot, even though he knew that by doing so he would crash to his death on the jagged rocks below. His mind was weak, as was his will power, and he couldn't stand the pain any longer. There was little to be gained from prolonging the inevitable, passing traffic couldn't see him and the police would not return until the morning, by which time he would either die from burst blood vessels in his brain or freeze to death. Constable Thomas took a deep breath of cold Welsh air and thrashed his body against the mountain. The wire mesh sliced through what remained of the fleshy part of his heel and he thought about his wife again as he plummeted toward the cruel rocks below.

# CHAPTER 57
# THE QUARRY

Omar pulled the stolen police car over to the kerb. He picked up the map that he had found on the floor of the Brigade van and looked at the markings that someone had made on it. He followed the promenade road on the map with his bony finger, and then traced the line of the quarry access road to its conclusion at the base of the mountain. He looked across the marina toward the breakwater and then back at the map. Beyond the breakwater was the Irish Sea and total blackness. To the left was the looming shadow of Holyhead Mountain. It somehow seemed to be darker than the night that surrounded it. In between the mountain and the breakwater were a copse of trees and the ruins of a building. Behind that ruin was the entrance to the quarry road, and that's where it appeared the Brigade men were heading before he had scuppered their plan.

"We follow this promenade to the end, init, and then we are going to drive down this track here. We'll see what happens when we get there. They're going to be expecting their men in that van and they definitely won't be expecting the law to be behind them, init," Omar put the police hat on and laughed. His gold teeth glinted in the glare of the yellow streetlights.

"What are the Brigade doing down there in that quarry man, there isn't nothing down there on this map."

"They don't do anything for free, that's a fact, anyway that's not important. They came through my Gemma's window man, that's not cricket. It's payback time man, we're going to give them the fright of their lives," Omar gunned the engine and banged his hand on the door. "Let's go, put those ski masks on and drive in front of me. When I flash my headlights come out shooting at anything that moves."

All bar one of the Yardies climbed into the Brigade van, and the other sat in the passenger seat of the police car next to Omar. The three hatchbacks had been dumped in a twenty four hour supermarket car park further up the coast. Omar checked his appearance in the mirror and he winked at his reflection and grinned. The gold teeth glinted in the darkness like two jewels surrounded by decay. He switched on the flashing blue light and pulled away from the kerb, following the Brigade van closely.

As the stolen police car reached the end of the promenade, and drove into the copse two military Land Rovers rounded the bend five hundred yards behind them. Tank was sitting in the passenger seat of the first vehicle.

"What the fuck is plod doing here?" Tank said as he watched the police car heading toward the quarry road with its blue light flashing.

"I'm assuming that the local uniformed division were informed that we have an operation underway here," Chen asked. Chen was part advisor and part agent, although he spent more time advising than Tank cared for these days.

"If you haven't got anything sensible to say then just shut up," Tank said reaching for the coms unit and passing it to Chen. "Pull over here, we need to see where they're going, Chen find out from the Major if either the police or the Security Services are messing about in our operation." The van disappeared into the tree line and the police car followed it, only the blue flashing light betrayed its position. They waited in silence as Chen relayed the information to headquarters and waited for a reply. The uniformed police divisions were always suspicious of the counter terrorist units operating on their turf, especially when they were ordered directly to avoid the area at all costs. The Security Services, MI5 and MI6 were a law unto themselves, and in this instance were not aware that the Terrorist Task Force were about to snatch one of their informers from underneath their noses.

"Pilgrim one," the coms unit crackled.

"Roger, we're receiving," Chen replied to the call.

"We are negative for any uniformed traffic units in that area," the Major's voice informed them. Chen looked at Tank and they both mulled over the possible scenarios.

"It wouldn't be the first time a police car was somewhere it shouldn't be," Chen said.

"Ask the Major if all their units are accounted for," Tank frowned.

"Pilgrim one, are all the police units accounted for?"

"Roger that, they're all on trackers now, they know where every unit is at any time."

"Well that can only mean one thing then," Chen said nodding sagely.

"Go on, share your wisdom with me," Tank said dryly.

"Either that isn't a police car at all, or it's not from this uniformed division, and it has come from further afield," Chen shrugged.

"We need to stick to the plan and cover that exit from the quarry, we'll find out what they're up to soon enough," Tank wrapped his knuckles on the dashboard as he spoke. The driver selected first gear and the two Military Land Rovers followed at a safe distance behind the mysterious police car.

# CHAPTER 58
# THE BRIGADE

Two Brigade men dragged Sergeant Hickey's limp body up a footpath and dumped him in the long grass that grew prolifically along the old railway embankments. His prosthetic legs clattered together as his body hit the ground. They would have to deal with him later on. He wasn't a priority right now. Terry Nick picked up the key fob and thought about moving the sergeant's vehicle. He had to think about the mental state of the sergeant, and when he did he realised that anything could happen. If it was rigged to explode on the touch of a button then it was probably booby trapped. It could be wired to a digital timer that would trigger the bomb after a stipulated period of time if the device's creator didn't return to it. He was debating what to do with it when a hushed whisper came over their coms.

"Two vehicles are approaching the first bridge."

Terry ran up the footpath and ducked behind the footbridge wall next to the two snipers.

"Roger that, can you identify them?"

"Roger that, we could have an issue. The first vehicle is plated as one of ours, but the second is a traffic cop."

"What?"

"You heard me correctly, our van is being followed by a traffic cop, blue lights flashing and the works," the voice said.

Terry looked over the wall into the darkness. Sure enough he could see two sets of headlights and the silhouette of a van, and behind it he could see the blue flashing strobe of a law enforcement vehicle.

"What do you want me to do? Do I let them pass as planned or take them out now?" the voice crackled.

"Don't shoot you bloody idiot, we're not in the business of killing our brave boys in blue, shut up and let me think," Terry hissed in reply. The Brigade couldn't risk any further encounters with the police. It would jeopardise their credibility and attract unwanted attention upon the organisation. The slightest controversy could compromise any further foreign contract tenders.

"Are there any other vehicles behind them?" Terry looked over the wall again and tried to see the vehicles, but they were covered by the series of footbridges. All he could make out were the lights.

"Negative, there are no other vehicles on the quarry road."

"Where are they exactly?" Terry was debating stopping them before they reached the quarry yard.

"They're approaching bridge three," a different voice answered this time. "When did you last speak to Jay or the driver?"

"It was a while ago, but he did say that his cell phone battery had gone flat. Why what's the problem?" Terry was curious.

"Something isn't right here boss, I'm looking at our men in the van through my scope, and they're both wearing combat ski masks," the sniper on Bridge three reported.

"What? Why would they be wearing them?" Terry asked out loud.

"Look at the traffic police man," Terry hissed down the coms unit.

"Roger that, got him."

"What colour is he?" Terry asked.

"He's a black traffic cop, what's the problem?"

"He's not a traffic cop, that's the problem, and that isn't Jay in the van either," Terry alerted his men. The snipers next to him chambered rounds into the breach.

"Hold your fire, I repeat don't open fire," Terry hurried the order. The two vehicles passed beneath the third bridge and motored steadily toward the quarry unhindered.

# CHAPTER 59

# THE REGIMENT

The SAS men approached the remote mountain residence like ghosts. The Unimog had managed to traverse the shoulder of the mountain undetected in less than half an hour, which was well ahead of schedule. They deployed the unit half a mile away from Rashid Ahmed's hideaway, and crawled silently through the thick foliage without incident. Each man knew his role inside out and back to front. Each man in the unit could have pulled off the extraction mission on their own without giving it a second thought. The combined strength of the men in the Regiment unit made them almost indestructible. When it came to Special Forces the SAS were the best in the world, bar none.

The unit approached the mountain residence with the cliffs and the Irish Sea behind them. Their view of the building from the headland was through the wide panoramic windows which wrapped around the first floor. It was clear that there was no one moving around inside the living room or the kitchen area beyond. It was also clear that the 18th Brigade snipers were positioned six hundred yards across the headland above the quarry walls. There were no Brigade personnel paying any attention to the rear flank, which gave the Regiment unhindered access to the building.

The snatch squad prepared to enter the dwelling. One man covered the living room with a rifle from the headland, ready to drop anyone presenting a clear and present danger to either the primary or their unit. Two more men set up a 'v' shaped field of covering fire, which incorporated the entire headland in front of the house. It would be impossible for anything but an armoured division to encroach the building without being cut down as soon as they were in range.

The set up was prepared and the rest of the unit entered the unlocked front door of the residence unchallenged. The men moved like one slick well oiled machine, taking up covering positions and overtaking the man in front. Once each section was deemed safe they began the process again until all the ground floor bedrooms were cleared. There was still no sign of life in the living room. They moved up the stairs in complete silence and swept the living room and kitchen areas.

"One x-ray located but there is no sign of the primary," the unit leader whispered hoarsely into the coms unit.

They stood gathered around the unconscious body of a Brigade man. He was lolled across an armchair like a giant baby. His eyes were open but unfocused and they rolled back into his skull when a Regiment man flipped his eyelids, looking for any sign of intelligent response. There was none. The Brigade man opened his mouth wide and his tongue dangled out dripping saliva onto his chin.

"This guy has been slipped a Mickey Finn," the unit leader said using military colloquialism for an incapacitating drug.

"He's no use to us, leave him there. We're out of here. Alert the taskforce that the primary may have been moved down the mountain," the unit leader ordered.

The Regiment were about to melt back into the undergrowth and exit the mountain the same way that they came in. Suddenly the sky lit up with a red glow, and the deafening sound of a huge explosion rocked the mountain. They looked toward the headland where the snipers were positioned. From the top of the quarry walls they could see the muzzle flashes of at least six sniper positions. The explosion had prompted the Brigade sharpshooters to open fire on the quarry below.

# CHAPTER 60
# THE QUARRY

Omar kept the police car close to the back of the Brigade van. The old railway track was cut deep into a narrow embankment, and there were passing areas built at regular intervals to accommodate tourist traffic through the busy summer months. The passing areas were lay-bys just big enough to fit one car, which would allow any oncoming vehicles to pass. They drove beneath a series of brick built foot bridges as they progressed toward the mountain. The brake lights of the van illuminated brightly and the vehicle slowed. Omar couldn't see any reason why. His passenger had a better view of the scene from his side of the police car.

"There's a car parked in a lay-by. I can't see anyone inside it," the passenger said.

"Check it out and then catch up. We're only a few hundred yards from the quarry," Omar said.

His passenger clicked the safety of his Mach-10 machinegun and opened the door of the police car as it slowed to a crawl.

"Later," he said as he closed the door. He ran to the back of the Brigade van and banged on the back doors. He yanked open the door and barked orders at the Yardies inside. Two of the Somalis jumped out of the van and ran toward the abandoned vehicle. The Brigade van and the police car trundled on down the access road.

"There's no one here, it's been left," the first Somali said.

"Is there anything inside worth taking," said another. He opened the driver's door and the vehicle exploded in a huge fireball.

Sergeant Mel Hickey had wired the vehicle to blow. He'd used the six kilos of Semtex that he had stolen from old Jim, and packed gas canisters around it. Taped to the gas tanks were twelve kilos of six inch nails. When the Somali opened the door he triggered the device. The resulting explosion was a pyrotechnic bonanza. The vehicle was catapulted twenty yards into the air, and was ripped apart by the force of the blast.

The gas canisters ignited and were propelled hundreds of yards in every direction, turning the six inch nails into an Omni-directional shrapnel shower. Nails and metal shards were launched high into the night sky, glowing red against the darkness. The car wreck arced through the air and crashed onto the footbridge where Terry Nick was taking cover. The vehicle smashed the brick structure to pieces and it collapsed onto the road below in a huge plume of smoke and flames. The Brigade leader knew little of his fate. The initial impact crushed him, and his two snipers, breaking their bones and smashing internal organs to pulp. Seconds later their bodies were incinerated in the firestorm that followed. When the brick structure collapsed their remains were squashed beyond all recognition beneath tons of burning debris.

The Brigade leader was dead, and the situation was still unclear to the rest of the 18th Brigade troop. None of them were one hundred percent sure whether the police car was the genuine article or not. Without their leader the Brigade was transformed into a group of individuals that reacted to violence with more violence, and the snipers opened fire on the vehicles below.

The driver of the Brigade van felt the back end of the vehicle lifted slightly by the force of the blast wave. The rear windows shattered as a maelstrom of red hot six inch nails sliced through the cold night air. One of the Somalis screamed from the rear of the van as two searing nails pierced the side of his skull just above the left ear. His colleague next to him grabbed the head and shaft of the deepest nail, trying to yank it out, and the skin on his fingers sizzled like a sausage on a griddle. He yelped and pulled his scorched digits away. The man with the nails in his skull bounced off the interior of the van desperately trying to remove the burning metal from his brain. The driver caught sight of his hideous injuries and panicked. He floored the accelerator. The van lurched forward tossing its occupants around like a paper bag in a wind tunnel.

Omar had ducked as the concussion wave shattered the rear window of the police car. Red hot nails were embedded in the headrests and dashboard of the vehicle, glowing in the dark, and causing the plastic to melt. The acrid smell of burning acrylics filled the vehicle instantly. The Brigade van launched into a wheel spin as the driver reacted to the explosion behind them, and took evasive action. Gravel and dirt splattered the police car as the van accelerated away from the explosion. Omar followed suit and stamped on the accelerator. The powerful police car roared as it sped forward behind the Brigade van. Omar whooped with glee as the vehicle fishtailed toward the quarry. His celebrations were brought to an abrupt end when the first high velocity bullet exploded through the windshield, spraying shards of shattered glass through the interior of the vehicle, slicing long cuts across his face.

# CHAPTER 61

# TANK

Tank had lifted his night sight binoculars and focused them on the quarry access road. He still wasn't sure if the vehicles that had entered the quarry were a part of another agencies operation, or if they had stumbled into the scene by accident. Whatever the outcome was, they had to secure the only escape route. If the 18th Brigade were spooked into bringing the primary down from the mountain then Tank and his team would be ready to intercept them.

The mystery vehicles passed beneath the first footbridge and the blue strobe light illuminated the area as it progressed. Tank could see a sniper positioned on the bridge. He shifted his position as the vehicles drove underneath, and appeared to be talking into a coms unit.

"The Brigade are expecting company, all the bridges are covered by their men," Tank said as he followed the action through the field glasses.

"I can see men positioned on every bridge," Chen concurred, as he looked through his binoculars.

"You had better alert the snatch unit that the Brigade are expecting trouble, and they may have been tipped off about our operation," Tank said.

Chen picked up the coms unit and was about to contact the Regiment on the mountain when the set crackled into life.

"Pilgrim one," the SAS leader said.

"Roger that, we're receiving," Chen answered.

"The primary has been moved, the residence is empty, over," the snatch unit reported.

Chen was about to reply when Tank grabbed his arm and put his finger to his lips to hush him. He pointed toward the two vehicles. The police car had slowed down to a crawl and the passenger got out. He was joined by two more men from the van and they seemed to be approaching a lay-by which was hidden from Tank's view. Two seconds later a fireball exploded into the air. Five seconds later the cliff tops above the quarry lit up sporadically.

"Muzzle flashes," Tank said. "Who are they firing at?"

"Whoever was driving those vehicles," Chen said as the van and the police car sped down the quarry road away from the explosion.

"We have to assume that they are firing on the police force," Tank said. "Order the Regiment to take those snipers out,"

"Pilgrim one," Chen said into the coms.

"Roger, receiving."

"Can you take those snipers out from your position?"

"We're already on it," the reply came followed by silence.

Tank pointed the binoculars up toward the quarry walls. The muzzle flashes stopped almost simultaneously. There was one persistent sniper at the far edge of the cliff wall, and his muzzle flash continued for a few second longer than his affiliates had. Eventually it too was extinguished.

"Pilgrim one, the situation has been neutralised," the Regiment leader reported nonchalantly.

"I guess they met the Regiment then," Tank smiled.

# CHAPTER 62

# OMAR

The van swerved violently as it reached the quarry yard. The back doors were flailing open as the vehicle rocked unsteadily, and Omar could see his men being tossed around like ragdolls in the back. He braked hard trying to avoid smashing into the rear of it. Bullets smashed into the bonnet of the police car ripping huge rents in the metal hood. A torrent of steam hissed from the engine block through the bullet holes and Omar knew that the vehicle was on its last legs. The van hit a low wall with its back wheel, launching the rear end of the vehicle high into the air. The body of a Somali was catapulted out of the back doors, and it landed across the bonnet of the police car. Dead eyes stared at Omar accusingly, and he winced when he saw two nails embedded deep in the man's skull. Omar slammed the vehicle into reverse and floored the accelerator pedal. The police car raced backward screeching its tyres as it tried to gain purchase on the gravel. Bullets pinged off the road as he reversed at speed, and the dead Somali was tossed clear.

The driver of the van opened his door and jumped clear of the vehicle. A tyre exploded as a high velocity bullet punctured it, before another ripped through the body of the vehicle and penetrated the floor plan. It pierced the fuel tank and the van exploded in flames. Two Somalis spilled out of the back doors and staggered across the quarry yard with their hair and clothes alight. One of them fell to his knees as the flames engulfed him completely. The second ran toward the dark waters of the quarry lake and hurled himself over the low stone wall. There was a huge splash and smoke hung on the water where the Yardie had entered. The black water smoothed over but the Somali never resurfaced.

Omar thrust the vehicle into first gear and the police car sprang forward. The van driver cocked his Mach-10 and sprayed the cliffs with nine millimetre bullets. Sparks flew all along the quarry walls as huge chunks of stone were blasted off the cliffs. The driver didn't stop shooting until the machinegun clicked empty. Omar felt blood trickling down his face as he waited for the snipers to return fire, but none was forthcoming. The cliff tops remained dark and silent. The van diver looked at his machinegun in amazement, thinking that he had silenced the sharpshooters with a single burst from his Mach-10. The police car rattled and the engine started knocking noisily. Smoke and steam billowed from beneath the bonnet, and then the engine died completely.

Omar sat holding the steering wheel tightly; his knuckles were almost white with pressure. The van driver staggered toward him, his legs were weak with fear. He was still clutching the machinegun despite the fact that it was empty. He was shaking his head and smiling, delighted and surprised to be alive. Omar smiled back at him and his gold teeth glinted in the dark. He relaxed his grip on the steering wheel a little.

A single shot rang out from behind them somewhere. The van driver's face was hit by a fat .50mm high velocity bullet. It punched a ragged hole the size of a walnut beneath his left eye on entry, and removed back of his head on exit. He looked shocked as he toppled over face first onto the gravel. His dead eyes were full of blame as they drilled into Omar.

# CHAPTER 63

# TANK

Tank and his team mopped up the remaining Brigade men without any further loss of life. They were not bad men; they were mercenary soldiers being paid to do a job. Once it had been established that Tank and his men were British forces they relinquished their weapons without any resistance. Uniformed police divisions were called in to secure the area from further intrusions, while the situation was assessed.

Omar had been found sat in the driver's seat of the police car, dressed in a police constable's uniform. He was staring at the remains of his friend's brains which had been sprayed over the front of his car. The Taskforce men laughed as he was led away in handcuffs because he'd soiled his trousers. The fear of being taken out by a sniper had forced him to stay in the car, even when the shooting had stopped. Something had finally snapped in his mind. The stolen police uniform that he wore was used as evidence to prosecute him for the murder of Constable Thomas. He'd been found guilty and was sent to a high security facility for the criminally insane, with a recommendation that he was never to be released.

When daylight arrived the true carnage was plain for all to see. What had started as a turf war had ended in multiple deaths. The figureheads of both organisations had been killed. There were always others who would be eager to take their place though. A daylight sweep of the house and the interrogation of the Brigade men didn't reveal what had happened to Rashid Ahmed. He had simply disappeared.

# CHAPTER 64
# RASHID AHMED

Rashid estimated that twelve hours had gone by. He had been hiding in the panic room while all the action went on around him. The Brigade man that he drugged had been hauled off with everyone else for interrogation. Rashid released himself from the panic room and then scanned the headland. There were no police and no Brigade men. He had dressed in a ski jacket and jeans, before he pulled on a woolly hat to help conceal him. He walked down the mountain path and greeted the odd tourist ramblers that he met along the way. The area was popular with walkers and bird watchers alike. The quarry yard was busy as police forensic scientists tried to protect and gather evidence. There were several areas cordoned off with yellow tape, but it was impossible to stop tourists from entering the reserve completely. Press teams and tourists were ambling around the quarry, some looking for a story, others for a rare sea bird or two.

Rashid decided to skirt the edge of the quarry lakes which would take him behind the railway embankment and into the nature reserve footpaths which crisscrossed the coastline. He was quite sure that he wouldn't be recognised by the general public, but not sure about the police. Rashid reached the black lake and skirted the edge away from the quarry. He was home and dry. The most perilous part of his journey was the path down the mountain, but no one had challenged him. He didn't look out of place amongst the sprinkling of hill walkers. As he walked along the quarry lake he noticed a blond man walking toward him from the opposite direction, but didn't think much of it. He had a strange limp.

"Hello Rashid," Sergeant Mel Hickey said. Rashid was surprised.

The blond man grabbed him in a vice like bear hug. Rashid struggled but he couldn't break the man's grip.

Mel had been stopped dead in his tracks when Terry Nick fired at him with the shotgun round. The makers of the Taser stun guns had developed an 'Extended Range Electron Muscular Projectile' round, which could be fired from a shotgun. It would stop an elephant in its tracks. The sergeant had no idea how long he had been unconscious, but when he woke it looked like all hell had broken loose. His chest was black and blue were the paralysing round had hit him, but otherwise he was fine. There was activity all over the quarry yard but no sign of any Brigade men. There was a set of field glasses in the long grass near him, and he used them to look up the mountain. He had spotted Rashid walking down the mountain path, and made up his mind in an instant. This time he was taking his target down permanently, and no mistakes.

He held Rashid in a vice like grip and walked toward the edge of the deep black lake. There wasn't even a flicker of doubt in his mind as he stepped off the edge. Sergeant Hickey and Rashid plummeted through the icy black waters. The freezing temperature of the lake sent their bodies into shock, forcing the air from their lungs. The sergeant's metal legs acted as a dead weight, dragging them down faster and deeper. In reality Sergeant Hickey wished that he had died in Nisour Square, at least as he died now he felt that he had redressed the balance of justice. He could hear Rashid Ahmed scream, which turned into a gurgle, and then the sergeant, was finally at peace with himself. A small raft of bubbles formed on the surface of the lake, and then the dark unforgiving water was still once again.

# CHAPTER 65

# ECHOES

Tank and the Taskforce informed the Minister of Defence that Rashid Ahmed was in the wind. His bank accounts were eventually traced and there was never any activity reported. Two years later he was finally recorded as missing presumed dead. The final arms deal with the Taliban was cancelled, and the directors of the security services were severely reprimanded for working with Rashid Ahmed at all. The investigation into the fire fight in the quarry was handed over to the uniformed divisions, and smoothed over as part of a turf war for the club land of Manchester.

The 18th Brigade were removed from the government's preferred supplier list, and they never deployed mercenaries on their behalf again. They did however deploy mercenaries through other giant security companies across the globe. Nothing had changed except uniform.

Omar was confined to a psychiatric ward where he continued to convince the doctors that he was mad. He had planned to continue the pretence until the time when security around him would be relaxed, and the opportunity escape arose. Unfortunately after a prolonged series of chest infections he was eventually diagnosed with full blown aids. Like millions of his African cousins he had carried the virus undetected for decades. Six months after the diagnosis he died from chronic pneumonia. His girlfriend Gemma never saw him again after the night at her flat. He had thrown her out of the hatchback onto the pavement, which to her was unforgivable. She claimed criminal injuries for the damage to her apartment and was awarded thousands of pounds in compensation. Gemma slipped back into her party girl lifestyle and she lived well for the next five years, although the advancing wrinkles and the increasing number of grey hairs were a constant worry. It was only when one of her many sexual partners spotted odd looking black growths on her spine that she went to her general practitioner to be checked over. The results confirmed that she had contracted the HIV virus from Omar, and that it had turned into full blown aids. Recording the details of her sexual history had raised a few eyebrows. The information then had to be investigated to track the possible infection of her sexual partners. The whole investigation took a considerable length of time, and destroyed a number of marriages. The echoes of Omar's life resounded through her present. She died alone a year later.

The Terrorist Task Force were put on red alert the same day, because MI5 had uncovered a safe house belonging to a right wing extremist cell. Paperwork and maps found in the dwelling indicated that a possible chemical terrorist attack was being contemplated. It looked like there was more trouble on the way.

# BLISTER

CONRAD JONES

GerriCon Books Ltd

# CHAPTER 1
# BLISTER AGENTS

The city of Liverpool was once the busiest port in the world, and the centre of the terrible human slave trade. Most of the historic dock buildings are long since gone, but some of them remain and have been turned into a tourist hub along the banks of the River Mersey. The Terrorist Task Force are also based on the riverbank. They occupy the top floor of a fortress-like building known as Canning place. The remainder of the building is occupied by the county's uniformed police divisions. The taskforce had been called to an emergency meeting.

"The sulphur mustards, of which mustard gas 2-chloroethyl sulphide is a member, are a class of related cytotoxic, vesicant chemical warfare agents. They have the ability to form large blisters on exposed skin, both internally and externally. In spite of the name, technically they are not actually gases, but are liquid chemicals which turn into vapour. Pure sulphur mustards are colourless, odourless, viscous liquids when they are at room temperature. However, when used in impure form as warfare agents they are usually yellow-brown in colour and have an odour resembling mustard plants, garlic or horseradish, hence the innocuous name. Mustard gas was originally assigned the name *LOST*, after two men called Lommel and Steinkopf, who first proposed the military use of Sulphur Mustard to the German Imperial General Staff during the First World War", Chen nodded to the audience of taskforce agents that had been summoned to an extraordinary meeting.

Chen was of Chinese origin, and was an information guru for the Terrorist Task Force. The taskforce was set up as an elite counter terrorist unit that operated outside of the usual military jurisdiction, and they answered directly to the Minister of Defence. When incidents were escalated to the level of the Terrorist Task Force involvement, then all other avenues had already been exhausted.

"Is there a reason behind the chemistry lesson?" John Tankersley asked impatiently, rubbing his aching neck. He had been lifting heavy weights in the station gym prior to the meeting, but he had pushed his limit too far and torn a muscle. It was Chen that had been spotting him as he lifted the last heavy set, and he had failed to provide enough support, which had caused the injury. Tank was pissed off with him.

"Please be patient Tank, I'm getting to the point but you will need all this background information to understand the implications of what I'm about to tell you," Chen replied holding his palms downward in a calming motion.

John Tankersley was the lead agent of the taskforce. He was an ex-Special Forces operative and had been decorated more times than an artificial Christmas tree. John Tankersley was a brute of a man, six foot tall and seventeen stone of solid muscle, it wasn't difficult to understand why his colleagues shortened his name to `Tank`.

"Okay, but get to the point please, the German high command are not really on my need to know list," Tank snapped back. The muscles in his wide jaw twitched and the veins in his massive neck throbbed visibly.

"I'll be as brief as I can," Chen smiled and his oriental features were exaggerated, narrow eyes and high cheek bones. His smile was brilliant white and had a very disarming effect on everyone he met, especially women. He continued. "Mustard agents are regulated under the 1993 Chemical Weapons Convention. Three classes of chemicals are monitored under this convention, with sulphur and nitrogen mustard grouped as substances with no use other than chemical warfare. Mustard gas has extremely powerful vesicant effects on its victims. Additionally, it is strongly mutagenic and carcinogenic, due to its strong alkaline properties."

"Will you get to the point Chen," Tank said under his breath. He rubbed his hand over his shaved head.

"People exposed to mustard gas rarely suffer immediate symptoms, and mustard-contaminated areas may appear completely normal, victims can unknowingly receive high dosages. However, within six to twenty four hours of exposure to mustard agent, victims experience intense thirst, itching and skin irritation which gradually turns into large blisters filled with yellow fluid wherever the mustard agent contacted the skin. These are severe chemical burns which are slow to heal. If the victim's eyes were exposed then they become sore, starting with conjunctivitis, after which the eyelids swell, resulting in temporary blindness. There are many recorded incidents of the thirst being so intense that it causes a type of delirium, or madness. Victims can become extremely violent," Chen smiled again as he continued the presentation. He could see that Tank was becoming agitated, which amused him. Chen had told Tank not to go too heavy on the weights but he never listened, and he often teased him that if Tank's brain was a big as his bicep, then he would be a genius.

"At very high concentrations, if inhaled, mustard agent causes bleeding and blistering within the respiratory system, damaging the delicate mucous membranes and causing the victim to drown on their own bodily fluids. Severe mustard gas burns are usually fatal. The mutagenic and carcinogenic effects of mustard agent mean that victims who recover from mustard gas burns have an increased risk of developing cancer in later life. Furthermore, mustard gas is a persistent agent which would remain in the environment for days and continue to cause sickness. If mustard gas contaminated a soldier's clothing and equipment, then other soldiers or medics he came into contact with would also be poisoned. Towards the end of the war it was even used in high concentrations as an area-denial weapon, which often forced soldiers to abandon heavily contaminated positions for months," Chen sat down at the long meeting table and looked at the gathered agents. The gathering remained silent. No one was quite sure where the meeting was heading.

"Thank you Chen, most interesting, and also very concerning," Major Stanley Timms broke the silence.

The Major was the director of the taskforce. Before he had been selected to operate the covert unit, he had been a high ranking officer in the Royal Marines with a military record that would make Rambo blush.

"I'm sure that you can appreciate the dreadful implications of a `blister agent` falling into the wrong hands. MI5 has received information that a right wing extremist group is intending to attack the 2012 Olympics with such a chemical," the Major explained. The credit crunch of 2008 had sent the economy into melt down, which had pushed unemployment up and house prices down, leaving many in a desperate financial position. The effect increased racial tensions nationwide as immigrants were still flooding in and taking indigenous British jobs. It was fuel to fire for the right wing Nazi parties.

"How solid is the information?" Tank asked. The intelligence agencies often scare mongered. The greater the perceived threat, the higher their government budget was.

"Solid enough to have been put onto the Minister`s desk," the Major replied.

"What do we know about the protagonists?" Grace Farrington asked. Grace was the taskforce`s number two. She was of Jamaican decent and looked more like a pop star or a beauty queen than a Special Forces operative.

"We don't know a great deal about them at all I`m afraid, except they preach the usual anti-immigration nonsense as the rest of the neo-Nazi groups," the Major answered. He stood up and walked to the head of the table. On the wall behind him was a bank of screens. He picked up a remote and the largest screen flickered into life. The face of a handsome young man appeared. The photograph looked like a school portrait.

"This is Christopher Walsh aged sixteen, and this is the only photograph that we have of him. He is now twenty seven and a very successful business man, but he is also a recluse. The information that the intelligence agencies have received puts Christopher Walsh on centre stage as the brains behind the proposed attack," the Major sat down again.

"What is his background?" Grace asked.

"Chemicals, believe it or not," Chen answered the question.

"Well, chemical weapons to be more precise," the Major added. "We think that he was behind selling mustard gas formulas and production methodology to at least half a dozen rogue governments, and god forbid, several extremist organisations, but nobody knows where he is or why he would be involved in an attack on the London Olympics."

Tank picked up a paper file from the desk and flicked through the pages. Chen had compiled some of the basics about chemical production. He stood up and walked toward the meeting room window. The chemical formulas and technical information blurred onto the page. It made no real sense to Tank, but he knew that to some people it would be only too easy to manufacture chemical weapons. Tank looked out of the window. The River Mersey was only a stone's throw away from the taskforce headquarters at Canning Place. It looked dark grey and angry as it flowed on its way to the Irish Sea. Across the road hundreds of tourists ambled around the historic Albert Docks, once the centre of the slave trade, Liverpool had now become a huge tourist destination. Tank wondered just how much of Chen's blister agent it would take to attack a `Soft Target` like the docks.

"How easy would it be to manufacture this stuff," Tank asked, placing the file down on the window ledge.

"It would be difficult," Chen answered. "All the ingredients required for the manufacture of chemical weapons and homemade explosives are monitored. So if someone bought enough of the individual ingredients required then the intelligence agencies would be alerted."

"We think that Christopher Walsh is involved because he may already possess the ingredients required, therefore no one would be any the wiser if he made a chemical agent. Every chemical plant with any association to him is being investigated by MI5," the Major said.

Tank looked out of the window again. It had started raining and the sky was obscured by dark low clouds. The Liver buildings on the riverbank looked bright and clean against the grey clouds. There were two huge bronze birds perched on top of the building. They had become the emblem of the historic port.

"We are looking into how easy it would be for anyone to get hold of a blister agent, but my concern is this," Chen approached the bank of screens and the school portrait changed. The black and white image of a naval ship appeared. Judging by the style of the uniforms worn by some of the sailors in the picture, Tank reckoned that it had been taken during the Second World War. The deck of the vessel was covered with artillery shells. There was barely an inch of the deck that didn't have ordinance on it.

"This is a British Royal Navy vessel shortly after the Second World War. I can`t tell you what it was called or exactly when the picture was taken because the information was so classified that it was destroyed. To all intents and purposes this picture is the only evidence that this ship ever existed." Chen moved across the room and the picture changed again. Two mini submarines appeared on the screen.

"The navy ship was carrying an unknown number of mustard gas shells. In your files are the details of a chemical weapons disaster which occurred during the Second World War in the Italian port of Bari, 1943. The incident was so bad that the allied leaders conspired to destroy their entire stocks of the chemicals. The British government scuppered the ship and pretended that it had never been contemplating the use of chemical weapons against the Germans. They scuppered a total of sixteen similar vessels at various points around the British Isles," Chen explained.

Tank could see what was coming. The mini-submarines in the picture had either been stolen or purchased by someone on the MI5 watch list, and when you combined that information with the fact that a known chemical weapons dealer had been implicated in a terrorist plot then it all added up. Someone was trying to recover mustard gas shells from the bottom of the ocean.